PEN

A PARADISE OF ILLUSIONS

Laurie Hashim lives with her husband, three boys and two dogs in Santa Barbara, California. Laurie graduated many years ago with a degree in economics from Tufts University. She has worked in management consulting in Boston, advertising in Kuala Lumpur, and software in San Francisco. But these days, when she is not writing or doing research for writing, she is hiking, biking and travelling.

The island of Penang has captivated the author ever since she married into a sprawling, multicultural family from this metropolitan mosaic almost thirty years ago. She is grateful to the Penang Historical Society, fastidious colonial records and a generation of Penangites devoted to writing memoirs which have helped her place her imagined characters in their proper time and place

A Paradise of Illusions

Laurie Hashim

PENGUIN BOOKS

An imprint of Penguin Random House

PENGUIN BOOKS

USA | Canada | UK | Ireland | Australia
New Zealand | India | South Africa | China | Southeast Asia

Penguin Books is part of the Penguin Random House group of companies
whose addresses can be found at global.penguinrandomhouse.com

Published by Penguin Random House SEA Pte Ltd
9, Changi South Street 3, Level 08-01,
Singapore 486361

First published in Penguin Books by Penguin Random House SEA 2022
Copyright © Laurie Hashim

ISBN 9789815017366

Typeset in Garamond by MAP Systems, Bangalore, India

www.penguin.sg

Penang 1966

Rizal paced the concrete sidewalk outside the bustling Penang airport. The morning storm clouds had retreated and the sun was beginning to make its penetrating presence known. He reached into his pocket to pull out a handkerchief and wipe the moisture above his upper lip. Where were they?

Finally, he spotted a sweaty porter huffing with exertion as he pushed a trolley with a familiar set of canvas bags on it. Shaun followed behind; his arm draped the shoulders of a young woman with ink black hair trailing to her waist.

'Bapa,' Shaun said and threw his arms around his father. His cheek grazed Rizal's temple. Had his son grown taller in the last year or was Rizal already starting to shrink like an old man? Shaun pulled back from the embrace to present his future bride to his father.

'This is Sheila.' He placed one hand protectively around his fiancée's waist while the other fiddled with the belt loop of his pants. That he should still require his father's approval at his age was endearing and perhaps a bit burdensome. Who was Rizal to judge the appropriate spouse for anyone?

'Pleased to meet you, Mr Mansour,' Sheila said. She hesitated, trying to determine the appropriate gesture, a handshake, a tentative hug, or perhaps a peck on the cheek.

'Please, call me Bapa,' Rizal insisted as he embraced her slender shoulders. 'We'll be family soon.'

A white Mercedes pulled up to the curb. The driver, with his khaki uniform and waxed mustache, hopped out of the car and loaded the luggage into the trunk. He held the door open for Shaun and Sheila, smiling in approval of the prospective bride.

'Welcome home, sir.'

'Thank you. It's good to be back.'

'Are you tired?' Rizal asked. He helped himself into the front passenger seat, giving the couple their space in the back. 'I thought we could do a quick tour and then stop at the club for lunch.'

'We had a long rest in Singapore yesterday. I think we're ready to see a bit of the island before we collapse,' Shaun said, eager to show off his hometown.

The road from the airport flowed through tender green rice paddies dotted with wrinkled ladies in sun hats and sarongs, bent over watery fields. The air shimmered with rising steam. In the distance, lush tropical hills spilled into emerald waters. Feathery clouds drifted like rice powder tossed across the azure skies.

As the Mercedes drove north from the airport, the rural beauty slipped away and they became immersed in the dense concentration of human activity clustered at the tip of the island. The driver made his way through the unruly traffic of the port city of Georgetown. Automobiles, buses, bicycles, motorbikes, trishaws, and pedestrians charged down makeshift lanes on impossibly narrow roads lined with Chinese shop-houses, modern offices, and colonial buildings.

They travelled along the coast, cluttered with clan jetties and colonial piers, to the edge of the island, where the promontory stretched to within two miles of the Malayan mainland. The driver turned down Beach Street, with its prestigious trading houses, banks, and law firms. Rizal pointed out his office, a three-storey Art Deco building facing the ferry terminal.

They rounded the tip of the promontory to the north shore, which was adorned with monuments to the colonial past—the grassy Esplanade parade grounds where loyal subjects once celebrated the coronation of British kings and queens; the cannon of Fort Cornwallis pointed toward a tranquil sea; the Queen Victoria Clock Tower still leaning from the impact of World War II bombers. They passed a row of dilapidated mansions perched along the seaside with boarded up windows and toppling roofs.

'What happened to these houses? They look deserted.' Sheila asked. 'That's Millionaire's Row, where the Chinese tycoons built their castles at the turn of the century,' Shaun explained. 'A lot of the owners died or lost their money during the war.' Rizal noticed that Shaun did not go into detail about the largest one, its broken glass canopy glistening in the afternoon sun.

The car passed the last of the crumbling estates and turned inland toward the city.

They passed a Hindu temple, its tiered tower cluttered with colourful gods and goddesses, then a majestic mosque with a domed top and lofty minarets. Within minutes, they were on a street filled with Chinese signboards, lanterns, and clouds of incense.

'Are you ready for some lunch?' Rizal asked.

The car travelled to the coast before turning down a paved drive lined with stately royal palms. A turbaned Sikh saluted as they passed through the security gates of the Penang Club. The car pulled to the curb and a gloved attendant rushed to open their door. They entered and made their way through the empty lobby to the verandah, where families gathered for a casual lunch by the beach. Ceiling fans creaked overhead, creating a scant breeze in the clammy air. A distant ocean liner drifted toward the horizon.

The club was once the exclusive preserve of the Europeans, but these days, the children jumping in and out of the pool were English, Australian, Chinese, Malay and Indian—the privileged children of elite Penang families. Rizal had known most of these children since they were born, just as the couples who stopped by their table had known Shaun since he was a baby. Georgetown was a sprawling urban city, but in many ways, the island was a small town. Everyone knew everything about everyone else.

Nobody had to ask, for example, how a Chinese boy had become the youngest son in a Malay family. At least they knew the public version, as scripted by Rizal and Anna, his wife. How they had found the baby abandoned during the Occupation, his parents likely victims of a late-night Japanese death squad. Naturally, it was impossible to track down the identity of an infant in the chaos of the war. The orphanages were overflowing. What was to be done but take the child in?

Rizal stole glances at his lanky son heartily consuming his curry laksa, from across the round table. He looked more like his father every year, a lighter, more jubilant version. The same narrow eyes with heavy lids, a long angular face that could look thin at times but opened beautifully when he smiled.

Shaun introduced his girlfriend to everyone who approached the table to welcome him back. Occasionally, he included her surname. Rizal remembered the first time Shaun had pronounced the name of his girlfriend over the crackly static of the international phone line.

'Her name is Sheila, Sheila Yamamoto.'

'Yamamoto,' Rizal coughed out. 'I thought you said she was American.'

'She is American. I mean she was born in America. Her dad's family is from Japan and her mom came from China.'

'I see.' Rizal searched for a neutral response. 'That's an unusual combination.'

'It's not so unusual here,' Shaun said. 'You're not going to have a problem with her name, are you? I mean, Sheila's great. I know you're going to love her.'

'Of course I'll love her,' Rizal had said, absorbing the irony of this particular child marrying a girl with a Japanese surname. 'I'm just so happy you've decided to settle down in Penang.'

Nobody at the club seemed shocked by Shaun's Japanese fiancée. They did not gasp or clutch their chests when he introduced her to them. Maybe there would be hope for Rizal's children. Maybe society would open up and make allowances. Not for the unlucky with transgressions as aberrant as Rizal's, but maybe for young people, who just wanted to marry the person they loved.

Why not a Chinese–Japanese–American daughter-in-law? His eldest son had returned from London with a blond, freckled bride. The two had settled down in Penang and produced a beautiful little boy with green eyes, tan skin, and a shock of copper hair. They called him Red, in honour of Red Parker, Rizal's father-in-law, a crimson-headed legend whose portrait still hung in the hallowed halls of this and many other clubs in the city.

Part I

1

June 1919

Two o'clock in the morning. Over three hours since the midwife had arrived and still nothing. Red Parker perched on the edge of his rattan chair, straining to hear sounds from the bedroom. A damp wind blew across the verandah, disturbing the bamboo chimes. Their tinkling mingled with the symphony of the nocturnal crickets. Doors opened and closed. A weary maid shooed the children back to their rooms.

Red had waited on this same verandah four times before, listening for the angry cry of a bewildered newborn. Only once had the outburst failed to come. His first had been a stillborn. A few years later, Adi had arrived red-faced and wailing, followed in due time by Faisal and Sofiah. But it had been almost ten years since Sofiah was born and four since the accident that had taken Adi. This unexpected child would be welcome compensation.

His wife Zaharah prayed openly for a son to replace her beloved Adi. Red wished in silence for a girl. He couldn't bring another boy into the world at his age. He might live long enough to see a girl to marriage, but boys required more time to mature. Red hadn't settled down until he was thirty-four. Even then, the urge to marry had caught him entirely unprepared.

Marriage had been the last thing on Red's mind that evening over twenty years ago, when he had climbed the steps of Ibrahim Hamid's raised wooden house. Shipping was the purpose of his visit. Ibrahim, a social acquaintance with promising entrepreneurial instincts, wanted Red to invest in his new venture, a passenger ship that could provide comfortable transportation on the Hajj to devout Muslims. Ibrahim's contacts among the Malay and Indian Muslims would be useful. The figures Ibrahim had presented were impressive and the assumptions behind them, solid. More importantly, he seemed to Red to have the skills needed to oversee the new business. Though still young, he had a reputation as a shrewd and intelligent businessman.

As a tepid Protestant, Red had only peripheral knowledge of Islamic pilgrimages, but a speculative spirit flowed in his blood. He came from a line of intrepid Scots who had sought their fortune in the East. He had gambled successfully before, converting his parent's sugar crop to rubber trees in time for the ascent of the motorcar. He had diversified his earnings by financing other growers; selling, shipping and insuring their crops. The wager had paid off, allowing him to grow his profits regardless of the fluctuation of commodity prices. So why not pilgrimages?

A toothless servant opened the front door. Leathery skin flapped against her arm as she motioned for Red to remove his shoes.

'Please, shoes here,' she mumbled in her best English, gesturing to the collection near the door.

'*Selamat pagi, Tuan ada di rumah?*' he asked.

'Yes, he comes already from prayers,' she said, refusing to take the hint that he could speak Malay.

She led him across the sitting room and pointed to a rattan sofa with rose-coloured chintz cushions. 'Sit,' she commanded.

Her mouth moved as if to try another English phrase but she changed her mind and held up her hand instead, like a dog trainer commanding him to stay. Satisfied with his compliance, she slipped out of the room to find her boss.

Ibrahim's family home was a confused combination of cultures. Bright Indian silks draped the side tables, English lace framed the windows, and embroidered Arabic script decorated the walls. An army of diligent servants kept the persistent red dust at bay, but their zealous attention had left the wooden floors lined and blanched.

'Mr Parker, thank you for stopping by,' Ibrahim called as he entered. 'You look well. I hope that you've escaped this latest round of illness.' He offered Red a firm handshake instead of the traditional salaam.

'I've remained stubbornly healthy. And your family? How have they been?'

'We've been spared, praise be to Allah. My wife is expecting, so we've been especially worried about the fever.'

Ibrahim reclined in a rattan chair, his bare feet peeking out from under a plaid sarong. Red usually saw Ibrahim with a western suit jacket over his sarong, his black hair topped with a songkok, the flat oval cap that Mohammedans wore in public. Today, he was dressed for the comfort of his own home in a collarless shirt and knit prayer cap.

'You've been a busy man, Ibrahim. How many children do you have now?'

'This will be our third. My wife seems to be blessed with remarkable fertility.' He leaned toward Red and winked. 'What about you? Raising a family is a man's most important responsibility. You can't put off your obligation forever.'

'Maybe not forever,' Red laughed. 'But for as long as possible. My mother was fond of telling me what a horrible husband I'd make. Perhaps I'm reluctant to inflict that curse upon some poor, unsuspecting creature.'

'Any mother in Penang would be thrilled to place their daughter in your care,' Ibrahim insisted.

'It's not the mothers but the daughters that I'm worried about.'

'That's where you're wrong,' Ibrahim winked. 'It's the mothers that should concern you.'

Red humoured Ibrahim and his gentle teasing. He was used to this kind of talk. An unmarried man in Penang society was a blemish that the entire community seemed eager to rectify. Every citizen felt a responsibility to see that all available girls were yoked to someone, even if it meant saddling some poor guy with several wives. Red suspected a societal conspiracy. Those already bound in captivity couldn't stomach the sight of a man enjoying his freedom.

The conversation continued on its predictable course with Red half-listening to the usual series of reprimands. The tingling aroma of chillies penetrated his thoughts.

Finally, the kitchen doors opened and the earthy aroma of curry poured into the room. Two women emerged carrying trays loaded with cakes, fruits, and curry puffs. Colorful shawls draped the girls' hair for the benefit of this male visitor; floral batik sarongs wrapped their waists. A fitted kebaya hugged the younger girl's chest, and the older girl wore a loose tunic that protruded around her abdomen.

'Ah, Red, you've met my wife, Aisha. This is her sister, Zaharah.'

The girls squatted in unison to place their bounty on the table between Ibrahim and Red. Zaharah's bangles clanged against the pewter trays as she lowered her slender arms. Relieved of their weighty offerings, the sisters turned toward Red. They took turns greeting him by touching his hands and then their hearts. As their palms brushed, Zaharah's eyes floated up from the floor, barely catching his before darting back down.

Aisha moved closer to her husband and whispered in a mixture of Malay and Tamil, 'Will Mr Parker be joining us for dinner? Cook is wondering whether to go easy on the chillies.'

Red almost begged them not to reduce the spice on his account but he didn't want to embarrass his host. Everyone assumed his lingual ignorance based on the colour of his skin.

'I haven't asked him yet,' Ibrahim said to his wife. 'I was waiting to see if Father would be joining us.'

'I believe he's staying out for the evening.'

'Perfect, I'd like to finish my chat with Mr Parker before the old man gets involved. Give us about an hour. Tell Cook to reduce the chillies. But make sure that I have plenty of sambal to flavour my own food.'

As Ibrahim and his wife continued their conversation, Red took the opportunity to study the younger sister who remained standing by his side. Zaharah's features reflected the best of her Indian and Malay heritage. She had a well-chiselled nose and high, angled cheekbones. Her kebaya blouse curved just enough to suggest firm, rounded breasts. Her clear skin, the colour of a roasted coffee bean, was unmarred by distracting powder except for the thin outline of a kohl pencil around her eyes. She was the most beautiful creature he had ever seen. Her cheeks flushed with the knowledge of his attention but her eyes remained rooted to the floor.

Aisha and Ibrahim finished their discussion and the girls returned to oversee the dinner preparation. Red's eyes followed Zaharah's swaying hips all the way to the door. He tried to focus on his conversation with Ibrahim but was distracted by the giggling sounds coming from the kitchen.

Red and Ibrahim chatted for over an hour without mentioning shipping. The polite banter was a necessary part of doing business. These preliminaries eased the tension of future negotiations. Red didn't mention Ibrahim's proposal until the subject became a natural extension of the conversation.

'Your figures were impressive,' he said. 'Perhaps I could send one of my accountants to review a few of the details.'

'I'd be happy to share any insights,' Ibrahim responded as if Red had commented on the weather. 'But let's not talk about business now. You'll join us for dinner, won't you? Our cook is famous for her rendang.'

The servants filled the teakwood dining table with bowls of fish curry, beef rendang, whole sardines with tomato sauce, eggplant floating in thick gravy and a heaping platter of biryani rice. Red's place setting comprised of a fork and spoon, though he would have happily eaten with his hands like his host. Ibrahim's younger brothers joined them, embroiling the diners in a passionate debate over the relative merits of their favourite cricket teams. No further mention was made of the shipping venture.

Aisha appeared several times to refill their drinks and replenish the platters of food. He wanted to ask about her sister, but he didn't want to alert the family to his interest. He needed time to regain control of himself before determining his next move.

That night he dreamt of Zaharah's body. His arm wrapped around her waist, his fingertips caressed her soft breasts. Their bodies pressed together, straining for release. He woke in the middle of the night with his nightgown soaked in sweat. Something needed to be done.

The next day, he walked through the gilded gates of a pale-yellow bungalow and sought out the one woman who could help him with his predicament.

'I hope I'm not disturbing you,' he said to the enormous matriarch filling the chair on the verandah.

'So nice of you to stop by.' Achi extended a puffy hand for him to kiss. 'I haven't seen your charming face for ages.' She motioned for him to sit and then placed her bloated leg on the chair next to his. 'You don't mind if I prop up my foot, do you? My ankles get so swollen in this humidity. The doctor says that I must keep them elevated.'

'I'm sorry you aren't feeling well.'

'It's just my usual condition. I've long since learned to live with it. I try to suffer in silence for the sake of my anxious husband. The poor man worries over me.'

'Someone should worry over you. You spend so much time attending to the needs of others.'

'Not at all. I get great satisfaction from helping others.'

Puan Rahila, otherwise known as Achi, or elder sister, was the self-appointed matchmaker of the Jawi Peranakan of Penang. Achi knew every Muslim girl of marriageable age in Penang. She had a keen eye for the subtle signals that men send out when they're in the first flush of infatuation. No matter how crowded the room, she could spot a young man arching his neck to catch sight of a fleeting maiden. Her ears were always ready to take in any relevant gossip. Which parents were anxious to see their homely daughter secured with a wealthy, nearsighted man; what new business alliance could be sealed with the convenient coupling of two hapless children? Perhaps she adopted this occupation to compensate for her own dismal marriage.

Achi couldn't help but take an interest in Red. He was a puzzle, she thought. Not unpleasant to look at, despite his shock of bright red hair and pale freckled skin. He had a solid build, well-proportioned features, and a rather lovely pair of blue eyes. But the way he dressed! His ill-fitting suits were frightful. He had the finest tailors at his disposal, yet he couldn't stand still long enough for them to take proper measurements. And his shoes, custom-made from imported leather but always scuffed, the soles caked with red dirt. If anyone was in need of a woman's touch, it was this hopeless maverick. She had assumed he would eventually settle down with a suitable English girl—likely one of the privileged daughters of the British ruling class that paraded around Penang.

'Miss Whitcomb is looking lovely these days,' Achi hinted as the lady in question passed by in a rickshaw. 'I've heard she has many inquiries from the more discerning bachelors in town. But she's saving herself for someone who can keep her in high style.'

'I pity the man who has to fund that wardrobe,' Red replied. 'Someone should tell her that expensive window dressing can never conceal an unattractive view.'

Red would never be interested in those spoiled girls who whined about the heat and pined for their pilgrimages back to civilization. His mother had dragged him too many times to England, where he was forced to sit in stuffy parlours sipping tea, while she paraded him in front of relatives. He understood that the itchy blazer and pinched shoes were part of the performance. His mother might be living in a barbarian, malaria-infested jungle, but she had as many servants as the finest families in London, and could afford to dress her son like a refined gentleman.

'I actually stopped by to ask you about A.S. Ibrahim Hamid's sister-in-law.' Red felt Achi would appreciate a straightforward approach.

'Do you mean one of Aisha's sisters?' Achi said. 'Syeikh Mohamad Ismail has five daughters. The oldest, Fareeda, is married to C.H. Abdul Omar. Aisha is the second. The younger three remain at home. They're all lovely girls, very well-mannered and disciplined. Which one are you referring to?'

Red pronounced her name for the first time. 'Zaharah.'

Of course, the pretty one. Zaharah had turned many heads in Penang. Achi had tried to match her up several times but most prospective mothers-in-law had rejected her haughty behaviour. Her poor parents were beside themselves with this beautiful, rebellious girl. Her hips swayed too much when she walked. Her voice was too loud and her laugh too boisterous. Achi was beginning to suspect the nature of Red's visit but she wasn't sure about his intentions. Was he asking about her for himself or someone else?

'She is a lovely girl indeed. I know the family well. What is the nature of your inquiry?'

'I thought you might know whether she was . . . well . . . promised to anyone.'

'She's not yet engaged,' Achi assured him. 'There have been several offers, of course. But her parents have been very picky about their favourite daughter. Syeikh Mohamad Ismail is an extremely attentive father. He has taken a keen interest in his daughters' futures.'

'I'd like to ask for her hand in marriage. Would you be willing to speak to her father on my behalf?'

Just like Red to get down to business. He was known for his single-minded approach to success, be it business or pleasure. Achi hesitated before answering. She was confident in her matchmaking abilities but she had serious concerns about this match.

'I'd have nothing but praise for your character, Mr Parker,' Achi said. 'You know how fond I am of you. But there is a problem.'

'What kind of problem?'

'Her father is one of the most respected Islamic scholars in the region. I can't imagine he would allow his daughter to marry outside the faith.'

'I understand.' Red had obviously anticipated this possibility because he answered without hesitation. 'You can tell Syeikh Mohamad that I'd be pleased to study under his guidance. He need not consent to the marriage until he is satisfied with my full conversion.'

'You'd be willing to convert?' Achi couldn't stifle the surprise in her voice.

'More than willing.'

Western men often enjoyed the exotic pleasure of a local mistress but they rarely married outside of their race, and they certainly did not convert. Such a union would be scandalous to the Christian colonialists and a remarkable coup for the Muslim community. For Achi, it would be the crowning achievement of her life's work.

'In that case, I'll speak to her father,' Achi promised, rising as if to execute the task immediately.

Red caught her arm. 'You should also know that I'm planning on investing in a new venture with his son-in-law. Ibrahim and I will be opening a shipping line that will transport the devout in comfort to the Hajj. I thought you might want to mention this, if you think it would be useful.'

Achi's smile bubbled over into ebullient laughter.

'I think that information might be very helpful.'

Red submitted to six months of religious training under Syeikh Mohamad's zealous instruction. He suffered in agony waiting for the day he could hold his beautiful Zaharah in his arms. As the time for their marriage approached, he was allowed some limited contact with her, but he was never permitted a moment alone with her to speak of his passion or touch her lovely body. Every glimpse of Zaharah strengthened his resolve to possess her.

Finally, after days of exhausting marriage festivities, they were alone together in his bedroom. When Red was finally free to slip off her layers of clothing, he discovered a body even more bewitching than he had imagined. At first, his young bride was understandably timid. The poor thing had never seen a man's body. She had never been offered even the most basic facts about her own. But in time, she proved to be an eager and able pupil.

A piercing cry punctured Red's reverie. He threw down his book and entered the bedroom. A midwife stood in the corner, wiping layers of blood and mucus off a tiny, wrinkled body.

'She's perfect,' the midwife pronounced, 'absolutely perfect.'

She handed Red a delicate bundle swaddled in white gauze. His other children had inherited Zaharah's coffee-bean complexion, dark hair and brown eyes. But this little girl had skin the colour of light toast with pale freckles scattered across her nose. She peered up at Red with her hazy eyes, silently contemplating her new surroundings.

'Hello, Anna,' he whispered. 'Welcome to your new home.'

2

August 1925

Anna's braid bounced against the back of her floral frock as she skipped barefoot down the hall. She ran into the bedroom and threw her arms around Sofiah's waist.

'The musicians are here!' she announced.

'Anna, please don't wrinkle my sarong.' Sofiah took her sister's wrists in her hennaed fingers. 'Give me a minute and I'll come have a look.'

'Hurry and finish, Auntie,' Sofiah begged. 'I can't hold my head still any longer.'

'I need more pins. You don't want your hair to fall, do you?' her Aunt Aisha scolded.

Aisha reached into a silver case on the dressing table and pulled out two more golden pins. She twirled the loose tendrils around her fingers and then shoved the pins into the black bun.

'There, that should do it. Come, have a look.'

Sofiah stepped into the frame of the dressing mirror, turning from side to side to examine the artistic creation on her head. The shimmering pins framed her bun like the rays of the sun. Her aunts gathered around her, straightening the hem of her sarong, their fingers picking at loose gold threads. For her bersanding, she wore a traditional knee-length tunic made of a woven green and gold fabric over a matching ankle-length sarong. This was the fifth outfit she had donned for the week-long wedding festivities, including two saris and two other *baju kurungs*. A white wedding gown and pale pink Western frock waited on their hangers for an appearance during the reception and dinner party, later in the evening.

'Do you think it will hold?' Sofiah asked, placing a finger on top of the bun.

Her aunt slapped the hand away.

'If you don't touch it.'

'Almost perfect. You just need one more piece,' her eldest aunt Fareeda declared. She unwrapped a braided chain from the cloth in her lap. 'This is from your new mother, my beloved sister-in-law.' She dabbed a handkerchief at the black streaks forming below her eyes. 'I'm sorry. I'm just so happy.'

The other aunts began wailing. They hugged each other, then Sofiah, and then each other again. Anna was tired of witnessing these emotional outbursts. She slipped out of the room before she became the victim of a suffocating embrace.

She ran through the house searching for her father. He would have found a safe haven away from all these embarrassing women. She checked the front yard, where a group of foul-smelling men were setting up an outdoor stage. Her father and brother stood in the corner smoking, overseeing the placement of the tables and chairs.

'Can I have gold pins in my hair, too?' Anna tugged at her father's dinner jacket.

He stopped his conversation and turned his attention to his youngest daughter. 'Have you soiled your dress already? You have curry stains all over your front.'

She looked down at the splattering of orange oil on her chest. 'Cook let me try the mee.'

'Go tell your amah to get you cleaned up. And put on some shoes. You look like a street urchin.'

'But Mama said no shoes in the house.'

'You tell your mother that this is not a backward kampung house. That frock looks ridiculous without shoes.'

'Okay,' she said, delighted at the opportunity to challenge her mother. 'But Papa, can I have gold pins for my hair?'

Red picked up his daughter and examined the loose braid holding her wavy hair.

'I don't see why not. Ask your amah to put up your hair. Tell your aunties to find some nice pins for you.' He kissed her on the forehead and set her back down. 'Now, as for you,' he turned back to her brother, 'I don't see what use a degree from England would be. You won't waste my money on philosophy and classics. I have plenty of books you can read if you want. Philosophy won't help you balance books. You need to finish your apprenticeship. If Rogers treats you like an imbecile, it's probably because you're acting like one. When he tells me that you've mastered the basics of accounting, we'll move you to another area. I'm not going to live forever and I don't want you to run my businesses to the ground as soon as I'm gone.'

Poor Faisal always seemed to be getting into trouble these days. Anna couldn't even recognize her soft-hearted Papa when he spoke to her brother so harshly. As far as she could tell, Faisal did everything Papa asked, and yet he never seemed satisfied.

Faisal bowed his head. 'I'll talk to Rogers on Monday.' Then he turned to Anna and patted the top of her head. 'Get your hairpins and then we'll go see the musicians before the guests arrive.'

Hours later, with her hair coiffed and her dress cleaned, Anna walked behind Sofiah as she descended the stairway, pretending to fuss over her hair and skirt. The seated guests turned to admire the bride as she joined her new husband on a raised platform in the sitting room. The bride and groom perched like exotic birds on the gilded bridal dais, while Anna and a boy cousin fanned them with exaggerated strokes. One by one, the guests of honour approached the platform to offer their blessings.

Poor Sofiah seemed to be wilting under the spotlight. Her nose was turning red and her eyes brimmed with tears as she tried to control the quiver of her lips. Anna aimed her fan at her sister's face, hoping the cool air would calm the flush of her cheeks. The hour stretched on until the last guest finished. Finally, they all poured outside.

Round tables with white linens covered the front yard. The guests murmured their approval of the garden, transformed into an oasis of jasmine blossoms and twinkling lights. A band plucked out a tune and a crew of turbaned waiters emerged from the house, bearing trays of Western, Malay and Indian dishes.

It was well past midnight when the last guests went home. Anna's amah snatched her up and rushed her to bed before she had a chance to say goodbye to her sister or even goodnight to her father. She waited for her amah to leave the room before sneaking downstairs. Red sat hunched over his desk in the library. His hands filed through stacks of paper as he reviewed notations in a black leather notebook. The sleeves of his dress shirt were rolled above his elbows. His gold cufflinks shared an ashtray with a smouldering cigarette.

Anna tiptoed across the room. She had to move quickly before her mother or amah caught her and scolded her for disturbing her father. As she stood on her tiptoes to throw her arms around his neck, his chair swiveled round and knocked her off balance.

'Are you alright?' he said, catching her before she fell. 'What are you doing up so late?'

'I wanted to give you a kiss goodnight,' she explained, confident that he would understand the importance of the interruption.

'Of course, a goodnight kiss.' He planted a soft peck on her nose. 'Now go to bed. It's been a long day.'

'I can't sleep,' she pouted. 'My room is too quiet. I want Sofiah to sing me to sleep.'

'Sofiah's a married woman now. She needs to stay with her husband. Maybe your amah can sing you a song.'

Anna thought of her poor sister spending the night in a strange house with those horrible people. She detested Sofiah's new in-laws. They always pinched her arm and told her what a big girl she was. She didn't want to become a big girl if it meant getting married and moving far away to live with people who pinched your arm.

Her papa turned back to his papers, assuming the nightly ritual was finished. But Anna wasn't ready to return to her empty room. She had never slept without Sofiah's warm body next to hers.

'What are you doing?' she asked.

'I'm just going through the accounts. You can't be too careful. People are always trying to skim a bit for themselves.'

He examined the stack of bills in his hands and then looked at Anna.

'Promise me that when you get married, you're not going to be so frivolous as to demand seven gowns for a single wedding.'

Anna followed her father's eyes from her head to her feet. 'What am I worried about?' he laughed. 'You're more likely to insist on getting married in your play clothes, aren't you?'

She thought of her sister crying herself to sleep every night for the past month.

'I never want to leave you to marry a silly boy like Zainal,' she said.

He picked his daughter up and placed her on his knee.

'Don't worry. When it's your turn, I promise, you will marry for love. Your mother may feel some misplaced obligation to these relatives. But I don't need to barter my children away. Sofiah was a fool to agree to the match. You'll find a young man who can appreciate you. He'll worship you like the morning sun. You won't leave home crying. You'll run to your new life with open arms, forgetting all about your poor old Papa.'

'I don't ever want to get married,' she said. 'I want to stay here with you forever.'

'You can stay here as long as you like,' he told her. 'But right now you need to go back to bed.'

Anna's amah appeared in the door, flustered from the search for her wayward charge.

'Anna, why are you bothering your father?' she scolded in a mixture of English and Malay. 'You must go to bed. It's past midnight.'

Satisfied with her father's promise, Anna kissed his cheek, took her amah's hand, and allowed herself to be led back to bed.

3

June 1934

At the Kedah bus terminal, Rizal hired a car to take him the last few miles home. As he approached the gates of the compound, he rolled down the window to inhale the heady perfume of the frangipani trees lining the drive. The garden was a colourful palette of copper pods, flame of the forest, coral trees, and lilac bungor, all gleaming against a jade jungle backdrop. Ripe rambutan and mangosteen dangled from heavy branches.

Rizal's mother stood watch on the porch of their graceful bungalow, shielding her eyes from the noonday sun. She ran to the edge of the walk and threw open the car door, enveloping her youngest son in a desperate embrace. Then she clasped his face in her hands while her eyes absorbed the changes in her child. He was no longer the scrawny schoolboy who had left for England, seven years ago. Now a grown man of twenty-four, his body had lengthened and fleshed out to full maturity while his round face had stretched to reveal cheekbones with high angular planes.

Her metamorphosis had not been as flattering. Her petite frame had shrunk to the point where Rizal had to wonder about the reliability of her fragile bones. In the years that Rizal had been away, his mother had gained two daughters-in-law and three grandchildren, but lost a husband. Each occasion had been communicated to Rizal through the long-delayed post. The letter informing him of his father's illness contained no indication of the seriousness of his condition. He couldn't remember his father spending even a day in bed. But he accepted the possibility that a man his father's age might be temporarily set back by a chest cold. When the news of his death came, Rizal was entirely unprepared. His brothers, the letter informed him, had performed their funeral duties admirably. They would be taking command of the family business. He was to continue with his studies and complete his law degree at Cambridge. The family was expecting great things from him. His prestigious Queen's scholarship provided him with the opportunity for an education abroad that would have been well beyond his family's means.

His father had earned a respectable living from the store, which supplied European planters with imported necessities such as Belgian chocolates, London papers, girly magazines, and their favourite brands of beer and whisky. Though the planters never blinked at the price of satisfying their eccentric whims, they procrastinated mightily when it came to paying their accounts. As a brown-skinned local, his father could not be so bold as to cut anyone's credit. Instead he became an expert at seeking the patronage of scrupulous payers, cajoling others for installments, stocking the shelves, and modifying his responsiveness according to each customer's creditworthiness. Rizal's brothers did not inherit their father's social or managerial skills. The family business was suffering in their hands.

Everyone sidestepped the issue of Rizal's employment for now. His imported law degree was useless in Kedah, where few businesses could support a full-time lawyer. As a Queen's scholar with a first from Cambridge, he was expected to pursue a career in Singapore or Penang. But he was owed a few months of leisure first.

Rizal spent the next few days trying to connect with his family. In the evening, he chatted with his brothers in the sitting room while their toddlers clung to his legs and their wives plied him with food. None of these interactions served to bridge the divide that had always existed between him and his family. A familial sense of belonging continued to elude him.

On the third morning, the gardener left him a basket of his favourite fruits. He ate mangosteen, durian, rambutan, and langsat until his stomach rebelled. Rizal searched the yard to thank the gardener for the fruit and to find his childhood friend. The gardener's son, Arun, was a few years younger than Rizal, and they were both significantly younger than any of the other boys in the compound. Naturally, they had been childhood playmates. From the time Arun had learned to walk, he had trailed after Rizal. They speared catfish in the stream, shimmied up coconut trees, and went on jungle treks to collect butterflies. Once, they caught a monkey and tied him to a post until he managed to escape by chewing through the rope. The memory of those adventures had sustained Rizal during his bleakest moments away from home.

When Rizal was about twelve, Arun had wandered into the kitchen, hoping to entice him into an afternoon swim. He had found his friend hunched over schoolwork at the dining table. Arun had plucked the book out of Rizal's hands and begun flipping through the pages, examining the illustrations.

'What's this about?' Arun had asked.

'It's a history book about a bunch of dead white kings and queens in a place called Europe.'

Arun had stared at a picture of a fat man in a puffy gown and tights. 'Can you read it to me?' Arun had asked, handing back the book.

Rizal had considered his friend's request and then his impending history examination.

'You need to learn to read. I've got too much schoolwork to do.'

'How am I going to learn to read?' Arun had asked, and his situation struck Rizal for the first time. How *could* he learn to read and write when he was stuck working in the garden all day?

'Maybe I could teach you,' Rizal had offered. 'It's easy once you know the sounds the letters make.'

'What are letters?'

'You see these shapes on the page?' Rizal had said, pointing to the text. 'Each of them is a letter. Letters represent a sound or in some cases several sounds. The letters or sounds form words. Would you like to see your name?'

Rizal had then torn off a sheet of paper from his composition book and written in block letters: 'A R U N. That spells Arun. That's your name.'

Arun had stared at the paper in awe.

'Can I keep it?' he had asked.

'Of course. But it won't seem so special once you learn to write.'

The history exam hadn't been able to compete with his friend's enthusiasm. Rizal had brushed his schoolbooks aside and begun Arun's first lesson. They had spent the next few evenings squatting on the floor of the servant's quarters, writing letters in the dirt. When Arun had learned the entire alphabet, Rizal had presented him with his very own ink pen and composition book, pilfered from the family store. Arun went on to use his prized possessions to record his new vocabulary words with the concentration and precision of a religious scholar.

His math lessons had also begun the day Rizal decided to earn some money selling fruit on the roadside. Rizal taught Arun to count the rambutan as they plucked the hairy red fruit off the trees and piled it into a wheelbarrow. Later, he explained how to add up the charges and count out change.

Arun's father would squat in the doorway and chew his evening betelnut while the boys read together in the fading light.

One evening, as Rizal had been running toward home, late as usual for his evening meal, he had noticed Arun's father hovering in the yard. He had stood near the path but not so close as to be in the way if Rizal cared to pass by without comment. The old man had wanted to say something but wouldn't dare have addressed the little master until he had been spoken to.

'Good evening, Pak,' Rizal had said, using the respectful term for uncle.

'Good evening, Tuan Kecil,' the old man had said, chewing a red wad of betelnut as he considered his words, looking toward the house to make sure that no one was listening. 'I thank you for helping my boy. You have given him a great gift.'

The old man's gratitude had embarrassed him. Rizal hadn't known what to say. School had been his sanctuary. He had been happy to share that world with his best friend. He remembered the first time the schoolmaster had praised his work in front of the class. After years of feeling childish and inept, Rizal had discovered that he was smarter than his older brothers—smarter, in fact, than all the other kids.

'I wish he could go to school with me,' Rizal had said.

Arun's father had smiled. 'You're a good boy,' he said.

Rizal spotted the father and son turning the soil in the vegetable garden. They speared their shovels in the blazing heat, naked except for the cotton sarongs tied around their waists. Sweat glistened on their bare backs. The old man had withered from years of labouring under the hot sun, but his son had grown into a striking, handsome young man. For some reason, Rizal hesitated before making himself visible. He couldn't account for the odd ripple in his chest. The two men finished their work and the father left, wheeling a pile of compost.

Arun leaned on his shovel, watching Rizal approach. He offered no gesture of greeting or benevolence.

'Does Tuan want something?' Arun asked in English.

'Don't call me that. I'm not your master.' Was this a joke? Why was he talking this way?

'Tuan has returned from studies. You are a master of the house.' His words were humble but his tone was almost haughty. Perhaps he was offended that Rizal had never tried to communicate from abroad or that he had waited so long since having returned to seek him out.

Rizal reached for some symbol of connection to apologize for his long absence. 'Tell me, how many tomatoes did you plant?' he asked.

'Thirty-one,' Arun responded, a puzzled arch in his forehead.

'If I were to remove ten of those, how many would be left?'

Arun suppressed the upward curl of his lips. 'I have no time for math problems, Tuan,' he said, his face returning to its blank state. 'I must go to the post office for your mother.'

Arun picked up the dusty shovel and strode off toward the servants' quarters.

The dismissal stung.

4

July 1934

Anna sat at the kitchen table under her mother's watchful eye, embroidering stitches onto a lace handkerchief.

'You see how much your sewing improves when you concentrate?' her mother said. 'A few more practice pieces and you'll be ready to work on your trousseau.'

The hairs on Anna's neck fluttered at the word 'trousseau'. But her lips remained pursed in a mask of concentration.

'Cik Zaharah,' a maid interrupted, 'the men have finished their meal. They're retiring to the front room,' she announced in Malay.

'You sit here and continue with your stitching. I need to go serve the tea.' She flashed a distrustful glare in the direction of her daughter.

When her mother was out of sight, Anna placed her sewing in a basket then lifted the spools of thread hiding a leather-bound novel. She could hear her mother's unspoken lecture, 'You're almost sixteen. Future mothers-in-law are beginning to take notice. How will you ever get married if you can't even sew a handkerchief?' She slid out the kitchen door, past the wet kitchen, and into the back garden. Her eyes scanned the yard for any tattletale servants before settling on the wooden bench under the casuarina tree. She reclined on the bench, arranging her sarong across her curled up legs. Her mind drifted away from the tranquil afternoon setting, into the chilling plot unfolding in the novel.

'I'm sorry, I didn't know anyone was out here,' a voice called from the side gate.

Anna scrambled to her feet. Couldn't she have one moment alone without being discovered? Now her mother would probably confiscate the book and she'd never be able to finish it.

'I didn't mean to interrupt such earnest concentration.' A young Chinese man blinked in the sunlight behind a pair of wire-rimmed spectacles. 'What are you reading?' He let himself in through the side gate and approached her.

'Nothing, just a book.' Her fingers spread across the cover to conceal the lettering.

'A rather engrossing book, it looks like. Can I have a look?'

She inched her fingers away so that he could read the title.

'*Crime and Punishment*.' he laughed. 'That's quite a dark novel for such a fair lady.'

The selection had been unusual. She normally chose her reading from her Grandmother Parker's section of the library. A woman she knew only as a floral scrawl on the nameplates, her grandmother must have shared her weakness for romantic novels. Anna loved fantasizing about her own Mr Darcy or Heathcliff. But lately, she had been trying to expand her horizons, as much as one could in a walled garden, by reading some of her father's favourites.

'My father lets me read all the books in his study,' she said. 'I've already read several books by Dostoevsky and Tolstoy.' For some reason, she wanted to impress this young man with her worldly knowledge.

'I see, a fan of the Russians. Have you read *War and Peace*?'

'Not yet.' She made a mental note to find that one next.

'I haven't read it either.' He stretched his hand to meet hers. 'I'm Boo Tong.'

'Pleased to meet you. I'm Anna.'

'I know. Your brother Faisal and I were classmates. It's lovely to finally meet you. But I didn't mean to disturb you. Please continue with your novel. I'll just stand here and admire the scenery.' The motion of his arms indicated the garden but his eyes remained fixed on Anna. She couldn't continue reading with this young man staring at her.

'Wouldn't you prefer to be inside talking about important things with the men?' she asked, lowering her feet off the bench into a more ladylike pose.

'What important things? All they talk about is money. My father drags me to these meetings every now and then, to try my patience.'

'Aren't you interested in business?' She'd never met a man who wasn't.

'No, I'm a doctor, or at least I will be, soon,' he said.

'You're too young to be a doctor.' Doctors did not have unlined faces, clear brown eyes, and thick full hair.

'I'm in medical school in Singapore. I'm on holiday for a few weeks, visiting my family.'

'Your father let you go all the way to Singapore to study?'

She clutched her book to her chest, imagining the freedom to wander into lecture rooms and engage in stimulating discussions. What she knew of school, she had learned from her brother. She had attended the Convent Light School for Girls for just two years until her mother had decided that the nuns and all those Christian girls were corrupting her morals. Zaharah had insisted that her daughters be taught at home by teachers who cared more about their posture than their perceptions. Her brother's education fell firmly in her father's domain. Faisal did not attend his grandfather's madrasah, as his mother would have preferred. He received a superior Western education with the elite of Penang at St. Xavier's Boys' School.

'He's more than happy to get rid of me. He already has one son and a nephew embroiled in the family business.'

'I wish I could study in Singapore,' Anna said. 'I think I'd study literature. Are there any courses that let you read all the great books?'

'Some schools offer a degree in the classics, but that really only covers European classics. They leave out some of the most important books in the world.'

'Like what?' she asked.

'Like Chinese literature, for example.'

'I've never read any Chinese literature. Is it interesting?'

'Some of it is breathtakingly beautiful. But it's hard to find good translations. I have a few at school. I'd be happy to send you some, if you'd like.'

'Annnnnaaaaa,' her mother called from the kitchen, 'where are you? I can't leave you alone for two minutes.'

'Excuse me,' Anna said, as she hopped to her feet and ran into the kitchen. 'Nice to meet you,' she called over her shoulder.

5

July 1934

'It's time we talked about your future,' Rizal's mother announced. His brothers sat supporting her like bookends, their arms folded across their chests, their heads bobbing up and down.

'Your brothers and I discussed possible positions at the store.' His mother turned to her eldest son for reinforcement. 'But any work there would be a waste of your degree. Your father's dying wish was that you return home from your studies and find a suitable job in a prosperous firm.'

Rizal sat back in his chair glancing from his pensive mother to his silent brothers, waiting to hear about his future. The decision about his employment would have been finalized long before they would have decided to speak to him about it.

'I've written to my brother, Ibrahim,' she continued. 'He says that he can put your talents to use at one of his companies. He offered a generous salary and even suggested that you stay in his home.' Tears threatened to break loose but she forced her way through the prepared speech. 'You wouldn't need to leave right away. You should stay until the end of the month, at least.'

There was no use fighting the inevitable. But maybe he could find a way to make the prospect more palatable. He couldn't stay in his uncle's compound with all those relatives. What he wanted was to be alone, to make his own home where he wouldn't have to answer to anyone.

'That's very generous of Uncle,' he said. 'I'd be happy to accept the position but I wouldn't want to inconvenience his family. I can find my own accommodations.'

'He'll insist,' she said, 'And rightfully so. It's only proper that you stay with family. We can't have you living on your own like an orphan.'

Well, perhaps it would be better to fight this battle from afar. He agreed to stay with his uncle until he settled into his new job. He offered his mother a willing smile. The maid, who had been eavesdropping from the kitchen, cleared her throat to indicate that their dinner was ready. They ladled out a steaming bowl of his favourite laksa noodles, a loving apology from his heavy-hearted mother.

Before he could finish his dinner, a nagging pain inched up his spine in the direction of his neck. He turned his head from side to side, trying to loosen the stiff knot forming in his shoulders. After dinner, he retired to bed, hoping a good night's sleep would ward off the growing tremor in his limbs.

By morning, a fever had transformed him into a limp rag. When he didn't come down for breakfast, his mother sent Arun to tap on his door. Rizal tried to answer but his tongue wouldn't form the words.

'Tuan is *sakit*,' Arun pronounced as soon as he saw Rizal's pale figure. 'I'll get your mother.'

His mother begged his brothers to call a doctor. The haughty Englishman showed up thirty minutes late, still in his polo breeches, and demanded payment before demonstrating any value. After a cursory examination, the esteemed physician informed the family gathered in the sitting room that Rizal had a fever, a fact that had been obvious even to the uneducated maids. He provided them with pills to bring the temperature down but they had no effect. Dissatisfied with the Western medicine, his mother decided to call in a *bomoh*. The bomoh with a trailing gray beard accepted her monetary offerings on behalf of the spirit world. He sat cross-legged on the floor behind a haze of incense and chanted incantations to the spirits. When he was finished, he promised her that the spirits would oblige and Rizal would be healed by morning, but he only grew worse.

When he wasn't delirious from the fever, he was immobilized by abdominal pain. A rash covered his chest and limbs. He tried to get out of bed but he couldn't move his arms or raise his legs. His throat was parched but his mind seemed disconnected from the hand that needed to reach for the carafe on the nightstand. The sudden betrayal of his body filled him with terror. He had spent his life obsessed with maintaining control over his every thought and action, and now he couldn't even force his eyes open.

By the third week, he lost his grip on his mind as hallucinations merged with lucid moments. His mother huddled by his bedside, weeping into her hands. Arun came and went with trays of untouched tea and rice. Finally, one morning, he woke with the remarkable sensation of a cool breeze drifting across his body. The darkened room held no clues as to the time of day. He raised his arm to see if it was still trembling. He placed his bare feet on the floor and slowly lowered his weight onto them. His legs managed to carry him to the washroom, where he peeled off his damp clothes. Then he ladled cold water from the washbasin over his head, rinsing away the layers of sweat.

After his bath, he stretched out naked on the bed, reclaiming his body from weeks of inactivity. He was still shaken by the sudden turn in his health. And yet, the experience left him strangely exhilarated with an overwhelming sense of gratitude for the wondrous serendipity of his own existence. Life was brief, capricious and magnificent. He would make the most of whatever time he was granted.

Arun entered the room with a pot of tea. He moved toward the bed and studied his friend's form. 'Good morning, Tuan. You look much better today,' he whispered in Malay.

Rizal reached for Arun's waist and pulled him onto the bed. His fingers loosened the bothersome sarong and tossed it onto the floor. Arun's cool, damp skin extinguished the last flames of the stubborn fever.

6

September 1934

In the stifling air of the sitting room, Anna couldn't be sure whether it was the oppressive heat or her mother's suffocating presence that caused the bead of sweat to trickle down the bridge of her nose onto the embroidery hoop. She pushed a damp curl away from her eyes and anchored it behind her ear.

Her mother had insisted on another round of beadwork. Anna was expected to complete two practice slippers before moving on to the more complex patterns purchased for her trousseau. Those ridiculous slippers were entirely impractical to walk in. Nothing held the shoes to the feet except a little strap of beadwork at the toe so a clomping heel announced your presence wherever you walked.

At least Penangites didn't go in for foot binding. She occasionally caught sight of old Chinese ladies shuffling along the street on tiny stubs, requiring the assistance of their daughters to manoeuvre from their chauffeur-driven cars to the entrance of shop houses. On the other hand, the notion of a feeble mother did hold a certain appeal. She stabbed the beading with such ferocity that her needle slipped and poked the end of her finger.

She licked the drop of blood it drew.

'Open the windows, Mama, I can't breathe.'

'The rain will blow in,' her mother said. 'Just focus on your stitching and stop biting your nails. Your fingers look like shredded rags.'

Anna felt the rush of fresh air as her father entered the room. A puddle was forming where water dripped off his suit onto the tiles below.

'What happened to you?' Zaharah asked.

'I got caught in the downpour. I came back to change before heading to the club.'

'You shouldn't go out on a night like this.' Her mother said the words with a sigh that betrayed the knowledge of how little weight her opinion carried.

Red dismissed her anxieties with a wave of his hand. Then remembering the stack of mail under his arm, he pulled out a package and handed it to Anna.

'This is addressed to you.'

Anna took the parcel from her father. It was still sealed. Her mother wouldn't have shown such restraint.

'Who is it from?' Zaharah asked as her suspicious eyes locked onto the package.

Anna unwrapped the paper in front of her parents because this was expected of her. Privacy was a privilege accorded only to the adults in the Parker household. Offspring, whatever their age, were never considered adults.

She removed the last layer of tissue paper to reveal a novel bound in red with gold lettering.

'*A Dream of Red Mansions*,' Red read the title over her shoulder. 'Never heard of it.'

'A friend recommended it to me,' Anna lied. 'I asked the bookstore to order it.'

Red seemed to accept the explanation. 'I've got to change,' he said. 'I'm already late and the road'll be hell in this weather. Let me know if it's any good.'

'What?' Anna asked.

'The book. Let me know if it's any good.' He shook his head but chose not to pursue the topic, for the moment at least. He climbed the stairs to his room with a maid trailing behind, wiping his watery footsteps.

Her mother continued to stare at the novel. She was generally suspicious of books and their indecipherable content, all the more so since her daughter and husband couldn't seem to keep their noses out of them. The only trustworthy book, in Zaharah's opinion, was the Quran, and even that hallowed text was best left to venerable religious scholars to interpret.

'I think I'll just take my stitching to my room,' Anna said. She threw the novel in her sewing basket and rose to make her escape. She walked to her room, closing the door on her mother's prying eyes. When she was satisfied that she would not be followed, she stretched across her bed and examined the book. Her fingers turned the pages, looking for a note or message. She found an inscription in blue ink scrawled across the cover page:

To Anna,
A beautiful novel for a beautiful girl.

Khoo Boo Tong

She read the words over and over, infusing them with wondrous significance. Nobody had ever told her she was beautiful. In her mother's family, it was considered bad form to compliment a child. Her mother said it was unseemly to dwell on something as shallow as one's physical appearance. Still, she sometimes wondered if others might think she was beautiful. She spent more time than she cared to admit staring in the mirror contemplating her physical merits. Sometimes she could be quite pleased with her reflection. She was not as fair as the European ladies but her eyes were unusually light. Paired with the right accessories, the blue-gray could look almost translucent. Her figure was still slender, not like poor Sofiah, who had puffed up after childbirth and never quite whittled back down. Her freckles were faint enough to ignore most of the time. If she had tried to cover them with powder as the English girls did, her mother would have called her out immediately.

It was her hair that pleased her most. As a child, her mother had tried to suppress the waves in braids, then later in a tight bun. But the curls would always break loose in messy clusters. In the end, her mother gave up and let her wear her hair down. The victory of Anna's curls marked her first real triumph over her mother's will.

7

February 1935

On the twelfth day of the Chinese New Year, Tong's family hosted their annual party at their seaside mansion. Tong's father and uncle, embracing the Western penchant for ostentatious displays of wealth, had built Seascape, their elaborate Italianate villa on Northam Road, at the height of their prosperity. A line of motorcars waited in front of the ornate wrought-iron gates for the privilege of dropping their bejeweled occupants under a glass canopy. The Khoo Open House was always a lavish affair that included several live bands, a marionette show and a Chinese opera. Guests gathered on the formal grounds, filling their plates from the extravagant buffet, their crystal glasses overflowing with whisky, fine wines and champagne.

All the important members of the Chinese community had arrived in their dark Western suits, accessorized by the vibrant kebayas worn by their wives. The usual collection of European administrators in white and cream silks meandered on the lawn, accompanied by their pale wives in pastel frocks. Members of the Kedah royal family strolled near the lotus ponds, all ablaze in robes of bright yellow. A few visiting dignitaries mingled with the Penang elite, including a Siamese prince, a Russian surgeon and two Japanese diplomats.

The sun began to make its westward slant, casting the party in golden hues. The lights of the mainland flickered across the water like fireflies in the evening sky. A westerly wind ruffled the ladies' dresses and a sudden gust sent a few scurrying after their hats. Tong spotted

Red and his son Faisal with an American hotelier near the western pavilion. Red's unbuttoned dinner jacket flapped in the ocean breeze.

'Tong, wonderful to see you.' Red seemed relieved by the interruption. 'I didn't realize you were in town.'

'I'm just back for the holidays,' Tong said.

'You must have been very busy assisting with the preparations for this grand affair.'

'I'm afraid I've been playing the dandy, lazing around the pool and catching up with old friends.'

'There's enough in this garden to keep a person entertained for days,' Red said. 'I just made my way down to the beach. There's a huge passenger ship coming into the harbour. Puts my little fleet to shame.'

'Those floating monstrosities never make any money,' Faisal interjected. 'I've always suspected that the men who strive to own the biggest ships, the tallest buildings, or the grandest mansions are just compensating for lack of size elsewhere.'

Red tossed a warning glance at his tipsy son. Faisal's remarks were perhaps insulting to a man like Tong, who inhabited such an opulent estate.

But Tong wasn't offended. 'How are you, Faisal? It's been awhile.' He offered his hand to his old classmate. Then, no longer able to contain himself, he asked the question that had been occupying his mind all afternoon.

'How's the rest of your family? Did your wife or Anna accompany you today?'

'They are in your mother's parlour, catching up with the latest gossip,' Faisal said.

Red looked like he was about to laugh. Instead, he put his hand to his mouth and coughed. The coughing overtook his body, forcing him to double over. Tong heard the distinctive wheeze of damaged lungs.

'You should see someone about that cough,' he said.

'Already did. Claims I'm healthy as an ox. But speaking of healthy oxen, I should find your father to pay my respects. Is he in the reception hall?'

Tong walked the Parkers to the west wing, where his father was receiving his New Year's guests. They passed the arched columns and entered the Chinese section of the home, with its Ming chairs of carved blackwood and inlaid mother of pearl, silk carpets, ancient scrolls and marble-topped tables. The family's two prized possessions flanked the hall: a portrait of Tong's grandfather seated with his friend, Sun Yat-sen, and a framed bill, reportedly the first dollar earned by his grandfather after he bought his freedom. Tong never liked that framed bill or the notion that money should be revered—no matter how tainted the source.

Tong's grandfather had arrived in British Malaya as a coolie, digging in a tin mine twelve hours a day. He was one of the few who survived long enough to buy his freedom, his ambition amplified by the fact that he was the last surviving son in his family. He needed to endure in order to guarantee that his ancestors would continue to be taken care of in the afterlife and the family line would remain unbroken.

After securing his freedom, he cultivated connections among the Khoo clan and the powerful triad to which it was allied. In return for his loyal service, he secured a major contract importing coolies from China, eventually expanding his business to finance gambling houses and brothels. But his real fortune was earned by securing a monopoly on the opium trade in the tin towns.

Tong's father and brother had solidified their standing by marrying sisters from an established Baba Nyonya family, who could trace their lineage in Malaya back to the seventeenth century. The brothers eventually diversified their inheritance into more acceptable pursuits such as banking and property speculation. But Tong suspected they were still involved in plenty of unsavoury enterprises.

Tong left the Parkers in the hall and made his way to his mother's parlour where most of the women had gathered. The heavy odor of imported perfumes greeted him as he entered the large airy parlour decorated with European fabrics, Victorian lamps and Venetian chandeliers. Feminine sounds filled the air: high-pitched laughter, the soft tinkle of jewelry and the clatter of teacups placed on saucers. Tong's mother held court in the centre of the room, her elegant beauty and refined manners on display for all to admire. Secure in her proud Nyonya heritage, she communicated in quiet gestures, leaving the clamorous conversation to the others. She wore a sheer lilac kebaya with an intricate butterfly motif embroidered on the collar, hem and sleeves. A floral purple sarong hugged her small waist. Delicate jewelry complimented her milky complexion and petite features. Her dark hair was piled high in a coiled bun secured with three golden combs in typical Nyonya style. Her dainty sister, Ah Ee, sat next to her in coordinated attire. Their mother-in-law, Tong's paternal grandmother, reclined on the neighbouring chaise, her glassy eyes fixed on a faraway vision. She wore the sickly complexion and sunken stupor of an opium addict.

The three matriarchs were surrounded by the aunties, his father's three sisters, who clung to his family's fortune like barnacles to an ocean liner. His mother tilted her head in Tong's direction, to indicate that he should join them. Tong reluctantly approached. He generally avoided his paternal aunts, the eyes and ears of his father's domain.

Tong's eldest and most ample aunt pulled a red packet of cash from her beaded handbag and dangled it in front of him. The children called her Tua Koh, or father's eldest sister, but behind her back, they referred to her as Tua Pek, father's eldest brother, because her broad face and beefy limbs were more suited to a man than a woman.

'Tong,' she teased, 'aren't you going to come get your ang pow?'

'Please, Tua Koh,' he said, 'save the packet for one of the children. I'm too old for that.'

'Nonsense. You're not married yet.' Her smile exposed red gums permanently stained from her betel nut habit. 'You should take your ang pow now because this may be the last year I can offer it to you.'

Tong blushed as he accepted the packet.

His second aunt, the most egregious of the informants, greeted him with a smile and a gentle bit of prying. 'How are your studies going? I hear you'll be opening your practice in Penang soon.'

His emotions felt so overpowering that evening, he worried his eerily perceptive aunt might somehow be able to decipher his clandestine thoughts. He decided it would be safest to throw her off the trail with a distracting bit of gossip.

'Actually, I'm not opening a private practice,' he informed her. 'I'm applying for a position at the Mission Hospital,' he clarified. 'I'm hoping to start with them when I return.' He let them chew on that unpalatable tidbit for a while.

The three aunts were visibly aghast at the unsightly prospect of their nephew humbly serving the poor and undeserving at a charity hospital. Before they could utter their objections, his little niece Mei appeared to collect her ang pow.

'Keong Hee Huat Chai,' Mei wished them a happy new year as she twirled to allow the women to admire her new red dress.

Tong waited until their attention was completely focussed on his precocious niece before slipping away. He continued to search the room until he spotted the back of a blue taffeta dress draped with auburn curls, headed toward the verandah. He checked to make sure his aunts weren't watching before following.

Anna stood on the porch, staring past the guests into the open sea as if searching for an escape from the tedium of her surroundings. He walked up behind her and stood for a moment, enjoying her scent, an alluring combination of jasmine and vanilla.

'Did you receive my parcel?' he finally asked.

Anna turned, startled by the interruption in her reverie. Was it his imagination, or did her eyes brighten when she saw him?

'Yes,' she told him. 'It was so thoughtful of you to remember our conversation.' She touched his arm with a gentle, unaffected gesture.

'I couldn't forget it even if I tried,' he admitted. 'I tracked you down to find out what you thought of the novel.'

'The illustrations were charming,' she said. 'And the prose was pure poetry.'

'But what did you think of the story?'

'Well, it was very rich in detail . . . and the characters were interesting . . .'

'You didn't like it?' He was surprised at the depth of his disappointment. How could she have been less than enthralled by his favourite book?

'Well, I guess I didn't like the ending,' she admitted. 'I thought it was silly that Daiyu died because Bayou married someone else. I mean, she was supposed to be an intelligent, noble heroine and she just withered away. It wasn't believable. People don't really die of a broken heart, do they?'

'It's not a condition we cover in medical school, if that's what you mean,' he laughed.

'Exactly. I mean in reality, life goes on, doesn't it. People make do.' She gestured toward the women in the parlour as if to illustrate her point.

'You might be right. But I don't mind suspending belief for a good romance. After all, isn't that what books are for? To allow the reader to experience a dramatic life without having to suffer the consequences?'

'Well, if I wrote a novel, my heroine would be stronger than that. She would know how to carry on. She would make the best of things.'

'If you wrote a novel,' he said, 'I would love to read it.'

Firecrackers punctuated the night with their explosive crackle. The smell of charred paper wafted toward them. She turned her head to watch the fireworks dance across the sky while he positioned himself so he could continue taking in her profile. He wanted to memorize her image to take back with him to school so he could conjure it up in the dismal quiet of his dormitory bed. The night air felt so charged, he almost feared an electric shock if he touched her. He wanted to tell her how he thought of her every day. He had prepared countless conversations in his head but in this moment, his voice refused to break the spell of their companiable silence.

He waited until the final rocket burst, then turned to her, determined to continue their discussion, when he saw Faisal's wife, Mina, heading toward them. He had to do something quickly.

'I'll tell you what,' he said. 'I'll send you some more of my favourite classics and then you can write to me and tell me what you think.'

'You don't have to go to all that trouble.'

'I'd like an excuse to write to you.'

Maybe he was being too forward but he couldn't go back to Singapore without making some stab at a connection with her. She didn't blush or shrink at his suggestion. Maybe she misunderstood his intentions or maybe she was used to the impertinent attention of bumbling suitors.

'There you are,' Mina interrupted. 'The fireworks have finished. We should go down and find Faisal and Papa on the lawn.'

Anna allowed herself to be led away, turning her head only once to offer Tong a parting smile.

8

Stacks of paper lined the mahogany conference table where Rizal sat with his Uncle Ibrahim. Next to them were Ibrahim's son Hafis and nephew Faisal, their heads bent over the pages of a bound report.

When Rizal arrived in Penang six months ago, Ibrahim had given him a small, probably hopeless assignment to seek damages for the loss of a light boat and its cargo after a collision with a Dutch steamer. Rizal was able to win a hefty settlement by showing that the steamer had not followed the required safety protocols when guiding the steamer to port. The favourable resolution and Rizal's triumph over the team of haughty European lawyers got Ibrahim's attention.

His uncle began inviting Rizal to join him at the club. Ibrahim presented him to the inner circle of businessmen as a Queen's Scholar with a first from Cambridge who was performing legal wonders. The men were impressed by his credentials and the exceptional endorsement. He knew that he should be more grateful for the attention from his uncle, but the more time Ibrahim spent with Rizal, the more he shunned his own son.

Two months ago, Ibrahim had asked Rizal to help draft a new contract with Red's shipping line. Hafis had worked on an earlier version of the contract, which Ibrahim had dismissed as a convoluted mess. The shipping line, now under the management of Red's son Faisal, was pushing for better turnaround times in the harbour. After weeks of negotiation, Rizal was able to reach an agreement that would benefit both companies. The two young men had come today to present their joint recommendations to their uncle and Hafis.

'Excellent work,' Ibrahim said. His fists tapped the table like an auctioneer closing a transaction. 'Thank you both for your input. I think this new contract will be of significant benefit to both our companies.'

He stood to shake hands with Faisal and Rizal, pointedly ignoring his own son.

'Rizal, I'd like you to come to a meeting tomorrow morning with the operations manager of my trading company. We could use your talents over there. We haven't had reliable counsel in years.'

'I'd be happy to meet him, but I'm not really a trading expert.'

'I don't need an expert,' Ibrahim said, 'just a little common sense.'

Hafis sulked in his chair. The trading company was theoretically his responsibility. Ibrahim was clearly pushing Rizal further into Hafis's territory by inviting him to look at the trading company. It was just a matter of time before Hafis sought his revenge.

'Enough of this work,' Faisal announced when the others had left. 'Let's go see the China dolls on parade.'

Faisal had become Rizal's guide to Penang nightlife. Faisal loved life with the compulsion of an addict, and his enthusiasm was contagious. He took Rizal under his wing and showed him all the rowdy island nightspots—dances, cabarets and boria shows. Though Rizal always returned with empty pockets, he never regretted the adventures. Tonight, Faisal had promised to take him to the famous Chap Goh Meh parade, where the Chinese maidens went on display on the fifteenth day of their new year.

The driver took them a few blocks toward the centre of town until the car couldn't go any further. They continued on foot to Bishop Street, where the industrious manager of Pritchard's department store had placed chairs on his pavement, hoping to draw parade watchers and their wallets inside. They found an empty table with two seats under the overhang.

A procession of cars and rickshaws paraded by, filled with the year's eligible Chinese girls arrayed in their finest clothing and jewelry. The crowds on the sidewalk threw handfuls of red confetti at the girls. A few of the bolder boys followed the floats, serenading their selected beauty with promises of undying love. The girls ignored the raucous suitors. They kept their eyes focussed on the oranges cradled in their hands.

Faisal spotted some friends in the crowd and motioned them over. Two dapper Chinese men approached the table, wearing the latest European styles—wide white trousers, silk shirts and Monte Carlo shoes. Rizal hoped they didn't look too closely at his attire. At least his old-fashioned loafers covered his tattered socks.

The proprietor promptly appeared with two more chairs for the young men.

'You two find any suitable brides tonight?' Faisal asked them as he adjusted his own chair to get a better view of the parade.

'Too many to choose from. I can't decide.' The speaker held out his hand to Rizal. 'I'm Boo Seng.'

'These are two of my old schoolmates, the Khoo cousins, Boo Seng and Boo Tong. They live in one of the castles on Northam Road,' Faisal said.

Seng and Tong were both tall and lanky, but Tong was fairer and more delicate-looking. He had a long face held together by a pair of wire spectacles.

'Rizal's been working with me at the firm. He's a lawyer. One of our Queen's Scholars,' Faisal said, winking at Rizal. 'These two went to school with me. Maybe if you're really nice to them, they'll invite you to play at their house. They have a swimming pool that looks like it belongs in the movies and a game room that would put most casinos to shame.'

'You're welcome any time,' Seng promised. 'But tonight the pleasures are to be found on the floats. Someone find me a girl, please. She must be dazzlingly beautiful, delicate and soft like the finest flower, sugary with a hint of spice.'

'You're married,' Tong reminded him.

'It's never too early to start looking for the next victim,' Seng joked.

'How about that one?' suggested Faisal, pointing to a rosy-cheeked girl with wide-set eyes. 'She looks promising. Nice complexion, pretty face.'

The girl in question was watching the crowd from the safety of an open car. When she noticed the group of men staring and pointing, she hid her face in her hands as though she might burst out crying.

'Never mind,' Faisal said, 'we'll find another for you.'

'Hey, did you hear the one about the disappointed bridegroom?' Seng asked.

'Which disappointed bridegroom? There are so many,' Faisal said.

'This poor slob fell head over heels for a beautiful maiden he saw in the parade. He took down her car number, looked up her family and asked his mother to send a matchmaker to her house. What he didn't realize was that the fair damsel he had seen was not the daughter of the house, but a niece. On his wedding day, the poor chap threw back the bridal veil only to discover that he had married the fat, plain cousin of the beauty.'

'Maybe he was better off with the cousin,' Tong said, 'rather than a piece of confectionery that would probably grow stale with age.'

'Must you always be so contrary?' Seng chided. 'There's nothing wrong with a little candy now and then. If it grows stale, you just go back to the store and pick another.'

Tong felt sorry for these girls, who spent all year hidden in their homes only to be thrust into this parade like caged birds on display. Anna would never allow herself to be part of such a humiliating event.

Where had this ridiculous tradition come from? Did they celebrate Chap Goh Meh the same way in China? Was Sze-yin being paraded in her neighbourhood that very evening? He had only seen her picture once, in a ridiculously formal photo. Her coiffed hair and thickly powdered face were so unnatural, he would never recognize her in person. Not that he would ever bump into her on the street. His introduction to his future bride would not be that spontaneous.

9

March 1935

Anna walked down the stairs, still groggy from her nap. Her hands gripped the teak railing. She had lost all her energy to the afternoon heat. Maybe a cooling bath would help brace her for the tedious music lesson.

'There's a package for you on the table,' her mother called from the sitting room.

Anna entered the room and picked up the brown parcel resting on a stack of letters. The return address was from Singapore. Anna's heart performed an involuntary flutter.

'What is it, Anna?' her mother called.

'Just some books I ordered.'

'Come say hello to Puan Sharizat,' her mother said.

Anna tucked the package under her arm and crossed the room.

'Salam, Auntie,' Anna murmured as she bent down and touched the woman's wrinkled feet. Puan Sharizat was the wife of a councilman, whose father was somehow related to Anna's grandfather. She could never keep track of these tenuous connections that everyone else seemed to have committed to memory.

'Salam, Anna. You're looking lovely as always.'

Sharizat's eyes swept up and down Anna's figure. She wouldn't be surprised if the old woman pinched her flesh like a piece of fruit at the market.

'Your mother was just showing me some of your embroidery. You have a good eye for colour.'

'Thank you, Auntie,' she answered.

'Would you like to hear Anna play the piano?' Zaharah asked. 'Her teacher tells us that she's a natural.'

Sharizat's eagle stare took in Anna's crumpled sarong and dishevelled hair before fixing on her chewed-up fingernails.

'I'd love to, but I'm afraid I must be getting back. Perhaps another time. It was lovely to see you again, Anna.'

Dismissed from the examination, Anna made her way upstairs, pausing at the top to eavesdrop on the conversation.

'Are you sure she's well?' Sharizat asked.

'Anna is the picture of health,' Zaharah insisted. 'She just woke up from a nap. The heat can be quite wearing.'

'I see. Nothing wrong with a little rest in the afternoon,' Puan Sharizat said, the condemnation barely concealed in her voice.

'It was very kind of you to stop by. Please give my regards to your family,' Zaharah said, bringing the failed interview to a close.

Anna slipped into her room and closed the door. Why did her mother persist in these pointless charades? She would never agree to marry any of the awkward men her mother kept dangling before her. They were all spoiled simpletons who wanted to lock her up in their house to wait on their mothers and produce their babies. Her father had promised that she could marry for love and that is what she intended to do. Tong would be graduating from medical school at the end of the year. She pictured herself as a doctor's wife ministering at his side.

Her fingers tore the brown wrapper from the package.

Dearest Anna,

I hope that you enjoy this selection of poems from the T'ang dynasty. I think this collection provides a flavour of the most celebrated poets of the Golden Age of Chinese literature. I love the reflective nature of the period. I sometimes worry that the more society progresses, the more we leave behind. I would not, for a moment, want to return to a time before modern medicine or motorcars, but all this rushing around does make it harder to stop and contemplate the simple beauty of life.

I think about our discussion often. I am perhaps guilty of overindulging my romantic tendencies, but I thought you appreciated our conversation as well. I would like to know what you think of the poems. Perhaps you could find a few moments to send me a reply. Even a line or two would immeasurably brighten my desolate days.

Yours Sincerely,
Khoo Boo Tong

10

April 1935

It took Anna two weeks to work up the courage to send a reply. She slipped out the door one morning, after her mother had left to visit an ailing relative. She ran down the street and ducked around the corner. A young rickshaw-puller bolted across the road, his cheerful expression belying the sorry state of his sun hat and sarong. He looked to be about her age, with deeply tanned skin and long wavy hair.

'I'd like to go to the post office,' she said in the most authoritative voice she could muster.

He stared at her blankly through a lock of mangy hair. So she tried again, this time in Malay.

'Saya nak pergi ke the post. Ke Downing Street.'

'Dua puluh.' He grinned as he pronounced the outrageous sum.

'Empat belas,' she countered. Still more than she should have paid, but she wanted to get off the street as quickly as possible and he did have a friendly smile.

He doubled himself over between the shafts in an exaggerated bow to lower the carriage for her. She climbed in and closed the bonnet to shield herself from prying eyes. He lifted the carriage, glanced over his shoulder, and then took off like a racehorse down the street.

The puller ran through the leafy suburbs, dotted with spacious bungalows and manicured gardens, his shoulders moving in smooth rhythmic motions, only the perspiration on his back indicating how hard he was working.

The exhilaration of the ride made her forget her anxiety until they turned onto Downing Street and her heart fell to her stomach. She had been to the post office several times with her father, but she had never before tried to mail her own letter. They arrived at the massive colonial complex on the edge of the promontory, an imposing concrete sentinel standing guard over the harbour. Anna paid the rickshaw driver, who flashed a smile and took off down the street. She walked to the entrance and stared at the arched double doors. A turbaned guard eyed her suspiciously. He had probably never seen a nervous postal customer before. She took a deep breath, then pushed open the doors. The noise from the street echoed through the chamber, causing a few customers to look in her direction. The cavernous space with its polished white floors and arched marble columns amplified the slightest sound. She crept to the back of the room and waited for her eyes to adjust. Fortunately, the building was fairly empty and she didn't see anyone she recognized.

'May I help you?' the speckled clerk asked as Anna approached the counter.

'Yes, I would like to mail a letter, please.' Her voice crackled with the fear rising in her throat.

He took the package from her and eyed the address.

'To Singapore,' he announced as he placed the parcel on the scale. 'First class?'

'Yes,' she said. She had no idea what the other options might be.

'Six cents.'

Anna reached into her purse and counted out the change. The clerk examined each coin then attached the postage and marked it with a red stamp.

'Will that be all?' the clerk asked as she continued to hover over his counter.

'Yes, that's all. Thank you,' she uttered before fleeing outside.

She leaned against the doors waiting for her hands to stop shaking and her breath to return to normal before she waved down another rickshaw to take her home. That wasn't so hard. No one had seen her come or go. No one would ever know, except Tong. The tremor threatened to return to her body. But it was not fear of discovery that agitated her now. It was the thought of Tong.

11

April 1935

Rizal tore open the envelope he had been anticipating for days. His mother must have consulted everyone in Kedah before deciding his fate.

Dearest Rizal,

I was so pleased to hear the news of your promotion. Your father would have been proud to know what an accomplished young man you have become. I have discussed your proposal with Ibrahim and your brothers. Ibrahim insists that your presence is no burden but he was not offended by the idea of you finding your own residence. I can imagine the house must be getting quite crowded with all his grandchildren.

The increase in salary should allow for modest accommodations but you must promise me that you will not spend all of your wages on rent. Remember to save for your future. Now that you have established yourself in your profession, it is time to think about starting a family.

Once you have found a place to live, I will send Arun, as you requested. He will make a fine houseboy. His parents have been loyal and hardworking contributors to our household. I will sleep well knowing that he is looking after you.

Please continue to write. I look forward to your letters and worry when I have not heard from you in a while. I thank Allah every day for your well-being.

Love,
Amma

12

August 1935

Anna waited on the portico every afternoon for the car to pull up to the circular drive. She greeted their driver, careful to sound as casual as possible, as if she just happened to be standing in the doorway at that moment, enjoying the breeze.

'I can take those from you,' she offered, holding out her hand to receive the stack of letters.

'Terima kasih. Does Puan Zaharah need me?'

'I'll check. Wait here.'

Anna slipped in through the door and riffled through the mail, willing her name to appear on one of the letters or parcels. Sometimes she found a book of poetry or a novel, always with a letter tucked inside. Occasionally, he sent a letter without the cover of a bound document. Today, her name was scrawled across a small square package. She tucked it in her sleeve and ran to find her mother.

'Mama,' she called as she walked to the kitchen. 'Chandru wants to know if you need him for anything.'

'Could you ask him to stop by the tailors' to see if Papa's suit is ready?' She looked up from her tea. 'Anna, are you alright? You look a little flushed.'

'I'm fine. It must be the heat.'

'Ask Cook to pour you some water. You really should stay inside this time of day.'

Anna delivered the message to Chandru and then fled to the garden to examine her package. She opened the parcel and found a white box with a silver necklace inside. The chain held a small pendant, the shape of a snowflake, with a dainty sapphire suspended in the centre. Anna had been surrounded by gemstones since birth. Penang women loved their jewelry. A husband might prove undependable—only gems could guarantee a woman's financial future. This necklace lacked flash, but to Anna, it was the most precious piece she had ever seen.

She checked the garden once more for servants and then clasped the chain around her neck, tucking the charm beneath her undergarments.

A piece of paper fluttered to the ground.

If I could be a single snowflake
Fluttering free in the currents of air
My destination would still be clear
Drifting, drifting, drifting—
Here on earth my place would be clear.

No forsaken lonely valley
No wooded hillside cold and still
Nor to the empty alley's chill
Drifting, drifting, drifting—
I'd have my destination still!

In my graceful airborne swirling
I'd spy the sweet place of her abode
Wait till she walked in a garden glade—
Drifting, drifting, drifting—
Ah hers the fragrance of plum-blossom shade!

At last in the liberty of my lightness
Gently I'd lodge in the bosom of her dress
And seek, the soft surge of her breast
Melting, melting, melting—
Melt in the soft surge of her breast!

— Hsueh-hua-ti k'uai-lo

13

October 1935

Rizal found a small, furnished duplex on the edge of town, conveniently located near the tramline. The house provided adequate space for a bachelor without requiring more upkeep than a single houseboy could handle. For the first time in his life, Rizal could finally enjoy the privacy he craved. No meddlesome roommates, parents, siblings, uncles or cousins to poke their noses in his business. In his house, he could forget about the expectations of others.

Arun loved Penang as much as Rizal. In the four months since he had arrived, he had learned his way around all the neighbourhoods. He had discovered the best markets to buy meat, produce and housewares. And he had become adept at bargaining with the more aggressive city merchants. His cheerful disposition rarely left him, except when Rizal became too engrossed with work or too busy with social functions, as had been happening frequently in the last few weeks.

One morning, Rizal came into the kitchen, where Arun was preparing breakfast. He sat down at the table in front of a waiting cup of tea. Arun diced the chilies, ginger and garlic, and sprinkled the mixture into the frying pan. A satisfying sizzle filled the air.

'I told the fish man to save a head so I can make a curry tonight,' Arun said as he pulled a chicken from the oven.

'Don't bother to cook anything for dinner. I'll be home late. I'm going to the cricket match and then the club.'

Arun's cleaver attacked the chicken on the cutting board as if it had just insulted his mother.

'Whatever you say, Tuan.'

'Don't call me that. You know I hate it.'

Arun continued cooking without speaking. He scraped the cut-up chicken into the frying pan and then added a few cups of cooked rice. He ladled the chicken rice onto a plate, which he plunked in front of Rizal with a loud thud.

'Breakfast for Tuan,' he announced and then stood over the table with his arms crossed.

'Look, I know I've been busy lately,' Rizal said to Arun's unspoken complaint. 'I'll try to stay home tomorrow. Maybe we can go for a bike ride.'

Arun smiled. 'Tomorrow is a nice day. We can ride tomorrow.'

* * *

Arun packed a knapsack with rice wrapped in banana leaf and a thermos of water. Arun's bike, which he used for most errands, was stored on the landing. Rizal had to pull his bike out of storage and spend several minutes wiping off the dust and cobwebs.

They left before daybreak to get past the thickly settled streets and into the seclusion of the jungle before nosy neighbours looked out their windows and wondered why a gentleman would be out riding with his houseboy. The morning mist still hung in the air as they left town and headed along the coast toward the uninhabited west side of the island. The road on this side was closed to motorized traffic during the rainy season, assuring them the privacy they required. They pedalled comfortably along the first 10 miles of paved road as it ran beneath a forest of palms and skirted the rocky coast punctuated with secluded patches of golden sand. A collection of small wooden boats dotted the sea, each with a solitary fisherman casting his wide net into the glassy waters.

The road began a steep ascent at Batu Ferringhi as it hugged the side of overhanging cliffs. Rizal stood on the pedals, forcing his weight from side to side, willing his bike to stay in motion. Sweat dripped down his forehead, blurring his vision.

'Wait, I need to rest,' he called before Arun pedalled out of sight.

'Already?' Arun stopped and pulled a thermos out of the knapsack and handed it to Rizal. 'Maybe you should spend less time behind a desk.'

'Somebody has to pay the rent,' Rizal said.

Arun shrugged, as if the consideration of rent was of no consequence to him.

The road became less dependable as it moved inland, away from the coast. They crossed two streams via narrow bridges before they came to a part of the road that the rains had left submerged. They had no choice but to dismount and carry their bikes on their shoulders. Rizal struggled to find a foothold in the mud, and his feet slipped out from under him. He and the bike tumbled into the water.

'Do you want me to carry your bike for you?' Arun teased.

Rizal felt in the mud for his lost shoe.

'Just keep walking. If we stop now, I'll never be able to start again.'

After several more miles of riding and hiking on washed-out roads, they spotted a stream.

They left their bikes by the side of the road and followed the trail of water deep into the jungle, where it emptied into a large rainwater pool.

'How about a swim?' Rizal suggested.

They peeled off their clothes and dove into the water, splashing like schoolboys. When Rizal had sufficiently cooled down, he climbed onto a boulder to dry off. The warm rays of the afternoon sun soaked his body, massaging his aching limbs as he closed his eyes to listen to the songbirds chattering in the jungle.

In the deep recesses of this hidden landscape, Rizal could almost believe that time had stopped, allowing them these stolen moments without repercussions. How long would he be able to hide from the real world? Sooner or later, his family would force their demands on him.

He couldn't deny the general appeal of a wife and kids. He imagined a house filled with the sounds of boisterous children and the gentle touches that only the fairer sex could provide. He would like more than anything to offer his mother a grandchild from her favourite son.

But how could he reconcile this dream with the impulses of his heart? There was no denying that a different kind of blood coursed through his veins.

Arun floated out of the pool and glided onto the rock next to him. How he loved that beautiful body, the feel of his skin, its perfect contours. Allah was a sadistic god to have created such a lovely creature only to have put him beyond reach.

14

November 1935

Red watched his daughter sprawled across the bed in a decidedly childish pose, stomach to the mattress, a book poised in her hands, her raised ankles crossed behind her. She was oblivious to his presence. He had knocked several times, a courtesy that was not required of him, but she had been too absorbed in her book to hear him.

He glanced around at the stacks of books on her desk, toiletries scattered on her dressing table, and knotted skeins of thread on her chair. The maids had long given up on her room. They entered only to dust around the clutter, strip her bedding and wash the dirty clothes they picked up off the floor. Zaharah sputtered and spewed about Anna's slovenly manners, but Red felt there would be plenty of time for her to learn decorum. She was destined to spend her entire adult life keeping a house in order. Why not allow her a little slack now?

The earnest concentration on her face reminded him of the expression she wore when he read her stories as a little girl. He could almost see the questions forming in her mind, endless questions about the whys and wherefores of even the simplest tales. She always wanted to know more than the words on the page provided. Sometimes he worried that such an inquisitive mind in a girl might be more of a liability than an asset.

But there was something different in her manner today. The familiarity had fooled him. She wasn't a child at all. Somehow, overnight, she had transformed into a young woman. The letter in his hand was proof of that. She had developed her first infatuation and dared to circumvent his authority by carrying on an illicit correspondence with a young man.

He should have been angry with her. If his other children had done this, he would have had their heads. Zaharah was right, he did spoil her. But she didn't seem any the worse for it. Unfortunately, there was a price to be paid for his indulgence. With love comes pain, and he would have to teach her that hard lesson now. He cleared his throat to get her attention. She looked up with a smile, which disappeared as soon as she saw the opened letter in his hand.

'I've written to Tong and told him not to send you any more correspondence.' He crossed the room and sat down in her desk chair. 'He had no business courting you.'

'He wasn't courting me.' She sat up, trying to adopt a more dignified pose. 'He only sent me a few books because I told him I was interested in Chinese poetry.'

'A man doesn't send poetry and love letters to a girl unless he's courting her. I'm sorry, Anna, but this has to stop.'

'But Papa, I love him.' Her voice cracked with heartbreaking sincerity. He never could hold up before a woman's tears. But this time he had no choice but to give her the hard truth.

'I'm sorry, but Tong was promised to someone else long before he met you. That's the way things work in his family. The bride's family is just waiting for him to finish his degree before claiming their prize. You'll have to forget about him. He never should have written to you in the first place.'

He could see the hurt ripple across her face. What could he do? She was past the age when he could give her a piece of sugarcane to distract her from a bruise.

'Don't be in such a rush,' he said. 'There's so much you need to experience before you can really fall in love. Tong is just an infatuation. Give yourself time and you'll forget all about him, I promise.'

What doesn't kill you makes you stronger, he thought as he kissed her cheek and walked out the door. *She'll get over it soon enough.*

* * *

Anna did not immediately accept her father's words as final. Her dreams had been filled with Tong for so long that she couldn't dismiss them overnight. A letter would arrive soon with an explanation. Of course, he would have had to pretend to go along with the marriage or his parents might have pulled him from school. Once he graduated, he would never go through with the charade. He would send her a note begging for a rendezvous. *Meet me at the courthouse at six, bring a suitcase.* They would elope and slip away to Singapore. He would practice medicine while she enrolled in college to study World Literature, maybe become a teacher. She would be the first in her school to include Chinese Literature in her syllabus.

But the days passed with no letter. She modified her explanations to account for the lengthy gap, until Tong's engagement was announced in the papers. The impending union of two prominent families was featured in both the society and business pages. Anna was not a regular reader of either, but the issue had been left on the breakfast table with the relevant sections in plain view.

Anna pulled *A Dream of Red Mansions* down from her bookshelf. She tore out the pages in handfuls at a time, tossing them into the wastebasket. Then she held his letters over a candle one by one, watching the black corner spread until a red flame consumed the offending pages.

After that day, everything in Anna's world became disagreeable. She couldn't find any joy in her favourite books. Her friend's chatter seemed pointless and juvenile. Even her reflection became unbearable. She hated the unruly waves of her hair and those coarse freckles.

She prayed that the upcoming visit from her sister Sofiah would pull her out of her dark state. She pictured them giggling together, shopping and chatting like old times. But she soon realized how misguided her expectations had been. Sofiah spent the whole time bobbing up and down like a jack-in-the-box to find a sock, get a spoon or wipe a mouth. Anna couldn't get a sentence out without Sofiah being interrupted by one of her children demanding food or drink or a kiss on an invisible scratch. Why couldn't her sister just tell them to wait, or ask a maid to help?

And why did she act so servile around her brooding husband? So what if Zainal was bored on the visit to his in-laws? Sofiah spent the rest of the year with his family. He could at least pretend to be having a good time. She watched with disgust as Sofiah tasted her husband's curry then added an extra pinch of salt. 'He prefers his food a bit saltier,' she explained.

When the conversation turned to Anna's rejected suitors, her sister smiled in commiseration with their mother. 'Anna is waiting for her prince to arrive on a white horse. Just give her time to grow out of her fairytale phase.'

Something in Anna snapped at this latest insult. 'Go ahead, take her side,' she shouted at her sister. 'I don't have to sit here and listen to this anymore.'

She stomped up the stairs to her room and waited for a knock at the door.

Finally, Sofiah appeared in her doorway. She crossed the room, sat beside her on the bed, and took her hand.

'I'm not taking Mama's side. There are no sides. We all just want you to be happy.'

'Happy like you, waiting on your in-laws and your husband like a servant? No, thank you. I'm in no hurry to enter that life. In fact, I don't think I'll ever get married.'

'Anna, don't talk like that. Of course you want to get married. What's gotten into you? Why are you acting so cross?'

Anna had been waiting to unburden herself to her sister the whole visit. It had taken a dramatic outburst to finally get some attention. She clasped Sofiah's hand and let the tears fall as she told the story of her humiliation. How she had fallen for the deception of a horrible young man. She had written of her love and had even allowed herself to dream of marrying him, and he had been engaged to someone else the whole time. Now she could never allow herself to fall in love again. How could she ever trust another man?

Her sister listened to the whole ordeal then hugged her to her chest.

'Anna, don't be so hard on yourself. Of course you don't understand men. What could you possibly know of them? I'm a married woman with two sons and even I don't understand them. You're too young to worry about choosing the right man. That's why it's best to leave the selection of your spouse to Mama and Papa. One must be practical about these things. Don't worry so much about love. If you believe in Allah's grace, he'll provide you with a man who can take care of you. Then love will come. I know you don't think much of Zainal. But he's a good man and we have three beautiful children. Really, I'm very happy with my life.'

'I do believe in Allah's grace, but I could never leave the selection of my husband to Mama. She doesn't understand me at all. I can't imagine who she would choose. And Papa doesn't seem the least bit interested in helping me find someone.'

'Well, maybe I can help. I think I understand your tastes fairly well. You need an easygoing man, someone who'll let you spend your days buried in a book. He must be smart or at least not intimidated by a wife with a quick tongue. And he'll need to have enough money to hire plenty of servants if he doesn't want to eat a burnt dinner every night.'

Anna smiled at her sister's characterization. 'Do you know anyone like that?'

'Not a soul, but we'll keep looking. Don't worry, Mama isn't going to force you into a match, Papa would never let her. Just trust in Allah, the right man will come along in time, I promise.'

Anna did trust in Allah's grace. But she couldn't trust her mother or her sister. Look at the poor specimen who had been chosen for Sofiah. And she could never again trust her heart. Look where it had led her.

15

January 1936

Tong dozed on the daybed in the game room, a book of poetry spread across his chest. The last few weeks had left him drained. Within days of finishing his exams, he returned to Penang to finalize his agreement with the charity hospital. Now, with his start date several weeks away, his body seemed determined to catch up on months of getting too little sleep.

'I've spoken with Dr Loh on your behalf,' his father's voice interrupted his momentary reverie. 'He's agreed to take you into his practice. He wants to retire soon. You'll start as his assistant and slowly take responsibility for his patients until he's able to leave the practice in your hands.'

Tong sat up straight and rearranged his spectacles, trying in vain to create a more dignified impression.

'I've already agreed to a position with the Mission Hospital. I can't go back on my word now.' Tong's voice contained more defiance than was suitable, but he was determined to see this responsibility through. Perhaps it was his education by nuns combined with the burden of growing up in an affluent household. He could never be happy while others around him suffered for lack of food, proper medical care and basic human dignities. 'If you watch a blind man fall in a well, whose fault is it?' Sister Margaret had asked his class.

The fact that his grandfather had built his fortune on the backs of the unfortunate only added to his culpability. His wealth was not his fault. He had never lifted a finger to contribute to the family resources. But that didn't erase the guilt he had felt even as a child, being chauffeured to school in his starched uniform, new pens in his breast pocket, while other children tapped on the window of the car, selling useless trinkets to fill their bellies. He felt compelled to redress these inequalities.

'You can't possibly earn an adequate living as a staff physician,' his father insisted. 'Once you settle into a private practice, if you still feel the need for philanthropy, you can always sit on the board of one of the orphanages or primary schools we support. It's much better to be able to give generously to these institutions than to slave away within them.'

Tong took longer to respond than he should have. Of what use was his hesitation? He had no experience confronting his father on even the most minor of issues. He had only gotten away with medical school because he was the second son and therefore, his future was of less importance. His father must have felt the need to intervene when he heard of Tong's plans to work at the Mission Hospital. Now that his father had an opinion, had got involved and had consulted outside parties, there would be no reconsideration.

He paused long enough to figure out how to maintain the kernel of his aspirations within the shell of his father's decisions. Once he owned the practice, he could set aside a portion of his time for patients who couldn't pay. The sums he could charge the wealthy could subsidize his work with the poor. The more he thought about it, the more logical the proposition seemed. One had to be flexible. He would bend like a reed to attain his just goal.

'Thank you,' Tong finally answered. 'Tell Dr Loh that I'm humbled by his willingness to take on such an inexperienced apprentice.'

'His decision is based on my recommendation,' his father warned. 'Don't prove me wrong.'

'Of course not.'

'You should start right away so that you can get several months under your belt before your wedding. The astrologer has selected a date in early May.'

Tong had yet to reconcile his dreams of Anna with the momentum of his impending marriage. He had studied Red's letter a thousand times, searching for a solution. He had to admit that Red's words lacked malice, and even contained perhaps the slightest hint of sympathy between the phrases, as if he were uncomfortable with the draconian role of an outraged father. It was not that Red objected to the liaison; he let that be known by the absence of an indignant tirade. It was society that would not permit it, most especially Tong's family, for whom, to be clear, Red had the utmost respect.

The words left little room for interpretation. Tong's behaviour, leading a young impressionable girl on when he was already committed to another, had been unconscionable. He would not be permitted to write again.

Tong hadn't meant to lie. He had truly believed that since his intentions were so pure and his desires so irrefutable, that somehow he would be permitted the one thing he wanted more than anything else in the world. His presumption seemed foolish now that Red had put the facts into plain words.

Tong did not fear the possibility of being disinherited. He could live happily on the meager salary of a doctor. The real threat, more sinister than any monetary loss, was the danger of shaming his family, or, to be specific, the ramifications of disappointing his father. If he dared cross him, the old man would cut him out like a tumor. *What son? I have only one son. The other was one of my few mistakes.*

This was no idle threat. The story of his disowned uncle had reverberated in his ear since he was a child, a stern warning by his family against any notion of defiance. The actual crime that his uncle had committed was never clarified, only the emotional drama of his grandfather compelling his grandmother to kneel with him at the family altar to inform their ancestors of the permanent removal of this son from the family. After this official and irreversible act, there would be no possibility of reconciliation and no member of the family would ever be allowed to see him again. Tong had always assumed that it was this traumatic severing that had broken his grandmother and left her the empty addict she was today.

And so he agreed to the marriage, or more accurately, made no objection. If he couldn't have Anna, what did he care who he married? His father's choice, some girl from China, a business connection sealed with his blood, would be as good as the next.

Part II

1

Xiamen, Fujian Province, China

January 1936

Sze-yin bit her lip when she learned that she would be marrying a sheep.

Her governess had been hinting all day about new and exciting developments, so when Sze-yin received word that her father wanted to speak with her in the ancestral hall, she knew he would be informing her of his choice. She had been preparing for this day all her life. She dressed in her most auspicious outfit, a red tunic with an embroidered dragon motif over a long silver skirt. Her governess took extra care in securing her tresses into two meticulous buns on each side of her head. When she was finished with her toilette, she took one last glance in the mirror to make sure every strand of hair was in place.

She could barely contain her excitement as she approached her father and stepmother in their high-back chairs. She counted out her steps, placing each foot like a soft pillow, just as her governess had taught her. She clasped her hands together and bowed, keeping her eyes firmly planted on the ground.

'The astrologer has selected a date in early May for your wedding.' Her father never wasted time on greetings or preliminaries with his children. 'We will leave for Penang by the end of March, as we want to have plenty of time to oversee the details of the ceremony. The groom is the second son of an important business partner of mine in British Malaya. As we have expended a great deal and time and energy on your preparation, I expect you to perform your duties well and make our family proud.'

She waited to be sure he was finished before she responded. Sometimes, he broke up his pronouncements into small chunks for people he deemed of lesser intellect, in case they needed time to absorb each of his profound thoughts. When he didn't continue, she decided to brave his wrath and ask a question.

'I am honoured with your choice, Father, but . . . if I may?'

'Yes,' he narrowed his eyes. Her stepmother folded her arms at the impertinence of a question in this setting.

'What is my future husband's birth date?' She held her breath in anticipation of the response that would determine the outcome of the rest of her life.

'Oh, yes.' His eyes crinkled as if he were amused by her concern. 'Don't worry, we have consulted the astrologer to ensure that everything is in order. He is a sheep, which will be a good match for you.'

She caught her breath and steadied herself before answering, lest the tremor in her voice betray her disappointment. 'Thank you, Father, for securing this honourable match that I do not deserve,' she replied.

Her father seemed satisfied with her response and dismissed her with a wave of his hand. Tears rushed to her eyes as she fled to her bedchamber. She ran past her inquisitive governess, knowing she would be punished later for her rudeness, but she needed to be alone to get control of herself.

She didn't mind being sent away to another country. Whether she married a man in town or a man on the other side of the world, she always knew that someday she was to leave her childhood home. But she had assumed she would be departing for a better future. She had worked so hard to guarantee the best possible outcome for herself. Why had they matched her with a sheep?

When she was a little girl, she had no thoughts about her marriage; perhaps she believed she would stay a child forever. As the third daughter in a house with twelve children, she had been largely ignored and left to idle away her time with her sisters in the upstairs children's area. Their amah allowed the girls the freedom to play as much as they wanted, as long as they displayed good manners and proper behaviour whenever an adult was around.

As she grew older, she felt a stirring change occurring in her body, as if the gods were brewing an extraordinary destiny for her. She could tell that she was becoming beautiful, by the way adults looked at her whenever she was paraded in front of family. She could see by her uncles' approving glances that her appearance pleased them.

When she was twelve, her stepmother appeared in the children's area and handed Sze-yin and her two older sisters new embroidered gowns. Her stepmother, who had never before assisted Sze-yin with her coiffeur, carefully plaited six strands of hair and rolled each into a spiral, securing them with pins from her own collection. Their amah repeated this procedure on her two sisters. After a careful inspection of eyes, ears and throats, her stepmother shooed the girls downstairs and lined them up before a wizened matchmaker, who paced the reception hall as if she were already late for another appointment. Their needlework was displayed on the family's best bench, which had been moved for the occasion from the ancestral hall.

The matchmaker took several minutes to assess each girl and her handiwork. It was obvious to Sze-yin that her embroidery was far superior to that of her sisters. They were even better, so she thought, than the sample work that her amah had provided. The matchmaker nodded and the girls were dismissed without a word.

Two days later, her lax amah disappeared and a governess with a new set of stitching patterns and a rattan cane arrived. From then on, Sze-yin spent several hours a day with the new governess, working on her needlework and practicing her culinary skills and her deportment. She learned how to walk with pillow feet, speak in pleasing tones, and cover her mouth when she smiled. The strict governess rarely had to use her cane because Sze-yin was a diligent student, determined to master each lesson. Her sisters watched without complaint, until the governess began picking out the best pieces of meat at mealtime and putting them in Sze-yin's bowl. Then the battles in the upstairs rooms began in earnest. Her sisters would hide Sze-yin's sewing needles, call her names and pull out her hairpins. But their opinion was of no consequence to her. She was filled with pride at her importance and her ability to secure a good bride price.

Her father was a high-ranking government bureaucrat, who was treated with deference by everyone who came to the house. But Sze-yin could tell that the family's fortune was not what it had once been. The reception hall contained intricately carved antiques inlaid with glistening mother of pearl, but the furniture in the rest of the house showed signs of wear. Their new porcelain and silver pieces were clearly not of the same quality as the inherited ones. When her parents had a dinner party, her stepmother would sort through the cupboards with the maids and inspect each dish for chips, to make sure they didn't invite more guests than the remaining number of unblemished place settings.

Sze-yin worked hard to master the skills necessary to help her family obtain the best bride price possible, but she also persevered in order to ensure that she would be worthy of a dragon. In her husband's house, she would be at the mercy of her mother-in-law. Her own stepmother lorded over her daughters-in-law, requiring them to comb her hair with two hundred strokes every morning, wash her undergarments and serve her at mealtime. So Sze-yin was determined to marry a dragon, who would be ambitious and strong and protect her from an overbearing mother-in-law. Instead, she had been matched with a sheep, which meant that while he might be gentle and soft-hearted, he would be indecisive, timid and weak-willed when it came to standing up to his mother on her behalf. Worst of all, he was a second son, which meant her rank would be inferior to the wife of the first.

So on this day, she escaped to her bedchamber to allow herself a few silent tears before emerging and sharing the 'joyous' news with her sisters and governess.

The next three months were a whirlwind of preparation. A tailor prepared twenty-six outfits for her trousseau, cut of the finest black, blue, red and purple silk. Her governess drilled her in table manners, tea preparation and flower arranging. An English tutor arrived to teach her a few basic words and phrases. Sze-yin approached all these lessons with the same level of determination. She would not be deterred but would strive to make herself the best bride possible.

2

Penang

May 1936

May descended with the force of a typhoon. Sze-yin's family arrived with an entourage from China for the month of festivities. They rented a mansion on millionaire's row to house the bridal party and all their trappings.

The gift exchange took place three days before the wedding. At his parent's instructions, Tong spoke as little as possible, allowing others to answer questions on his behalf. His future father-in-law appraised him with the discerning eye of a businessman, looking for a fair return on his investment. Though the gift exchange represented the formal acceptance of the marriage proposal, the bride was not involved, nor was she present at the signing of the marriage contract. Tong would not see the woman with whom he was expected to spend the rest of his life, until the wedding ceremony.

On the morning of the wedding, Tong's mother handed him a new morning suit, a starched shirt and an embroidered handkerchief, presumably stitched by his future wife. His valet stood at attention, ready to assist him with his attire, but he waved the boy off, wanting to dress himself.

He stood in front of the mirror and put on the pressed trousers slowly, trying to postpone the moment when he would be bound for life to a complete stranger. He managed the studs on his shirt but the monogrammed cufflinks kept slipping from his fingers and dropping to the floor.

His aunt, Tua Koh, came in to check on him.

'Not ready yet?' She clicked her tongue. 'What's the matter with you men? It's always the same, as if you're facing a firing squad instead of a bride.'

She fastened his cufflinks with her beefy hands, then tied his bowtie. He submitted to her grooming with the will of a rag doll.

'There,' she said. 'Finally, the groom is ready.'

His brother, Boo Kian, stuck his head in the door. 'What's going on in here? Mother sent me to check on you. You better hurry before she comes up here to get you herself.' Kian was annoyed by the nuisance Tong's wedding had become. He preferred to focus on his own important affairs rather than his younger brother's inconsequential life. He spent as much time as possible away on business in Singapore, which he considered to be infinitely more sophisticated than Penang. He had arrived home at the last possible moment to perform the smallest possible role in the ceremony. His wife, Jade, had arrived even later. As a born and bred Singaporean, her distaste for Penang was even more pronounced. The two of them couldn't keep their disgust over Tong's mainland bride to themselves. As the family emissary, Kian had been allowed a sneak peek at Sze-yin, and he had thoroughly enjoyed terrorizing Tong with his negative reports.

'If anyone had asked me, I could have found you a much more appropriate bride in Singapore. But you know how backward Father is about these things. He still looks to that out-of-date continent as some beacon of civilization. Oh, well, you're stuck with her now. Maybe you can teach her some English and proper manners. She acts like a village bride.'

Boo Kian, the handsome eldest son of one of the most prominent families in Penang, had had no trouble securing a spectacular bride, the glamorous Jade, the daughter of a Singaporean tin tycoon and his socialite wife. The matchmakers practically fell over themselves to lay claim to this couple, who were so obviously meant for each other. The two shared a passion for pretense that transcended both sets of parents.

Firecrackers exploded around the car as they turned into the circular driveway of the bride's residence. Two boys in red brocade tunics grabbed his gloved hand and pulled him out of the car. Jade and Kian's three-year-old daughter, Mei, dressed as a little princess, tossed flower petals at him as he walked through the front door. They marched him into a sitting room that had been converted into a bridal chamber for the wedding. The room, filled with waiting guests, reeked with the stagnant tang of perspiration and sandalwood incense. His bride stood in the centre of the smoky room, an ornamental statue buried beneath a veil of pearls.

The master of ceremonies motioned for him to join the girl who was standing in front of the canopied bridal bed. The two bowed to each other. Tong moved through the ceremony like a precious puppet. He could almost feel his father's fingers bobbing his head up and down as he enacted his prescribed role. Not once did he imagine the possibility of standing up to this self-assured assembly, announcing his love for Anna, and calling the wedding to a halt. Other men might have rebelled, but Tong held no illusions about his heroic qualities. He would submit because that was what he had been trained to do his whole life.

To the strains of Chinese flutes, Tong unveiled his new wife. She didn't flinch when he lifted the tassels from her face. While she was expected to keep her eyes lowered throughout the ceremony, his eyes were free to roam up and down her frail figure. He had been told that she was sixteen, but her petite, flat frame made her look more like twelve. Her pale skin had a smooth, translucent quality, as unblemished as a porcelain doll. Her features were well-proportioned and delicate. Most people probably found her beautiful. Tong did not.

When they were finished, the bride and groom knelt before their parents to pay their respects. Tong wondered what his new wife would make of his relatives, with their hybrid ensembles—Chinese silks on kebayas, short, beige men in penguin suits puffing on Cuban cigars? The Khoos' ancestors would not have been deemed worthy to sweep the floors of Sze-yin's family mansion. Now that his family had earned their fortune, one that could rival the best families back home, they seemed obsessed with earning the approval of these emissaries from their old world.

Long tables draped with red cloth filled the yard as the wedding party gathered for the reception at Seascape. Tong and his wife sat at the head table surrounded by guests of honour. Well-wishers came by to offer the couple their congratulations. Tong chatted with family and friends, consuming a shot of whisky with the men who wanted to toast him. His head wobbled and his stomach rebelled, but he couldn't refuse to drink without offending his guests. Sze-yin picked at her food, exchanging only polite nods in exchange for greetings.

Tong searched the tables for Anna. His aunts had delivered the invitation to the Parkers and returned with a positive response. He spotted their table in front of the Botticelli replica. Anna sat on the farthest end, next to her sister-in-law. She refused to look up and acknowledge his glances. Well, why should she? He had never attempted an explanation, no furtive farewell letters or pounding fists at her back door. What explanation could he possibly give that wouldn't disgust her? Better that she be left with the image of a callous brute rather than a simpering coward.

Red and Faisal made their appearance at his table to slap his back and shake his hand. Anna remained rooted in her chair, examining her empty soup bowl.

3

The morning after their wedding, Tong and Sze-yin went to Seascape to review their wedding gifts. The packages had already been catalogued so that thank-you cards could be sent and appropriate gifts reciprocated. A portion of the presents had been set aside for future weddings. Wedding gifts were passed around Penang like poor relations.

The remaining presents filled several buffet tables in the dining room. They were free to keep what they wanted and distribute the rest to siblings or servants who had helped with the festivities. Tong's niece, Mei, danced around the room touching all the shiny objects singing 'Pretty, pretty, pretty,' until her distracted mother offered her a pair of diamond earrings in exchange for momentary silence.

Sze-yin examined the silver trays, porcelain tea-sets, vases, scrolls, gilded ashtrays, crystal glasses, lace bedsheets, embroidered napkins and table cloths. Most of the gifts would be useless until after they set up their own household once their children were born.

She picked up a silver necklace resting on a lacquer tray.

'I found it among the gifts,' Jade explained. 'It couldn't have been intended as a wedding present. It's far too plain. Someone must have dropped it by mistake.'

'What an odd piece,' Tong's sister said. 'I think it's supposed to be a snowflake.'

Sze-yin lips curled in a show of distaste as she swung the chain in the direction of the hawk-nosed maid.

Tong intercepted the necklace. 'I'll make some inquiries to see if someone lost it. It might have sentimental value. We wouldn't want to dispose of it until we've done our best to locate the owner.'

Sze-yin moved on to the next gift, a pair of diamond watches. Her eyes sparkled as she held the gems up to the light.

'Who?' she asked, meaning who gave them such an obviously superior gift.

'Third Aunt,' Tong's sister explained.

She placed the watches in the pile of choice items by her side. The conversation continued as Sze-yin inspected and assigned each gift. Tong clenched the necklace in his pocket, pricking his palm on the sharp tip of the snowflake.

The next day, he gave his most trusted servant the wrapped necklace to take to the Parkers' home.

When the maid returned, Tong asked, 'Did you give her the packet?'

'I caught her as she was leaving the house.'

'Did she open it?'

'She shoved it in her pocket.'

'Did she say anything?'

The girl tried to force her face into a neutral stare, but she couldn't hide the knowing smirk in her eyes. 'You told me not to wait for an answer.'

'Right, thank you.' He handed her a few bills. 'There's no need to mention this to anyone.'

'Mention what?' she called as she ran back into the house to start her afternoon chores.

4

December 1936

After eight months, Tong felt no closer to his bride than when they had first met. Sze-yin spoke little English. She struggled to understand his bastardized Hokkien with his odd accent and Straits slang. Tong was disappointed to discover that Sze-yin had been given almost no education outside the sphere of domestic tasks. She could only recognize a few letters and numbers. She could count to 100 and do some addition and subtraction, but nothing more. She understood little of the outside world. She knew the names of the king and queen of England, but couldn't locate Britain or China on a map, much less Penang.

The couple moved into Seascape, surrounded by the same furnishings and servants he had grown up with. Sze-yin appeared to have settled into her new household. Their lives seldom intersected. Tong spent his days at the clinic, returning home for lunch and dinner. Their meals were usually taken separately; the men ate in the dining room or sun porch, and the women gathered at the table in the kitchen. After dinner, Tong visited friends or attended a function at one of the many sports clubs, social clubs, business associations, or charitable organizations that he was obligated to support as a member of the Khoo family. The women kept busy with their own social life. Most evenings, they gathered in someone's parlour to play mahjong. Sometimes they collected in the kitchen with relatives to plan festivals and gossip about the latest news regarding second cousins twice removed.

All of this activity kept Sze-yin occupied, leaving Tong time to focus on his career. Tong learned a great deal from Dr Loh about the practical side of the medicine, skills that medical school had ignored entirely: how to put a modest maiden at ease before an examination; how to humor an ageing patriarch who insists he is not sick; how to help a sick child forget about his pain; and how to comfort the family of a dying patient.

After a while, Dr Loh began sending Tong alone on most house-calls, except to the oldest of patients, who would never tolerate such a young physician. Tong found the practice to be more rewarding than he had expected. While he dreaded visits to the spoiled hypochondriacs whose ailments represented a desperate plea for attention, he came to realize that a sick person, however wealthy, was still in need of care. Money could never buy health.

One day, as Tong was reporting to Dr Loh on his latest house-call, the Parkers' driver entered the office and waited to be addressed.

'Good morning,' Dr Loh said.

'Good morning, sirs. Puan Parker said to please come. Tuan Parker is sakit. He stays in bed.'

Faisal led them upstairs while the women waited with their hands in their laps, perched on parlour chairs.

'What's this I hear about you refusing to get out of bed?' Dr Loh said as he entered the sick room. 'We'll see about that.'

'I told them I'm fine. But they seem to think there's something wrong with me.' Red's baritone had been reduced to a crackly whisper. His face was as white as his bed sheets. His damp hair clung to his scalp. He didn't even have the strength to lift his hand off the blanket so that Tong could take his feeble pulse.

Dr Loh made small talk with Faisal, who hovered at the back of the room while Tong conducted the examination. The doctors didn't need to compare notes in this case. They decided that Dr Loh should take his leave while Tong remained behind to break the news to the family.

Tong led his former classmate to another bedroom and closed the door. This was his fourth such conversation since joining Dr Loh, and it never got easier. He always felt somehow responsible for the news.

'I'm sorry,' he said. 'Your father has pneumonia. I can administer some pain medication to make him more comfortable. There's really nothing else I can do but let the illness take its course.'

'He's going to be alright, isn't he?'

Tong looked into his friend's eyes, but in his mind, he saw Anna's face. If only he could be allowed to lie, just this once.

'His lungs aren't in good shape. He's had that cough for some time and I've noticed that he's been losing weight. I don't expect a recovery.' Tong paused to allow his words to sink in. He watched Faisal's face register disbelief. 'I'm sorry,' Tong said. 'Do you want me to speak to the others?' He hoped that Faisal wouldn't take him up on the offer.

Faisal shook his head. 'I'll talk to them. But, Allah forgive me, I can't explain to my father.'

'I think he understands anyway,' Tong said.

5

Anna wouldn't accept Tong's diagnosis. Tong was a liar. Her father would be fine. He just needed to rest. She pushed her chair closer to the bed and opened a book to read to him, but Red placed his freckled hand over the page to stop her.

'Anna, I want you to be kinder to your mother.' He forced the sound through his strained vocal cords.

'Please don't tire yourself. We can talk about it later.'

'After I'm gone, your mother will need you. Sofiah is too far away and Faisal is too absorbed in his own life. I want you to try harder to get along with her.'

'It's not my fault. She's always trying to turn me into someone else.'

'That's not true. She only has your best interests in mind. Her children are everything to her. I'm the one who's been selfish. I never pushed you to marry. I didn't want to share you with anyone.'

Anna stared at her father's parched hand hovering over the book.

'You said I could marry for love,' she whispered.

'Yes, but you have to give love a chance. You never gave any of those boys your consideration. It's all very well for men to take their time. But after a certain point, it's too late for girls.'

A warm flush rushed to her face when she remembered how Tong had humiliated her. The painful memory of his betrayal hadn't subsided. She would never allow herself to be such a fool again.

'Papa.'

'Let me finish. Your mother has promised that she won't push you into anything. But I don't want you to go through life alone. Promise me that you'll keep an open mind.'

'I don't want to talk about this right now, I want to read. We can talk about it when you're better.' A tear trickled down her cheek and dripped onto the page. Red removed his hand from the book, satisfied that she would never deny him his last wish.

'My biggest regret is that I won't be able to meet the man you choose.'

6

Tong returned the next day to check on Red. The family was huddled together on the end of the bed. Red could no longer comprehend their words. His laboured breath came in long intervals. He wouldn't last through the night.

Tong went through the motions like an industrious physician, taking his patient's pulse and feeling his forehead. In reality, he was as helpless as everyone else in the room. He should instruct the family on how to administer the pain medication, offer his condolences and return to the office. But he couldn't bring himself to leave.

He kept vigil with them through the night, absorbing their grief. He played the part of nursemaid, rather than doctor, placing cold compresses on Red's forehead, fluffing his pillows, and opening the windows to draw out the stench of death that had settled in the room.

The call to prayer pierced the morning air like a songbird heralding the first sign of daybreak. Red seemed to take the call as a sign. He had made it through the night; nothing more could be expected of him. He gasped out one last breath, and then silence.

Tong paused a few minutes for the sake of decorum before feeling for a pulse. Anna didn't wait for his confirmation. She threw herself across Red's body and wept. Tong crept to the back of the room and began packing up the vials of medication and equipment scattered across the dresser. When he turned to extend his condolences, Anna had fled the room.

He picked up his medical kit and creaked down the stairs, his footsteps echoing in the silence of the hollow house. Tong entered the back garden, where two years ago, he had found Anna engrossed in her novel. She was sitting on the same bench under the casuarina tree, her head in her hands. Tong had some experience comforting grieving family members, a sympathetic furrow of the brow and a few phrases of condolence. These wouldn't do for Anna. He crossed the yard and sat next to her in silence. He wanted to touch her but fear stilled his hands.

She threw her arms around his neck and wept into his collar. The sharp point of a snowflake dug into his chest. He held her tight, stroking the back of her hair as the sun rose in the sky. Then suddenly, as if waking from a dream, she shook off his embrace, stood up and ran in through the back door, disappearing into the house.

Tong let himself out of the garden. He waved away the rickshaw-pullers. Today, he would walk.

7

May 1937

After a year of marriage, Sze-yin still struggled to find her place in this peculiar household. Her diligent preparations had proven completely useless. Nobody bowed, walked with feather feet, or covered their mouth when they smiled. Women in the Khoo house did not brew tea or serve anyone, as they had plenty of servants trained to perform these tasks. The women only cooked when preparing special Nyonya dishes for festivals and celebrations. Though all the women were capable of embroidery and beadwork, they rarely bothered with these pastimes. The sewing room served as a location for the tailor or cobbler to take their measurements and compile their orders.

She couldn't complain about her situation, however. Her in-laws were far from the tyrants she had feared. Her mother-in-law did not harass or even scold her. For the most part, she just ignored her. Sze-yin was not disappointed by the lack of demonstrative affection, quite the contrary. She respected her matriarch's regal bearing, her beauty and obvious intelligence, and the command with which she ran the large and complex household. The more her mother-in-law neglected her, the more determined she became to earn her respect.

Her sister-in-law, Jade, was rarely around as she found every possible excuse to return to Singapore, leaving her daughter, Mei, in the care of the servants at Seascape. Loo, Seng's wife, was a timid woman who spoke only when spoken to and answered with few words. She spent her time hovering around her baby in the nursery and attending to her husband's needs. Tong's unmarried sister Siew wandered around the house daydreaming, patiently waiting for her wedding day, when her life would begin.

Sze-yin was invited to join the ladies of the house when they went on social calls, but any attempt to open her mouth and speak was met with a furrow of annoyance from her mother-in-law. For now, she concentrated on absorbing the behaviours and mannerisms of the other socialites. She focussed on the nuances of their phrases and the subtle lilt in a phrase or tilt of a head that betrayed their true feelings. In this way, she became a reservoir of information when it came to local gossip, memorizing the names, lineages and scandals of all the prominent families in Penang.

Her father-in-law paid for her English tutorials and provided her with a generous clothing allowance. For every important social occasion—and there were several each month—a tailor would appear and willingly create anything she could imagine. Whether the cumulative expenses exceeded her allowance, she would never know, because no one ever presented a bill or spoke of costs, so she continued to grow her wardrobe without restraint.

She traded her chignon for a modern bob with a permanent wave and replaced her Chinese robes with sarong kebayas. Only the sinkehs, or newcomers, wore Chinese clothes, and sinkehs were clearly viewed as crude and inferior by the aristocratic Nyonyas. At first, she copied her mother-in-law's style, as this represented to her the high water mark of grace and beauty. But over time, she began modifying the designs to better suit her frame—short, hip-length kebayas showed off her petite waist better than the looser knee-length style. A sheer, pale kebaya over a camisole complimented her complexion better than the brightly coloured patterns that the Nyonyas seemed to favour. Through concerted effort, she managed to make herself less conspicuous than the backward Chinese bride who had arrived a year ago. But the role of wallflower could never satisfy her ambitions.

Today, the women gathered in the kitchen to prepare Tong's grandfather's favourite dish for his death anniversary. Siew pounded the shallots, garlic and coriander with a mortar and pestle, while Loo fried batches of the fragrant pork filling over the wood stove.

Sze-yin's mother-in-law spooned the cooked filling and glutinous rice onto bamboo leaves, which her sister, Ah Ee, wrapped into perfect triangles.

They didn't trust a sinkeh to prepare these special recipes, so Sze-yin was given the job of folding the golden joss paper into the shape of nuggets for burning at the altar, later that day. This would have been an easier task if Mei hadn't insisted on helping. Sze-yin watched in horror as her petulant niece mangled paper after paper. Tong's grandmother, Ah Ma, observed the activities from the wooden bench in the corner, lost in her memories. Her trembling hands rendered her useless in the kitchen.

'It shows a lack of respect,' her mother-in-law complained to Ah Ee, as she tied five packets together with string and placed them in boiling water. 'You know that I am the first to defend my son over my husband's tirades, but this time Ah Kian has gone too far.'

The family had been thrown into a tizzy because Tong's brother had extended his stay in Singapore on 'urgent business' and had not returned in time for his grandfather's death anniversary.

'Don't trouble yourself over it,' her sister replied in her gentle sing-song voice. 'Grandfather understands. He was a businessman as well.'

'No, it is unacceptable.' Sze-yin's mother-in-law pounded her fist on the table in a rare outburst that caused even the self-absorbed Mei to look up. 'Young people today don't understand the importance of these rites. If they're not more careful, our ancestors will begin to exact their revenge on our family. And we would deserve it for raising such careless children. What if our children decide not to honour our ways? Who will take care of us in our afterlife?'

Ah Ee placed a soothing hand on her sister's shoulder. 'Don't worry yourself. Your children will never abandon you. They are young and they know that for now, the older generation will take care of things. When it's their turn, they will not disappoint us. Please, don't let your ill temper enter the food or you'll give Grandfather indigestion.'

Her mother-in-law calmed down and no more mention was made of the disharmony caused by Ah Kian. The women finished assembling the dumplings and returned to their rooms to dress for the ceremony, leaving the servants to clean up the dishevelled kitchen. Sze-yin sat down next to Ah Ma on the wooden bench and began unfolding the disfigured nuggets and reforming them into their proper shape.

'Granddaughter,' the old lady said in a voice that vibrated as uncontrollably as her hands, 'please hand me my pipe.'

Sze-yin went to the cupboard and pulled out the red lacquered tray that contained Ah Ma's pipe and paraphernalia. She laid the tray on the bench between them and lit the oil lamp.

'My son always makes sure I have the best opium,' Ah Ma said proudly in her native Hokkien.

She was the only woman in the house with whom Sze-yin could converse comfortably. She understood Sze-yin's struggles better than anyone because she was also a sinkeh, who spoke broken English. She had been the Chinese village wife whom Tong's grandfather had married to take care of his parents back home in Xiamen. After their deaths, she resettled in Penang as the second wife. But when the primary wife died during childbirth, she found herself suddenly promoted to matriarch.

Ah Ma dipped the end of a long needle into a clay urn on the tray. She held the needle with trembling fingers over the waiting flame of her oil lamp. The thick syrup sizzled and popped, releasing a wispy trail of curling gray smoke that penetrated the air with its sweet, pungent aroma.

'Why do you smoke?' Sze-yin asked.

Ah Ma took a deep breath from the pipe and seemed to draw the smoky essence down into the depths of her soul. She closed her eyes and bowed her head, allowing the sensation to fill her limbs and quell the tremor in her hands. Once the drug had calmed her breath, she opened her eyes to respond.

'Do not judge until you have lost three sons. I am an old lady and the fates have chosen to keep me alive past my usefulness. My pipe allows me to experience a little bit of the oblivion of heaven here on earth.'

'Three sons?' Sze-yin had not heard this particular piece of family history. 'You had other sons, besides Father-in-law and Uncle?'

'Number Three Son is no longer a part of our family. Number Four Son fell off his horse when he was twelve. And of course, we don't count the ones that died before their first month.' She looked down at her hands and drew in her hollow cheeks. 'But a mother who loses her babies feels their weight in her arms for the rest of her life.'

'Ah Ma, I understand your sorrow but how can you feel useless?' Sze-yin asked. 'A mother-in-law should be the empress of the house.'

'These Nyonya girls don't see things that way. They don't bow to anyone,' she answered in a steadier voice. 'Nyonyas are not like the girls back home. The constant flow of men to Penang has created a shortage of brides, so the daughters in Penang believe they are precious. But what good are the two of them? Only three sons between them, one who lives for himself, another who lives in shadows and the last who lives in dreams.'

'Tong lives in dreams.' Sze-yin nodded her head with the painful realization of the truth in this statement.

'I know you are disappointed with your husband,' Ah Ma whispered, placing a withered hand on Sze-yin's shoulder.

'No, I'm not disappointed.' Sze-yin was shocked by the inappropriateness of this sentiment, the vague essence of which might have entered her head but would never escape her mouth.

'You should never rest your hopes on a spouse, they will always disappoint you. You must focus on your children. Only a son can bring you eternal happiness. Our life is short and of no importance, compared to eternity. You can collect all the treasures from the four corners of the earth but they will not feed you in the afterlife. Only a son can ensure your comfort there.'

Once again, Ah Ma spoke the uncensored truth. While her mother-in-law and aunt could never be accused of heartlessness—they doted on their granddaughters—it was also clear that they were holding out for a grandson. Ah Ma was right, a boy would be the answer to Sze-yin's prayers. By providing the family with their first grandson and ensuring the continuation of the family to the next generation, Sze-yin could secure her rightful place as a respected member of the household. Finally, she found an outlet for her ambition: She would have a boy to secure her future in this family and for all eternity.

8

August 1937

'I've come to kidnap you for lunch.'

Faisal swung into the office where Rizal was concealed behind a pile of papers.

Rizal hadn't seen his friend in a while. Faisal was spending more time at home since the death of his father and the birth of his daughter. He seemed to be taking his new role as head of the household quite seriously.

'I can grab a quick bite,' Rizal said. 'But I have to be back for a meeting in an hour.'

'Skip the meeting. I want to take you for a ride.'

Before Rizal could answer, Faisal stepped into the corridor and leaned on the secretary's desk.

'Please cancel all of Mr Mansour's afternoon meetings. And feel free to take a longer lunch yourself. You look like you could use a decent meal. I'm sure you're tired of eating rice at your desk.'

The young man turned to Rizal for confirmation. A long lunch was rarely an option with his boss.

'Fine.' Rizal said. 'But I really have to be back by two.'

They walked outside onto the crowded sidewalk of the financial district. A row of drivers in threadbare suits and sweat-stained hats leaned against immaculate vehicles, waiting to whisk their boss away to a meeting or a luncheon, or an afternoon rendezvous with a mistress. A few played a noisy game of cards on the hood of a Bentley.

On the other side of the street, a crowd of rickshaw-pullers jockeyed for position to win a fare off one of the workers emerging from the office. A cluster of men gathered around a blue-and-cream motorcycle with chrome fenders and whitewall tires. The crowd cleared a path for Faisal and Rizal as they approached the bike.

'Hop on and we'll go for a spin,' Faisal said.

'What's this?'

Faisal caressed the leather seat. 'It's my new toy, just arrived from England, a top-of-the-line Norton.'

Rizal wasn't a motorcar enthusiast like Faisal and his friends, who followed assembly-line trends as closely as their wives followed fashion. But even a Luddite like Rizal could appreciate this bike's aesthetic appeal. This purchase would surely put Faisal on top of the competitive speed-chasing heap. While all young men of means had opulent cars imported from Europe or America, there were only a few hundred motorcycles on the island, and none of them looked as impressive as this metallic sculpture.

'Come on.' Faisal threw his cigarette to the ground and straddled the leather seat. 'I'll show you how this beauty can fly.'

Rizal stared at the metal contraption. He wasn't at all sure he wanted to fly in a vehicle so obviously built for ground transportation. For his friend, Rizal had risked arrest at establishments of dubious reputation, nearly shot himself in the foot while snipe-hunting, participated in a drunken brawl with two oversized rickshaw-pullers, and practically drowned while island-hopping in a fishing boat with more holes than an old pair of socks. But flying down the congested, pockmarked streets on a vehicle with only two wheels and no carriage was quite another story. Before he could utter his protests, Faisal started the engine and Rizal found himself jumping on the back, clutching his friend like a lifebuoy with one hand, and grabbing his songkok with the other.

They sped through town, weaving in and out of the traffic before stopping in front of a Chinese temple with red-tiled gables suspended on colourful dragon pillars. The temple was mobbed with afternoon visitors; throngs of men drinking tea, playing cards and gossiping, while small children, the youngest of whom were naked from the waist-down, ran through the courtyard chasing metal hoops.

'You're going to love this place,' Faisal promised.

They hopped across the yellow stream of an open sewer and passed the marble lions guarding the entrance. A bowlegged man in a stained cotton shirt and rolled-up trousers motioned them down the side alley. He led them through the narrow corridor where the aroma of ginger and garlic competed with the stench of urine. Behind the temple, they found a crowded food stall filled with Chinese coolies wolfing down their afternoon meal.

The old man pulled two rickety wooden stools from behind his stall and placed them next to an overturned barrel that doubled as a table. His cracked hands wiped the tabletop with a stained rag.

'They have the best chicken rice in town,' Faisal said.

The man bowed to accept the compliment. He shuffled back to the stall and filled two tin plates with rice, bits of roasted chicken, slices of cucumber, and a bright chili sauce. He placed the plates on the barrel along with saucers of murky chicken broth and two steaming cups of tea.

'How'd you find the place?' Rizal asked.

'A Chinese tin man told me about it. Worth millions, but so miserly, he hates spending more than a few coins on a meal. I didn't get any business out of him. But I did discover this fantastic place, so it wasn't a complete waste of time.'

Rizal lifted his tea in a mock toast. 'I'm honoured that you shared your find with me.'

'Actually, I had an ulterior motive. But we can talk about that later. How's work these days? I hear you've created quite a stir in Ibrahim's empire.'

Rizal winced at the attention his latest assignment was getting.

'I pointed out the obvious siphoning. What Ibrahim does with that information is his business.'

'Precisely. You told Ibrahim, instead of demanding a cut from the culprits, as all of your predecessors had done. You're a brave man.'

'I'm just a salaried employee doing my job. Ibrahim asked me to look at the books and I told him what I saw. I have no idea why he gave me the assignment anyway. I'm supposed to be a lawyer. But the kickbacks were so obvious, a child would have found them.'

'I'll tell you why Ibrahim gave you the assignment. Because he knows you're the last honest man in Penang. I think it's great. Those monkeys had been growing fat for years. Maybe I should have you look at my business.'

'No, thanks. I'm done with the role of tattletale for a while.'

Rizal was embarrassed by the fallout his revelations had caused, but he didn't feel sorry for the managers who had been dismissed. He had no patience for corruption.

'I'd rather earn one honest dollar than a million tainted ones,' his father always said. 'Money can't buy Allah's grace.'

Rizal didn't inherit a family fortune like his peers. But his father died knowing that he had never compromised his scruples. Rizal intended to go the same way.

'How's fatherhood?' Rizal asked to change the subject.

'Fabulous,' Faisal beamed. 'Rozi's stolen my heart. It's remarkable how a tiny person can completely transform a man. But that's exactly what I wanted to talk to you about.'

'What? Babies? I don't know anything about them.'

'Maybe you should learn more,' Faisal said. 'I've noticed that you don't express any interest in settling down.'

Rizal shifted in his seat. What exactly had Faisal noticed?

'I don't have the inheritance or position to attract the ladies in Penang.'

'You can't fool me with false modesty. You know full well that you're one of the most eligible bachelors in town, up-and-coming, a Queen's Scholar from Cambridge, Ibrahim's protégé. You're every girl's fantasy. I'd marry you myself if I could,' Faizal winked.

Rizal blushed at the awkward compliment. 'No one's approached me, so the point is moot.'

'I'm approaching you.'

'You're already married,' Rizal laughed.

'True, but my sister's not.'

Rizal sat back, realizing for the first time where this conversation was heading.

'We're family, so I thought we could dispense with the formalities of a go-between,' Faisal continued. 'I've already talked to Ibrahim.

Since your father's dead, I assumed I should go through him. He's thrilled with the idea. He's always been fond of Anna, and you know how he feels about you. I won't feel offended if you have no interest. I know Anna has a reputation as a difficult girl. My father spoiled her. He never seemed in a hurry to fix her up. But she's eighteen now. My mother and I are getting worried that her best years are passing her by.'

Rizal was equally flattered and panicked by the proposal.

'I haven't really met her. I mean, she seems perfectly nice, but I never considered the possibility.'

'I have no desire to thrust two perfect strangers together. Believe me, Anna would never accept an arranged marriage. But she does respect my opinion. I was hoping that you might be able to stop by the house for tea one afternoon. You could see the baby and meet Anna. What do you think? No harm in a friendly visit, right?'

So that's what his mother was going on about in her letters, her allusions to milestones in his life, new chapters, grandchildren. How long had Ibrahim and she been plotting? Was the idea really Faisal's, or was he just the appointed ambassador?

He couldn't refuse the invitation without offending his friend.

'I'd be glad to come over sometime.'

'How about Thursday, around three o'clock?'

'Alright. Thursday then.'

Faisal checked his pocket watch. Rizal tried not to envy other people's material possessions, but he couldn't help admiring his cousin's watch, a silver marvel with a tortoiseshell cover.

'That's a beauty.'

Faisal considered the piece. 'It was my grandfather's. Papa gave it to me on my wedding day. It's probably too valuable for everyday use but I wear it because it reminds me of him.' He allowed his thoughts to drift in a reflective moment. Then he shook off the melancholy lapse. 'It's late. We'd better head back. I've got a meeting at three.'

He was not as irresponsible as he liked to pretend.

9

A rickshaw rolled down the driveway of the Parkers' stately house. A plaque marking the entrance was engraved with the name Rumah Merah, meaning Red House. The exterior of the house looked like a typical double-storey English bungalow modified for the tropical climate, with white stucco walls, a red-tiled roof, and large shuttered windows. Rizal had never been to Faisal's home. The Parkers didn't entertain, except for a few business partners and close family. Zaharah's aversion to people was well-known. Rizal heard rumours of an earlier time, when Rumah Merah had been famous for its parties that continued into the wee hours of the morning, but that was before the death of their son; before Zaharah slid into seclusion.

The puller stopped under the portico and Rizal climbed out of the carriage. Arriving in a hired rickshaw probably cost him enough standing to crush the deal. A car would be useful for situations like this, but he couldn't bring himself to spend his money on a useless status symbol.

A maid greeted Rizal at the door and led him past the folded partition at the doorway into a large, open sitting room. He had expected the inside of the house to be decorated in the same English style as the facade, but the interior was clearly Zaharah's domain. The house was furnished with local products, more comfortable than ornate. The floor was laid with green and white floral tiles; rattan couches covered with chintz cushions created an intimate seating area in the centre of the room, Dutch-colonial cabinets made with local fruitwoods lined the walls; and a baby grand graced a corner.

As soon as Rizal was seated on the couch, Zaharah and Faisal entered from the kitchen, followed by a servant carrying a tray of lime juice and sweet kueh.

'Thank you for coming,' Faisal said.

'Assalamualaikum,' Zaharah greeted him.

'Waalaikumsalam,' Rizal said, touching Zaharah's hands and then his heart. 'It's wonderful to meet you.'

The servant poured the lime juice into tall glass tumblers and handed them to the men.

The three made small talk about the weather, a light glossing of local politics, and a brief summary of Rizal's family, most of which Zaharah probably already knew. The conversation waned as they ran out of topics. As if on cue, Mina emerged from the kitchen with Rozi nestled in her arms, followed by Anna, who seemed to be focussed on her footsteps on the floor.

Faisal's chubby infant had a mop of dark brown hair, her father's large brown eyes, and dimples. Anna had the same shaped eyes, but hers were a translucent blue-grey. Her skin was fairer than the rest, with a collection of freckles like a starry constellation spread across her nose and the apples of her cheeks. She was tall for a girl, probably only an inch or two shorter than Rizal, with broad shoulders and slender hips. Her most remarkable feature was the long hair that fell in loose waves down her back. From a distance, the colour looked auburn, but on closer inspection, he could see that her light brown tresses were actually streaked with strands of red, as if her parent's genes couldn't quite mix into one coherent colour.

Anna sat in a chair and stared at her hands in her lap without uttering a word. The earlier topics were repeated for the benefit of the girls; weather, politics, Rizal's family.

'I understand from Faisal that you've moved into your own house,' Zaharah said. 'Living alone must get tiresome. Who cooks and cleans for you?'

'I have a houseboy who looks after things. I spend most of my time at work and in the evening, I find it relaxing to unwind in silence with a book. I guess I haven't quite given up my solitary student ways.'

Rizal thought he saw Anna's glazed eyes show a little life after this explanation. Faisal must have picked up on it as well.

'Anna's quite the bookworm,' Faisal said. 'She's been through all the novels in Papa's library.'

'What do you like to read?' Rizal asked her.

'Anything,' Anna replied flatly, 'I'm not too particular. It just passes the time.'

Faisal and his mother tried to resurrect the conversation several times, but it refused to come back to life. After an excruciating hour, Rizal took his leave.

Back at home, Rizal was greeted by a smiling Arun and the enticing odour of simmering lamb. He didn't mention his afternoon session at the Parkers' house. Anna's disinterest convinced him that nothing would come of it.

* * *

Anna picked up her niece and fled upstairs, leaving the others to murmur in her absence, but their grumbling floated to the second floor. Why was she so difficult? Didn't she want to get married? Rizal was perfect. Mina thought he had kind eyes and a handsome face. Zaharah was impressed with his manners and the tenderness he showed when he spoke about his mother.

Anna pulled her little niece into her chest. She hadn't meant to be rude. She had actually liked the young man. He had a nice face and a pleasant voice. Faisal was extremely fond of him and she respected her brother's opinion. He must be intelligent and very worldly to have earned a Queen's scholarship. He probably found her dull and provincial. Why had she been so boorish?

The conversation below finally stopped. Faisal trudged up the stairs to deal with his problematic younger sister.

'I take it that you weren't impressed,' he said as he entered her room.

'I thought he was very nice.' Anna stared at the infant in her arms as if explaining it to her. 'But he would never be interested in me. He's much too intelligent and sophisticated. I'm sure he thought I was an ugly simpleton.'

'Well, you didn't give him much to go on. Why did you have to be so rude?'

Anna started to cry. 'I wasn't trying to be rude. I just didn't know what to say. How would you like to be put on display like that? I felt like a trick monkey in a circus act.'

Faisal had lost his immunity to Anna's tears after their father's death. He crouched next to her, offering his finger for Rozi to clutch.

'I'm sorry if you felt awkward. I thought that was the best way for you to meet each other. Mina and I went through the same routine.'

'I know but you were the appraiser, not the object of scrutiny.'

'What if I try to arrange a different kind of meeting, some neutral territory where you two could talk alone together?'

'I don't see the point. I'm sure he's not interested.'

'You underestimate your appeal,' her brother insisted.

What appeal? How could she ever be sure that a suitor was interested in her and not her family's position, or money, or Faisal's connections? How could any girl understand what goes on in a man's head?

10

Rizal searched the crowd for his friend. He spotted Faisal toward the front of the stands, waving in his direction. Next to him, in a pale blue sarong kebaya, Anna gestured for the binoculars. So that was the purpose of this outing. Well, kudos to Faisal for his persistence. Rizal shuffled up to the pair. His pride forced him to give the day a chance.

He had expected to feel relieved when the first encounter with Anna had failed. Instead, he had noticed a nagging sense of disappointment. Her looks and her demeanour had pleasantly surprised him. He had even entertained for a moment the idea of this singular young lady taking a fancy to him. As the meeting had continued, her aloofness had needled him. Why shouldn't she have been interested? Was he that unattractive? Perhaps a glimmer of hope still remained—she must have agreed to give him another chance.

'Sorry I'm late. I didn't realize how mad the traffic would be,' Rizal said. 'I couldn't even find a bullock cart willing to take me. Hello Anna, good to see you.'

'Nice to see you again,' Her words were formal but her smile seemed genuine enough to allow him to relax a bit.

'I should have offered you a ride,' Faisal said. 'I forgot you still don't have a car. At least you made it. What do you think?'

Rizal scanned the crowd milling about in self-contained units. The lawn was filled with Europeans in the latest Paris fashions, completely unsuitable for the tropical heat. Oversized umbrellas protruded from the centre of their bistro tables, providing a modicum of shade from the morning sun.

Multicoloured locals filled the stands. The men wore suits and ties, with the occasional sarong wrapping the Malays. Fedora hats topped Chinese hair and songkoks covered Muslim heads. Umbrellas and canes wrapped their wrists. The ladies, clad in bright combinations of Western and local attire, balanced precariously on delicate, pointy heels splattered with muddy soil.

'It's quite a scene,' Rizal said. 'More like a carnival than a sporting event.'

'Haven't you been here before?' Anna asked. 'I thought everyone came out on race day.'

'No, this is my first time.'

He didn't have the means for the sport. He hadn't really wanted to come out today and throw his wages at a couple of horses but Faisal had insisted. Now that he understood the purpose of the invitation, he wasn't inclined to draw attention to his economic deficiency.

'Have you had a look at the spread yet?' Faisal asked. 'Are you ready to wager your fortune?'

'I wouldn't know where to begin. I don't know anything about horses.'

'Well, you can do what most people do and just pick a name you like.' Faisal said.

'Maybe you could pick for me?' Rizal suggested.

'I warn you, I'm partial to underdogs.'

'Go easy on me, please. I don't want to lose my shirt in an afternoon of fun.'

'Don't worry,' Faisal laughed. 'We'll make sure you have enough left for the fare home.'

He plunged into the crowd to place their bets, leaving Rizal and Anna without a buffer.

Rizal tried to break the ice. 'I understand that your family has a horse in the race. Which one is he?'

'Hephaestus. He's in the third race. Papa always kept at least one horse. He loved the track.'

'Your father must have had quite a sense of humor, naming his horse after a lame god.'

'Papa enjoyed cryptic irony,' she said, turning to look at him for the first time. 'Do you like mythology?'

'We studied it in school. I had a professor in England obsessed with the Greeks. He drilled all the gods into our heads.'

'What's England like?' she asked. 'I've read so many books about it. But I don't really have a picture in my head.'

He searched his mind for adjectives. How could he explain that other world to someone who had never left the tropics?

'It's cold and damp. Green, in its own way, but not lush like Penang. Instead of brief storms where the sun returns within the hour, England can be covered in clouds for days. In the winter, the sun barely reaches midmorning before disappearing.'

'You make it sound awful,' she said.

'Not awful. Just different. Living in the middle of all that history was amazing. England has castles, dungeons, clock towers and bridges that have been around for centuries. And the galleries are filled with ancient artifacts from all over the world. They have so many plays, dances and musical performances that an entire section of London is dedicated to theatres. One summer, I got a job ushering at a playhouse, so I could see all the performances for free.'

Why was he admitting to his poverty? He wondered.

'What are the people like?' she asked.

He stared at the self-important Europeans collected on the lawn. All the snubs and insults, the years of feeling like an unwanted intruder came rushing back to him.

'The British are well-bred monsters,' he said. 'Outwardly polite but cruel to the core. Having dark skin is worse than being a leper in Europe.' The words slipped out of his mouth before he had time to consider the implications for Anna. Faisal moved so comfortably in his skin, Rizal often forgot about his hybrid heritage. But Anna, with her fairer complexion, might have taken more pride in her English blood.

His outburst seemed only to amuse her. 'Europeans aren't any different from other people,' she said. 'We all have a basic need to feel superior. Some people focus on intelligence, looks or financial success. The less creative types obsess over skin colour or social background. It's all the same, really.'

'I'm not like that,' he said. 'I don't need to feel better than anyone else.'

'Really? Don't you take pride in your intelligence?'

'Who says I'm intelligent?'

'My brother. And you must know that you are charming.'

'Your brother said I was charming?'

'No, that came from me,' she smiled.

'Well, thank you, but I'm not especially proud of my intelligence, charm, or how I look. We're all born with different attributes. It's what we do with them that matters.'

And then she beamed with triumph. How easily she had flushed out his vanity. She could have been on the debate team at Cambridge.

'However you are able to justify your feelings of superiority,' she said.

'Okay, you win. And what about you? In what way do you believe yourself superior to others?'

'Well, isn't it obvious? I'm better at being me than anyone else I know.'

Faisal returned with a lime soda for Anna and a couple of beers for the men. Anna set aside her drink and sipped from her brother's cup instead.

The afternoon sun turned into a scorching fireball. Spectators sought relief under the shade of the stadium awning. A wide-winged hawk soared over the peaks of Penang Hill, inching closer to watch the amusing human spectacle. Faisal and Rizal lost the first two races. In the third race, Hephaestus came in a respectable third.

'I guess he's not ready for the glue factory yet,' Faisal said.

Rizal watched Anna as she sipped from her brother's beer. She shifted her weight from side to side. 'I've got to take these off,' she whispered to Faisal.

'Why don't you find a seat?' he suggested.

'And miss all of this excitement? You stand in front and cover me.'

She leaned one hand on Faisal's shoulder as she reached down to slip off the offending heels and tuck them behind her. Then she pulled her skirt a little lower so the hem covered the tops of her bare feet.

'Sorry, I just couldn't stand it any longer,' she giggled.

Their luck improved in the afternoon and they won several big races. Rizal went home at the end of the day with extra cash in his pocket and a bemused grin on his face. She certainly was different. If he had to marry, he could do a lot worse. Perhaps, they could have a pleasant life together after all.

Part III

1

September 1937

The office hummed with the clatter of tea-time. Typewriters ceased, replaced by clinking cups and the rattle of the tea cart rolling through the aisles. Faisal's office boy leaned into the doorway, a whisper of crumbs stuck to the sparse strands of facial hair he tried to pass off as a moustache.

'Encik Mansour is here to see you, sir.'

Rizal appeared in the doorway. There was something different about his appearance; polished shoes and the lingering whiff of cologne. He must have reached a decision. It was about time.

Faisal sprung from his chair. 'Hey, hey, my friend! You look spiffy but I can't go out dancing tonight. I've got to babysit my maiden sister.'

'Very funny.'

Faisal put on a somber face and mimicked his friend's wooden stance. He crossed his arms in front of his chest. 'So then. Shall we get a drink and talk this proposition through?'

They walked arm in arm out the door. Faisal resisted mocking his friend further, at least until they had crossed the street and entered the welcoming din of the Runnymede Hotel. They took their seats at the usual spot, just off the long bar, facing the sea front. It had been ages since they had gone out. This marriage proposition had placed an artificial wedge between them that they were both anxious to remove. The waiter appeared from behind the row of potted palms that separated the dining area from the gentleman's bar. His face was as polished as the wooden counter and his slick hair considerably more waxed. He blinked expectantly at his favourite patrons.

'I'll have a scotch with ice,' Rizal ordered.

'Make it a double, and I'll have one as well,' Faisal added.

Rizal took a long drag on his cigarette, waiting for the waiter to disappear behind the palms.

'So obviously you've ferreted out the reason for my visit.'

'You don't usually reek of cologne when you show up at my office.'

'Can we be serious for a moment? This is a rather important step for me.'

'I'm sorry. Really, I'm thrilled, you know I am. To tell you the truth, I'd begun to give up hope.'

'Well, your family doesn't make things easy. There's no protocol for heretics like you. I thought about sending Ibrahim.'

'No, this is better. This is wonderful. Really. I'm so glad you came to me. I've been on pins and needles for weeks. You two can be so stubborn. I thought you might thwart the attempt just to spite me.' Faisal leaned forward in his seat, all joking gone from his voice. 'She's a great girl, you know. You two will be perfect together.'

'So you'll talk to her for me?' Rizal asked.

Faisal hadn't yet determined the proper way to proceed. He had assumed, as Rizal must have, that the proposal should be carried to Anna through the family. But now he reconsidered.

'I think it's best if you talk to her,' Faisal suggested.

'What? Ask her directly? I can't do that.'

'Why not?'

'For one thing, I'd rather not be rejected to my face. There's a reason men use a go-between.'

'She's not going to reject you.'

'She's not?'

'Well, probably not. If she does, she'd be a fool.'

'Then she hasn't given you any indication?'

Faisal looked around for the waiter. Where was that drink?

'She keeps insisting that you aren't interested. And to tell the truth, after a few weeks went by, I started to believe her. I didn't push her for an answer because I didn't know how you stood.'

'Well, now you know. Can you push her, please?'

'No, I think you need to ask her. She's a modern girl. A direct proposal will appeal to her vanity.'

Finally, the waiter emerged, their drinks balanced on a silver tray. Faisal downed his in one gulp. The club watered down the drinks so much, he reasoned that the double was little more than a single shot. Besides, he wasn't going back to work after this. He was going straight home with the news. He needed time to work on Anna. He'd have to recruit Mina and his mother. No, better to leave his mother out of it. Her words could have the opposite effect. Women were so challenging. He couldn't wait to have another man in the house to balance the feminine drama.

2

Rizal dressed in a pale green baju with a plaid sarong around his waist. He frowned at the mirror. Alamak, this family was difficult. He stripped down to his underwear and reached for his beige suit. He hated uncertainty. This whole marriage idea had thrown him into a state of frantic indecision. Who was he trying to impress anyway? Anna, Faisal, the mother? Evidently, if he was going to have any hope of succeeding, he would have to appeal to Anna. The suit then.

Arun stooped to pick up the discarded baju from the floor. He hung the shirt back on the hanger and placed it in the armoire.

'The suit is nice. Does Abang have a special occasion?' He posed the question without a hint of irritation, using the pet term for elder brother. Rizal hated deception. But there was no point in alarming Arun unnecessarily. She might say no.

'I'm having lunch at a friend's. Faisal Parker, the rojak from the shipping company.'

If Arun had his suspicions as to why Rizal was worrying so much over his attire for a business lunch, he chose not to pursue them. Not that he ever questioned Rizal or pushed his point. They never discussed such things. Rizal's responsibility and Arun's loyalty were assumed. It had always been that way. It was, in many ways, the perfect relationship.

Arun plucked a cream tie from the wardrobe. He draped it around Rizal's neck. His studious reflection flickered in the mirror. 'This one is best.'

The guilt was difficult to bear. But they couldn't remain bachelors forever. Society would insert itself between them before long. Arun would have to understand.

And Anna? He could make her happy. He would be a good husband, better than most. He may not love her the way another man might, but most successful marriages, he had observed, were based on respect and affection, not passion. He felt a strong affinity toward Anna. Not attraction, certainly not ardour, but admiration mingled with the protective desire to be kind. Perhaps she could help him become a better person. He might even be able to modify his 'unnatural affliction'.

Rizal surveyed his bedroom. What would Anna think of this sparse abode? The cane armoire and four-poster bed had come with the house. The cast-off bedding, he'd carted from Ibrahim's house. The windowless servant's hovel remained bare and uninhabited. He didn't like to think of that room and the possibility of shutting Arun up in it.

Even worse, he might be expected to move in with the Parkers. Where would Arun sleep? In the back quarters with their driver? Maybe they wouldn't even let him keep his own houseboy.

He shouldn't be thinking of Arun. These thoughts were futile. He needed to make a new start, end his bachelor days. Perhaps even eradicate Arun from his life.

'Will you get a rickshaw for me? I'm running late now.'

Arun turned to execute the request. Rizal grabbed his arm and twisted it around his waist planting a kiss on his lips.

'But Abang is late?' he said as he touched his lover's cheek.

'Right. Late. Alright then, go get the rickshaw for me, please.'

The honourable path lay before him, but he knew he lacked the will to take it.

3

Anna stared at her complexion in the dressing mirror. 'I look ill.'

'You look beautiful,' Mina insisted.

'I look horrible.'

The sound of male voices drifted up from the sitting room.

'You have to go.'

Anna whisked off the yellow dress and pulled a lavender one over her head. She turned back to look in the mirror. They both noticed the smudge on the right collar.

Mina rushed her out of the room, rubbing the stain with a handkerchief. 'You've got to go. They're waiting,' she said, and gave her a quick squeeze on the shoulder.

Anna's foot hovered over the first step. What would she say? She felt wholly inadequate to make this momentous decision. She was terrified of accepting but even more afraid of letting the opportunity pass. If only her father were still alive.

The men hopped up from their chairs as Anna entered the room. Her brother looked as nervous as the potential groom. Poor Faisal. What an awkward position she had put him in. He really should have been more cross with her. She hadn't given him an answer because she truly had no idea what she would say. She changed her mind on the hour. *Yes, but I must marry. No, but I don't love him. He's a good man, everybody tells me so. What do I know of him? Nothing. What do I know of any man?* She actually envied the girls whose decision was made for them. How much easier to accept what fate had to offer than to take responsibility for charting your own course. She was too young for such a step. And yet, the others worried she was getting too old.

Faisal escorted the couple into the garden on some pretext of a lovely breeze. Her mother was nowhere in sight but her presence was evident everywhere. The encounter had been carefully orchestrated. A side table had been placed next to the bench with a pitcher of lime juice and two glasses.

Several pairs of eyes blinked through the slatted kitchen windows. The servants must be having a fine time. Then, without warning, her brother made an excuse and disappeared into the house, leaving the couple alone to pull a conversation out of the stifling air.

Rizal motioned for her to sit, which she did, in the most ladylike fashion possible. He took his place on the bench, in close proximity, but not so close as to be touching even the hem of her dress. He opened his mouth, clasped his hands, and then closed it again. Was she going to have to speak first?

'Looks like the rains have stopped,' he finally said.

Alamak, was he going to talk about the weather?!

'Yes, I think we'll have sun for a while,' she replied.

'In fact,' he continued, 'some of the seasonal birds are already arriving.'

He started rattling on about the effect of monsoons on migration patterns. She watched Rizal's lips as he babbled. What torment the poor man must be going through. He did have a kind face and pleasant voice. She liked the earnest spark in his eyes and the way he tilted his head as if considering his thoughts before he spoke. She couldn't care less about bird migration. But she liked that he spoke to her as someone who might be interested in such an academic subject. He spoke not as a lecturer but as a fellow pupil who had learned something fascinating about myra birds the other day and wanted to share his discovery.

He didn't flatter or humour her like most young men, like Tong, whose flowery words had sucked her in. Rizal seemed the picture of sincerity. She could imagine the possibility of being happy with someone like him. She liked the sharp planes of his cheekbones and the pleasant contours of his mouth. What would it be like to kiss those lips? As a married woman, she would be within her rights to find out.

She might even kiss those lips every day. She laughed at the impropriety of her thoughts. Fortunately, he seemed to just have said something that was funny, so he smiled along with her. It was a handsome smile. A rush of affection burned off her indecision. She might not love him now, but she could grow to, in time.

Just as Rizal seemed on the verge of losing his courage, Anna made up her mind. She communicated her decision by placing a palm on his hand. This seemed to provide all the encouragement he needed.

'Do you know why I came here today?' he asked.

'I'd like to hear it from you.'

He took hold of her hand but then couldn't decide what to do with it. He held it in the air as a visual aid.

'I came to ask you to marry me. I believe we could have a pleasant life together, if you would agree.'

The practiced tone of his speech could be forgiven. His eyes were sincere.

'I would be honoured to be your wife.'

They called the others outside to share the news. Faisal patted his friend's back with genuine relief. Mina giggled like a schoolgirl. Zaharah embraced Rizal with unaccustomed affection.

4

October 1937

The families selected a date in January for the ceremony. The women ordered the food, the flowers and decorations. The families decided to hold the smaller akad nikah ceremony at Rumah Merah and the larger bersanding and reception at the Eastern and Oriental Hotel, reducing the burden on Zaharah to entertain such a large crowd. Rizal's mother would stay with Ibrahim for several weeks to help with the preparations.

Rizal tried to ignore the frenetic activity, endless parties and persistent butterflies in his stomach. Everything would work itself out after the wedding. Things would return to normal, or as normal as they could ever be, once he and Anna settled down into a quiet life together.

He wandered into his office after lunch, his mind cluttered with work, crowding out any space for doubts regarding his personal life. He found Anna sitting in an armchair, her hands clasped in her lap.

'Is everything alright?' he asked. Had she changed her mind? Maybe she sensed his apprehension?

'We can't stay at my house.' She faced him as if for a confrontation. 'Mama says that your place is too small but I don't mind. I don't need a big house, really. We can't live with my mother. You don't know what she's like. We would suffocate.'

Rizal almost fell over with relief. He had been searching for a way to broach the subject for weeks.

'Have you spoken to your family about this?' he asked.

'Mama says that I'm being difficult. She insists that your place isn't suitable for a married couple.'

'What if I found a larger home? It wouldn't be as grand as Rumah Merah. But I could probably find something outside of town, large enough for a servant or two, and a small family.'

He stumbled over the word 'family.' They hadn't actually discussed children. The concept of marriage seemed foreign enough.

'Could you, really? I think Mama would agree if she approved of the house. She can't complain about being left alone. She has Faisal and Mina, and now Rozi.'

'I've already done a little research,' he admitted. 'Give me a week or two to see what I can come up with.'

She threw her arms around his neck and planted a kiss on his cheek, their first physical contact in all these weeks. The impression of her lips lingered on his face. He felt inexplicably proud of his ability to make her happy.

5

Rizal brought Arun to see their new home first, as a peace offering. Arun had sulked for weeks but he seemed to be coming around to the inevitability of the decision. He would also have to marry soon enough. Even servants expect their sons to procreate. The family line, however humble, must not be permitted to die out.

The two-storey cottage was nestled in the shade of rambutan trees surrounded by four acres of an abandoned fruit plantation. A small stream, perfect for fishing and swimming, bubbled through the backyard. Arun would appreciate the similarities to their garden in Kedah.

The fruit trees and the stream had initially attracted Rizal, and the bargain price had clinched the deal. The house was located miles from town, at the foot of Penang Hill, and thus was considerably cheaper than anything else he had seen. The owner's wife had died in her bed after a car accident. Though most people would never consider buying such a cursed home, but Rizal didn't harbour any irrational superstitions.

The small house was adorned with elegant details throughout. The raised wooden floors were polished to a high gloss. Intricate wood carvings framed the windows and accented the walls. Brown and black geometric tiles covered the sitting-room floor. Arun took a cursory look around, pretending to be disinterested. He ran his hands along the walls of his new quarters, a spare room located behind the garage. Rizal switched on the light and ran water in the faucet to display the modern amenities, far superior to those in most servant quarters. But Arun refused to be impressed. He strolled outside and climbed a sprawling rambutan tree, gathering a bundle of fruit in his arms. Then he squatted on the ground and began peeling the hairy skin to suck the juicy flesh off the pit. Rizal sat beside him, not daring to join him.

'I'll have to buy a car. Wouldn't you like to learn to drive?' he asked.

'What? Am I to be the driver now?'

'Well, I imagine Anna will prefer a girl working in the house. You'll love the freedom of a motorcar. After you drop me off at work, you'll have the rest of the day to cruise around town and do as you please. Just be careful that all that leisure doesn't make you fat.'

He pinched Arun's narrow waist. Arun, always ticklish, wiggled away. Then he turned the full force of his beautiful, trusting face to Rizal.

'When do we start the lessons?'

Anna loved the rustic charm of the bungalow that had been built as a country retreat by wealthy Malay. Their rural village provided a picturesque base to Penang Hill, an exclusive vacation resort for wealthy Penangites who sought the cool air of the higher altitudes.

She hired a craftsman from the village to build their furniture and selected styles similar to her mother's rattan couches and chairs, Dutch-colonial dressers and chests. She begged Rizal to come to the workshop and approve her choices. He was so busy with work and the various marriage preparations, the last thing he wanted to do was spend an afternoon looking at furniture.

'If you like it, then I'll like it,' he would say.

'No, but you must have an opinion.' She would throw her hands up in exasperation.

Finally, he agreed to accompany her to the house, to approve the layout. They walked the floors of the vacant home as Anna placed imaginary furniture in its proper location. 'I thought we could put the desk here.' She twirled in a semicircle around the envisioned spot. 'What do you think?'

'Sure.'

'Or would you prefer it by the window.'

'By the window is fine.'

'But that might be too much sunlight.'

'Really, Anna, I don't have the head for these things. Put it anywhere you like.'

Her shoulders fell, like sails emptied of wind. Rizal could feel his mood sink right along with hers. Their emotions were already eerily bound.

'It's a north-facing window,' he suggested. 'The sunlight would probably be just right.'

She ran to him and pecked his cheek. He was becoming accustomed to her spontaneous displays. Coming from a family that never showed any affection, he initially found her tenderness jarring. But now, he would be disappointed if he failed to draw out the occasional kiss.

'And the bookcases?' she asked.

'I think they should go in the nook between the kitchen and the sitting room.'

She squeezed his arm. 'That's just what I was thinking.'

*　*　*

Rizal drained his meagre inheritance to pay for the house and the furniture. Fortunately, Ibrahim gave him a hefty bonus as an early wedding present to cover the cost of a car. To save expenses, Rizal and Arun moved into the house as soon as the deed changed hands.

He took his future driver to a dirt road behind the house and parked the sedan under a canopy of trees. He spent several minutes explaining the function of the various mechanisms.

'Here's the clutch, the brake and the gas pedal. You start the engine by turning the key.'

Arun wasn't listening. He climbed into the driver's seat and began turning the wheel, like a child in a toy car.

'Okay, enough, enough, do you want to give it a try?'

He grabbed the key from Rizal's hands and shoved it in the ignition. After a series of abrupt starts that jostled them back and forth, his foot gained a feel for the pedals. The car glided down the road and progressed smoothly, until the first bend. Arun turned too hard and drove the car into a muddy ditch.

'Sorry, Abang.' He flashed a grin.

'Never mind. Let's get it out.'

They hitched up their trousers and waded into the mud to push the car back onto the road.

After a few lessons, Arun transformed from a cautious student into an aggressive speed demon. He put the pedal to the floor and swerved around any vehicle, bullock cart, or animal he deemed too slow.

'Alamak! These people move like tortoises,' He shouted as he passed an ancient lorry.

Rizal's lectures and curses did nothing to deter his reckless driving.

'You must drive with more respect for these roads. They can be treacherous. Didn't I tell you that the previous owner's wife died in a car accident on this very street?'

'No. On this road?'

'She was thrown from the car. They barely got her back to the house before she passed away.'

'She died in the house?'

'Yes,' Rizal told him.

Arun stared at him in disbelief. 'Why would you buy such a cursed home? How can you sleep at night with a ghost in the house?'

'You miss the point entirely. Her death had nothing to do with the house. I'm trying to tell you to be more careful on the road. Stop driving so fast and passing without looking.'

'Hmm.' Arun considered this alternative moral to the story. He eyed the house and then the parked car. 'I think we need a monkey or a cat to scare the ghost away.'

'We don't need any pets. Just stop driving so fast.'

The next day, Arun appeared with a mangy tabby in his arms.

'I found her out back,' he explained, rubbing the protruding belly of the pregnant feline. 'A very good omen. I think we should keep her. You can never be too sure.'

'You keep her. I don't need any kittens scratching up my new house.'

Arun folded an old sarong into a box that he placed in the corner of the kitchen for the mama cat. Every night he fried up a fresh fish, picked the meat off the bones, and placed it on a platter for her. Rizal chose not to comment on the indulgent behaviour. Arun was just trying to protect him from what he viewed as a very real threat.

Only once did Rizal allow himself to glance at the market receipts to see where the fish was coming from. He found no more than the usual amount on the accounts. But Arun couldn't have been paying for it himself; he didn't have any money. He must have been catching it in the stream out back.

Arun routinely ignored the stack of notes on the counter that constituted his pay. The cash would pile up until Rizal, concerned about the possibility of theft, would deposit the sum in an account he had opened on his lover's behalf. Arun bought himself nothing. He lived in Rizal's house, ate what Rizal ate, and wore Rizal's hand-me-down clothes. Once, Rizal tried to buy him some new clothes for the Islamic New Year but Arun seemed offended. He took the gifts back to the store and returned the money.

'Their Mama has left.' Arun stood at the door with four mewing balls of fur in his arms. 'What can we do? They won't eat the fish.'

They drove to the nearest market to purchase tins of milk, then sat cross-legged on the floor of the unfurnished sitting room, feeding the kittens from balled-up rags dipped in warmed milk.

6

December 1937

Tong joined the other men on the sun porch. The Khoo men dressed for breakfast in suits and ties, their place settings laid with pressed white linens, lacquer bowls and ivory chopsticks. The meal began at seven-thirty sharp and the food never varied: bowls of chicken congee, pork dumplings and a platter of steamed greens, downed with ample cups of strong tea.

Several papers circulated around the table—local papers in English, Malay and Chinese, as well as international papers from Singapore and London. The Penang papers were scanned for news on local business developments, municipal projects, announcements from club meetings, all spiced with gratuitously graphic descriptions of fires, accidents, deaths and dismemberment.

The English paper from Singapore did a better job of acknowledging events in the outside world. They focussed primarily on the menacing reports from Europe: daily updates on the Spanish Civil War, Stalin's horrific purge and Hitler's military build-up. Scant coverage was given to the carnage taking place in their own backyard. The Chinese papers did their best to report accurately from the frontlines, where the Imperial Japanese Army was advancing through the crumbling Chinese defenses. The information coming out of the area was spotty and unreliable, but it was clear that having captured Shanghai, the Japanese had quickly moved on to Nanking, the capital of the Republic of China.

The men read the papers in silence and discarded them as soon as they had consumed the news. They had an unspoken rule, strictly enforced: the women, particularly Sze-yin, were not to be exposed to these alarming reports.

Sze-yin had been so preoccupied with her new life that she had failed to notice the lack of communication from her family. The Japanese army was hopefully still months away from Xiamen, where Sze-yin's parents lived, but her brothers, uncles and cousins, leading members of the government who resided in the capital, were unlikely to have escaped the invaders' wrath.

Of course, she had no idea that she should have been concerned about her family's well-being. She knew nothing of the geopolitics, could never comprehend the hatred and violence ripping her homeland apart. The China of her cloistered childhood was a civil country filled with old families that dressed well, spoke politely and carried on the genteel cultural traditions of the last century.

After reading a particularly gruesome account of the massacre of Nanjing, Tong's father began lecturing his sons on their responsibility to their innocent brethren in China. While he was at the breakfast table, his views were given deference by the younger generation. *Of course, the Nationalist government would prevail. It was regrouping and would emerge victorious with or without the help of the indifferent Europeans. Of course, our brothers need our help. We will continue to support them in any way we can—ammunition, infrastructure, money and more money.* Nobody ever questioned their father's authority to his face. But as soon as he finished eating and left the table, Kian started in.

'Bloody corrupt and incompetent, the whole Nationalist government,' he muttered, careful to keep his ranting quiet and out of his father's earshot. 'Why continue to throw good money after bad? Who's to say where our funds are going? Probably lining some bureaucrat's pockets, shoring up his personal supplies or funding his escape route.'

Tong had to agree, but what was to be done?

'Someone needs to speak to Father,' Kian continued, as if anyone would take the assignment seriously. 'The war with Japan has nothing to do with us. We are British citizens now, and this island and Singapore are our home, our future, the place we're going to be buried—not some ancient plot with a bunch of ancestors.'

An ageing houseboy, immaculately attired in a crisp white shirt and black trousers, interrupted their debate with the morning mail. Kian riffled through the stack and pulled out an engraved invitation with gold lettering.

'It's for the Parker girl's wedding,' Kian said. 'We're going to have to send a representative. Father wants one of us to go. Jade and I have already accepted an invitation to the Cheong's wedding that evening. You should go, Tong. You were schoolmates with her brother, weren't you?'

Tong stared at the piece of paper, high-quality linen stock with gold embossing formally uniting Anna and Rizal's names in print. Their engagement had been the talk of the town, two of the most eligible youths in Penang: Anna, the beautiful youngest daughter of the Parker family, and Rizal, a rising star in Penang society.

Tong had only met Rizal on a few occasions. He had to admit that he seemed quite likeable. Though he had the credentials to exude arrogance, a Queen's Scholar with a first from Cambridge, he lacked the pretension of his lesser peers. Anna and Rizal were undoubtedly well-suited. Tong should be happy for her. But he couldn't bring himself to attend the wedding.

'I'm sorry. I have a meeting that day.' Tong tried his best to sound nonchalant.

'With whom?' Kian scoffed at the notion of his younger brother having an important commitment.

'With the PLK.' It was not the truth, but it was the best excuse he could come up with. His brother would have no idea whether there was a meeting or not, as Kian's interests did not overlap with a charity that helped girls escape the sex trade.

'Skip it,' his brother insisted. 'Those well-meaning sops never get anything done. They sit around and bemoan the fate of the poor exploited women while taking meticulous minutes of their findings.'

An apt description, perhaps, but insulting all the same.

'I'm chairing the meeting,' Tong lied. 'Seng could go to the wedding. He was also Faisal's schoolmate and he has more to do with the Parkers' business.'

'What do you think, Ah Seng?' Kian spun the lazy Susan to pluck a dumpling from a silver platter. 'Do you have any ridiculous charitable obligations on that day?'

'No,' Seng laughed, 'No charities here. I'd be happy to go. If I play my cards right, I might even get to dance with the lovely bride.'

7

The clamour of kampong drums signaled the groom's arrival. Someone thrust a bouquet into Anna's arms and led her out of the room, down the spiral staircase, past the grinning guests and up onto the bridal dais, next to her husband.

Family members came in pairs to sprinkle water on the couple and whisper their congratulations. The men gave long speeches followed by laughter and applause. Finally, Rizal and Anna were allowed off the dais to partake in the meal. Men in white coats placed course after course in front of her but her stomach would not cooperate. She picked at each plate as streams of relatives, friends and strangers filed by, kissing her cheek, hugging her shoulders, or shaking her hand.

Before the dessert plates were cleared, Anna was rushed back upstairs, changed into a Western bridal gown, and brought down to the ballroom. Guests spun to the sounds of a string quartet. Did she dance? She must have. But she couldn't remember. Where was her husband? Every time she looked for him, he was surrounded by a crowd of well-wishers.

Her aunts dragged her back upstairs. This time, they dressed her in a pink brocade jacket with a matching pleated skirt. The music stopped. The guests gathered around the stairs as she made her last grand entrance, walking slowly down the marble staircase, trying not to trip over her heels. Rizal stood at the bottom of the stairs, looking as shell-shocked as she felt. Somebody placed her arm in the crook of his elbow and shoved them toward the waiting car, a yellow Jaguar covered with coloured paper and flowers. Where had the car come from? Who had decorated it?

The car sped through the night to their new home. Her body melted into the molded contours of the leather seat. She must have fallen asleep because someone was shaking her shoulders and jostling her out of her dream. Crickets squawked in the night. In the darkness, she could just make out the outline of the fruit trees and the darkened bungalow.

She stumbled into the house, up the stairs and to their bedroom. Rizal was downstairs, dismissing the yellow Jaguar. She managed to remove her shoes. Where was her nightgown?

Her clothes had been sent over in the morning. Apparently, someone had unpacked her bags and put everything away. But where? She stretched out on top of the bed, fully clothed, trying to concentrate on where her nightgown might be. Her mind drifted in and out, refusing to focus on the task at hand. She didn't hear Rizal enter the room, change into his sarong, and fall asleep beside her.

8

Rizal hadn't been able to take time off work after the wedding but he tried to come home early, that first week. Each evening, they went to a different relative's house for dinner, ticking down the endless list of invitations. They returned home, late at night, exhausted from the hours of socializing.

Anna kept expecting Rizal to do whatever it is a groom is supposed to do in bed. But each night, he changed into his sarong, slipped under the covers and turned out the light.

On Sunday, Faisal dropped by the house to see how the newlyweds were getting on. Rizal had gone to the office for a few hours of paperwork. Anna took Faisal to a banana-leaf stall in the village for lunch, explaining that their new maid, Rosanne, had no idea how to cook. A shopkeeper had recommended the girl stocking his produce. It didn't occur to Anna that the shopkeeper was probably just trying to get rid of the hopeless thing.

'So,' Faisal smiled as he dug into his curry, 'how's married life? Are you and Rizal settling in?'

Anna stared at her plate of rice, unable to scoop another mouthful. How could she explain? What could she say? If only Sofiah were here. She could talk to her sister about these things. Why wasn't her husband interested in her? Didn't he find her attractive?

'I'm not sure,' she mumbled.

'What do you mean?'

'I'm not sure we're settling in.'

'Rizal's treating you alright, isn't he? He's not working too hard, leaving you alone in that house all day? I knew it was a bad idea for you to move out here. You should have stayed at home with us.'

'No, no. He's treating me fine. It's just that . . . I'm not sure that he's very happy with me. I think that he might be sorry that he married me.'

'What makes you think that?'

Anna shrugged her shoulders.

'I'm sure everything will work out. Married life can be a big adjustment. Just give it time,' Faisal said.

'I will,' she murmured.

As soon as lunch was finished, Faisal drove off to find Rizal. He'd better get to the bottom of this. Girls were so sensitive. He remembered Mina's pouting when they were adjusting to married life. He had learned how to walk the necessary line. Offer the compliments, the terms of affection that could get you through the day. Women were brooding, complex creatures. But once you got the hang of them, understood their individual needs, they weren't so different from kittens. Each had a spot that, if rubbed the right way, could make them purr.

What was Rizal doing at work on a Sunday anyway?

He took his new brother-in-law to the Runnymede Hotel for drinks. This time, Faisal downed several whisky shots before attempting to pry into the delicate matter.

'So, how's married life?' he asked, trying the same question on the groom.

'It's great,' Rizal beamed. 'Anna's been really wonderful. She's got the whole house put together, all those wedding gifts put away, and she hired a new maid to help around the house. The maid is a horrible cook but a nice enough girl.'

'You're not unhappy with Anna for any reason? I know that it can be tough getting used to someone else's constant presence.'

'No.' A furrowed brow darkened his usual smile. 'Why would I be unhappy with her?'

'I mean,' Faisal paused to find the right words, 'you're not dissatisfied with her? She's very young, you know, and hasn't had any experience with, well, life.'

He motioned to the bartender for another round.

'Anna's a great girl. I have no reason to be dissatisfied.' Rizal seemed overly defensive, so Faisal decided to stop meddling. They would figure things out.

That night Anna lay in bed listening for her husband's car. It was ten o'clock already. Rizal had sent a message that he was going out but hadn't mentioned where, with whom, or until how late. She had expected him much earlier.

Finally, the car pulled into the drive. She heard his footsteps echoing down the hall to their bedroom. The door creaked open and his figure appeared, shadowed by the shaft of light in the doorway. He undressed quietly, perhaps uncertain whether she was awake or not. She decided not to give him any clues.

She felt his fingers fumble with buttons at the neck of her nightgown. His lips pressed against her neck, shoulders, face and cheeks. His breath smelled of whisky and his hair of cigarette smoke. His hand reached down and pulled her nightgown up around her waist. She felt a piercing pain shooting through her body as he entered her. With each movement, the pain intensified until she was sure she would cry out. Just when she thought that she could not take it anymore, he stopped and collapsed beside her, falling into a deep sleep. She watched her husband's rib cage moving up and down beside her. Her body finally succumbed to exhaustion some time before the first call to prayers.

She woke, startled to find the room bright. It was nine o'clock. How had she slept till so late? What would Rosanna think? She peeked through the window to look for Rizal's car. He would have left for work hours ago. She changed out of her nightgown and threw the sheets into the bottom of the wash basket, trying to hide the bloodstains under a pile of towels. The foolish maid never noticed any of the other stains in the laundry. Each load came back as dirty as it left.

When she entered the kitchen, Rosanna offered her a plate of burnt rice, flavourless sambal, and a runny egg. Something needed to be done. She would go to her mother and borrow a maid for a few weeks to teach this hopeless girl how to cook.

Zaharah greeted her at the door and offered her a cup of tea and biscuits, as if she were an honoured guest in her own home. Everything seemed different. Her mother's voice was softer, the sitting room lighter, the maids kinder. She felt infinitely older than the young girl who was married in this house, just two weeks ago. She was a grown woman now, a married woman with a house of her own, a husband, and maybe someday soon, a baby to take care of.

'I think that you should take the piano,' her mother was saying. 'You are the only one who plays it. It would fit nicely into your sitting room, don't you think?'

Yes, a piano. She could almost picture her future children at their lesson.

Part IV

1

March 1938

After almost two years of marriage, Sze-yin had failed to produce an heir. Unaccustomed to failure, she was desperate to figure out how to accomplish her objective. Though she prided herself on her self-sufficient and resilient nature, in this matter, she lacked basic information. She had not even realized that it was the performance of marital duties that prompted the gods to provide children to couples. Tong's grandmother had to drop several hints regarding bed business before Sze-yin understood the connection between her marital and maternal responsibilities.

Ah Ma was the only person Sze-yin could confide in about this delicate issue. They had already engaged in several uncomfortable conversations on the subject. Ah Ma was a learned mentor who had been educated by her grandmother on the workings of the gods and spirits that governed one's fate. She gave Sze-yin advice regarding the location of the bed, the frequency of their 'interactions', the proper positions for their body parts, the foods she should eat, and the aphrodisiacs she should employ.

Sze-yin did her best to follow these prescriptions. As a woman, she couldn't suggest timing or position to her husband, but she could use her skills in manipulation to influence these matters. Ah Ma had suggested the placement of a talisman by the bed. She had given Sze-yin the figurine that she herself had used to give birth to eight children, a magnificent jade sculpture of a dragon tortoise with a baby on its back.

When all these recommendations failed to help her conceive, Tong's grandmother suggested that she go to the Snake Temple to pray to Zhusheng Niangniang, the goddess in-charge of assigning parents to souls who are ready to be reincarnated. Sze-yin waited until Zhusheng Niangniang's birthday on the twentieth day of the third lunar month. She decided to broach the topic of visiting the temple with her mother-in-law over breakfast.

The Khoo women were seated around the kitchen table as the morning sun filtered through the open window. Breakfast always began after the men left for work, as soon as the servants could shift their attention to the women's needs. The kitchen with its hanging pots, shelves of crockery, and seven-foot brick stove, served as the women's boardroom, the wooden table their conference area. During their morning meal, Sze-yin's mother-in-law would assign their social obligations, coordinate their errands and schedule the use of the driver. Everyone's attendance was required, except Ah Ma's, who was served a pot of tea at her bedside.

The serving girl with the pierced ears circled the table, ladling a portion of piping hot congee into every bowl. The girl had on a new pair of silver studs, probably gifted by Boo Kian. Their affair, so obvious to Sze-yin, appeared to have escaped Jade's notice. Sometimes Sze-yin envied others for their blissful oblivion.

After the congee was served and all the women were eating, her mother-in-law addressed Jade's latest ploy to slip off to Singapore.

'I don't understand why you need to leave for a whole month,' she said.

Jade, accustomed to getting her way, had been badgering her mother-in-law for the last two days. 'My father's sixtieth birthday celebration is going to be the event of the year in Singapore. The Governor and the Sultan of Johor will both be there. My mother is overwhelmed with the planning and has begged for my help.'

'And what about Ah Mei and Ah Fang?' her mother-in-law asked, trying to poke holes in Jade's plans.

Jade was ready with her reply. 'Well, of course, I could bring them. But I will be so busy; I won't be able to properly care for Baby Fang. And Ah Mei will be quite bored. I think it would be best if Ah Fang stays here with her amah and Ah Mei keeps her company.'

Mei's eyes darted back and forth between the women, waiting for her fate to be decided. She was spoiled enough to be sitting at the adult table for breakfast, but not so spoiled as to open her mouth while her elders talked.

'They are not expected at the party then?' her mother-in-law countered.

'I thought you might bring them along with their amah when you came down for the event.' Jade's eyes sparkled with the triumph of a player who had just revealed her winning hand. The mother-in-law had met her match with this daughter-in-law.

'Very well. You will need to wait until tomorrow so that we can finish with the shopping, unless you don't want to be involved in the selection of Ah Mei's outfit for the party.'

Sze-yin envied these two sparring women and hoped to one day be viewed as worthy of a match. But that would never happen, as long as she remained barren. She resented her inferior status. She had done everything within her power to improve her standing. She could now speak English with the lilted accent of an established Nyonya. She was just as attractive as Jade and was far better at accessorizing her features. Many of the younger socialites had even started to copy Sze-yin's dress styles. If Jade had bothered to ask, Sze-yin could have helped her select colours and lines to suit her lengthy frame and almond skin. Of course, a waist still thick from her last pregnancy limited her sister-in-law's current options. Sze-yin would gladly trade her wispy figure for a wider one, though. Those pregnancies were what gave Jade her preeminent position. She now had two healthy girls, and Loo had one. Only the birth of a boy would enable Sze-yin to surpass her sister-in-laws' accomplishments.

Sze-yin waited for the conversation to conclude. She would have preferred to catch her mother-in-law alone so as not to remind the whole family of her deficiencies. But protocol dictated that everyone remain as long as the matriarchs continued to eat, so Sze-yin had no choice but to make her request in front of the entire table.

'I was wondering if we might go to the Snake Temple today,' Sze-yin finally said.

Her mother-in-law's sharp mind took less than a moment to process the reason for the uncharacteristic request, but she would never address the issue directly. 'What a wonderful idea,' she responded. 'Perhaps Ah Siew could accompany you.' Tong's youngest sister would be married soon. It was never too early for a girl to pay respects to the One who watches over births.

Siew's teacup paused on its way to her lips. 'But Mother, you know I'm terrified of snakes.'

'All the more reason for you to go with Sze-yin and get over your silly fears,' her mother replied.

'Please don't make me go,' she begged.

'Then who will accompany Sze-yin? The rest of us are going shopping today to select fabric for the girls' gowns.'

'I can go alone,' Sze-yin suggested.

Her mother-in-law weighed the inappropriateness of this request with the importance of the mission. 'Very well, take my driver. He can come back and pick you up after he leaves us at Prichards.'

The driver dropped Sze-yin off at the base of the temple hill. She lifted the hem of her sarong and hiked up the stone steps embedded in the hillside. Lazy pit vipers slithered across the courtyard. Their scaly bodies were visible in every crevice of the temple grounds, curled in the eaves, resting on altars, and draped around statues and incense burners. Instinct told Sze-yin not to be afraid. These holy officers of the gods only wanted to encourage her to come forward with her supplication.

She purchased a package of joss sticks from a monk at the entrance of the temple and then approached the altar of Zhusheng Niangniang. Sze-yin knelt to pray. As she stood to place three joss sticks on the altar, an old woman touched her elbow. 'Is this your first time here, daughter?' the woman asked in Hokkien. 'Would you like some assistance?'

The woman's eyes were clouded with the milky film of the permanently blind. Her sparse gray hair was pulled up into a bedraggled bun, which exposed a bulbous growth on the back of her neck. Sze-yin did not recoil. The frail woman had spoken with power and purpose.

She had offered assistance, rather than asked for it. She was clearly a fortune-teller proposing her services.

Sze-yin had been taught as a child to revere the gifted soothsayers whose powers could command the gods to heap fortune on a worthy soul. But Ah Ma had warned her that the local fortune-tellers could not be trusted because they practiced the black magic of the Malays. So Sze-yin politely declined.

'Thank you, Auntie. I have finished my prayers now and am ready to go.'

The old woman did not press her case. She nodded her head and walked away.

2

June 1938

Anna made a little headway in mastering her daily routine. She gained some aptitude for the shopping, cooking and organizing required to get through the day. But she still made frequent mistakes. Dinner was never ready on time and the linen chest was always empty when she reached for clean towels. The maid, Rosanna, had learned to make a few dishes from Zaharah's cook. Her housework had improved, though her pace had not increased.

Thank goodness for Arun. Anna didn't like the moody driver but he was the only one with any experience running a household. She sent him to the market with lists, remembering to ask for fish, chicken and eggplants, but not for staples like rice, garlic and onions. He would return with the requested items as well as the essentials she had forgotten.

Rosanna looked to Anna, as matron of the house, for instructions on the laundry and cleaning. Anna didn't know the first thing about such skills. When she lived in her mother's house, clean clothes just appeared in her wardrobe and new sheets on her bed.

After stopping for tea, one day, at her cousin Nariza's house, she noted with envy the pristine state of the stately home.

'How do you manage everything, with the baby and your housework?' she asked her cousin, who was glowing with the news of her second pregnancy.

'A schedule, you must have a schedule,' Nariza informed her. 'Everything should be clearly spelled out for the maids—when to feed the baby, give her a bath, plan the meals, what linens to wash, and on what days. Then there can be no mistake about what should be done when.'

'But how do you create a schedule? How do you know what needs to be done when?'

'My mother helped me create one, though I have modified it over time. Of course, it helps that my Jena is an ox.'

Anna eyed the boxy maid dusting in the corner, oblivious to the English conversation. Jena did, in fact, look like an ox. She could probably snap Rosanna in two with her bare hands. But Anna was honest enough to realize that the fault did not lie with Rosanna's physique. What had she expected when she hired such an inexperienced girl? Well, she was stuck with her now. She knew less about firing a maid than she did about hiring one.

'May I have a look at your schedule?' Anna asked.

'Of course.'

Nariza produced a sheet of perfumed stationery with an elegant script listing the tasks for each day of the week. Anna didn't know what half of them were. How does one bleach sheets, and what is brining, and what kind of oil does one use on trim?

When Anna returned from her visit to Nariza's, she asked Arun to oil the banister. He gave her a queer look, but to her relief, he pulled tins of coconut oil and kerosene out of the garage and began rubbing the mixture into the wood in small circular strokes. She made a mental note of the labels on the tins and then asked Rosanna if she would help Arun finish the task.

Occasionally, Rosanna's arm would brush Arun's when the direction of her circles became confused. Her hand would fly to her mouth and she would let out a stifled giggle. Anna found the whole scene mildly distasteful. She returned to the kitchen and began her first draft of a schedule.

Arun rarely spoke to her or Rosanna, preferring the company of his kittens in the garden. He spent most of his spare time planting, weeding and pruning little patches of greenery in the yard. They hired a gardener to perform the weekly maintenance on the trees and hedges, but it was the driver who transformed the acres surrounding their bungalow into a tropical showplace with trailing bougainvillea, miniature pools with floating water lilies, and pebbled paths lined with lush ferns. She would have preferred if he had asked her permission or at least her opinion, but she was pleased with the result, especially the tranquil bench under the rambutan tree, where she could escape to read a book.

Rizal kept a consistent routine, rising with the first call to prayers, though she never actually saw him pray. He left for the office at seven-thirty, returning around six to eat dinner. When they did not have a social obligation, they talked or played cards or curled up together on the couch, engrossed in their separate books.

Anna read from her growing library of classics, while Rizal preferred books on history or science. She tried a few of his favourites, the most recent being Darwin's *Origin of Species*. Though Rizal argued vigorously for the scientific merits of the theory, she found the premise appalling. She couldn't imagine how he slept at night, believing as he did in the capricious presumption of natural selection. She preferred to rest her faith on the concept of a benevolent architect guiding his creations. Anna found comfort in the rituals of prayer, fasting and especially the sound of the imam's voice as he recited passages from the Quran. She held firmly to the reassuring precepts of Allah and his even-handed justice.

Still, she loved these philosophical debates with her husband and was not concerned about his analytical nature or his apathy toward prayer. She knew in her heart that she and her husband were good people who belonged unquestioningly among the faithful, destined for paradise. She couldn't help believing that Allah took a special interest in their well-being.

The couple's lazy evenings became fewer as their social circle began to assert itself. Nariza convinced Anna to join a few of her friends, who were forming a new ladies' auxiliary. The young women were all from more liberal homes, with husbands who didn't mind their wives venturing out of the house, provided they were working on charity projects. They gathered together to sew blankets for flood victims or pack donations for orphanages. Anna enjoyed the company of these high-minded, gossipy married women. The sessions gave her something to do on the evenings Rizal went out after dinner with friends or business associates.

Every Thursday night, he returned home late, the pungent smell of whisky and cigarettes announcing his presence. She prepared for these evenings with ritualistic intensity. Her new friends had taught her the value of perfumed baths and strategically placed aphrodisiac scents. After completing her toilette, she burrowed under the sheets and pretended to be asleep.

Rizal entered silently and undressed without the light before slipping into the bed next to her. His lips explored her shoulders, breasts, thighs, until her back arched, allowing the gown to slip up over her hips. She learned to respond to the rhythm of his body with her own.

She enjoyed the next part almost as much, the warmth of his body stretched out next to hers, the weight of his arm draped across her chest. She would lie awake, savouring the sound of his breath flowing like waves against her neck, until it slowed to the deep rhythms of sleep.

One morning, she woke feeling light-headed. Waves of nausea churned her belly. She raced to the bathroom and reached the washbasin just in time.

'Are you alright?' Rizal stood in the doorway, alarmed by the sight of his wife hunched on the bathroom floor.

'I'll be fine,' she said. 'I must have eaten something.'

All day, she lay in bed, immobilized by nausea. When Rizal came home from work, he insisted they send for a doctor.

Dr Loh entered the sickroom in great spirits, laughing and joking, as if on a pleasant social call. He felt her abdomen and prodded her with a few personal questions.

'What's wrong with her?' Rizal asked as he hovered over the bedside.

'Nothing's wrong. She's expecting.'

'Expecting?' Rizal repeated the word as if trying out a foreign phrase.

'Yes, your new addition will be arriving next year.'

'A baby?' Rizal asked. Now he looked like the one who could use a doctor.

'Yes, a baby. Congratulations!'

'You should be feeling better in a few weeks,' he told Anna. 'In the meantime, rest, stay in bed as long as you need.'

'But what should we do?' Rizal asked. 'Does she need any special food or medicine?'

'Why don't you talk to her mother? She'll know exactly what to do.'

Zaharah appeared that same day with a small suitcase and her most experienced maid, taking charge until Anna got back on her feet, several weeks later. Their Thursday night routine stopped but Anna didn't mind. She was too preoccupied with the changes occurring in her body, the tiny pooch in her belly that continued to expand, and the little butterflies that turned into insistent kicks. She lay awake at night watching her stomach move as the baby wiggled inside her, amazed that she could be so filled with love for a person she had never seen.

3

February 1939

Tong tapped his knuckles on the door of the sickroom. His wife lay curled in the fetal position, the back of her nightgown warding off potential visitors, her eyes fixed on the blank wall. A maid, the shape and colour of a brown mouse, held a teaspoon of chicken broth suspended in the air. She made clucking sounds with her tongue as if cajoling a willful child.

'How are you feeling this morning?' Tong asked as he approached the sick bed.

The question ricocheted off the walls and returned unanswered. The maid glanced from dejected husband to brooding wife and scurried out of the room.

Tong had purposely assigned her care to another physician in the hopes of reducing his perceived responsibility. Despite this precaution, Sze-yin still blamed him for the miscarriages. As a doctor, he should be able to prevent such medical misfortunes from befalling his own wife. This loss had occurred earlier than the last. The physical damage had long since healed but the mental scars ran deep.

His mother had engaged the family herbalist to prepare daily fertility brews for Sze-yin. But her problem was not easily solved with an herbal brew. If she did fail to conceive, he would be pressured to take a second wife. He didn't want to think of the possibility of adding another responsibility right now. He had capitulated to the family and married Sze-yin, but he refused to buy into their obsession with descendants.

Kian would eventually have a son and then the pressure would be off him to extend the family line. He wasn't particularly worried about ensuring his own progeny. He didn't know what he believed about death and the afterlife; he was more interested in the present. His primary concern was to help his wife stop suffering. He had tried to give her body a break, keeping his distance for a while so she could heal, physically and emotionally. But she wouldn't hear of it.

'You should try to eat something,' he murmured as he kissed her icy cheek.

4

July 1939

The driver dropped Anna by the stone pillars in front of Rumah Merah. Her nieces and nephews circled a mango tree in the front yard, throwing sticks in the air, trying to dislodge one of the fruits.

'Me do it! Me do it!' the littlest one clamoured, jumping up and down for emphasis.

'Hello,' she called. 'Doesn't anyone have a hug for your auntie?'

The kids tossed their sticks down and came running to hug her waist. They shouted greetings in unison.

'Where's your mother?' she asked.

'Mama's inside,' the oldest informed her. 'She said we had to play in the yard.'

'Be careful,' her little niece warned. 'She's very cross today.'

'I'll do my best to not upset her,' Anna laughed.

Her sister did look cross. Sofiah sat slumped at the kitchen table, her eyes red with tears. Zaharah and Mina were huddled around her, patting her hand.

'What's the matter? Is everything okay?' Anna asked.

'Everything's fine,' Zaharah said. 'Sofiah's just a little tired today.'

'How can you say that, Mama?' her sister hissed. 'My husband is marrying another woman and you act like it's nothing.'

'Zainal's getting married?' Anna asked. 'When? How?'

'In a few weeks,' Sofiah cried. 'He has apparently been planning this for months. He only just bothered to tell me.'

'Why would he get married again?'

'Why? Why?!' she screamed. 'Just look at me. I've given him five children. My breasts are saggy and my waist is thick. He wants a new wife. A young, pretty wife, not this old, used-up hag.'

'Sofiah, don't talk like that,' her mother scolded. 'You're as beautiful as the day he married you. Men just get tired of their wives after a while. Look at it this way, you'll always be the first wife, no one can ever take that away from you. And you've given him five beautiful children. What more could he ask for? Now, some young girl has turned his head. So what? Let her have him for a while. You had him in his youth, when he was still strong and handsome. Look at him now. Talk about a thick waist.'

Anna couldn't help but giggle.

'Fine, laugh at your poor sister,' Sofiah sputtered.

'I'm sorry.' Anna tried to control her laughter. 'It's just that, Zainal is looking rather round these days. And that hair growing out of his ears!'

This time, Sofiah smiled. 'He has hair on his back, too,' she admitted.

'You see,' Zaharah continued. 'He's no great prize. Think of that poor young girl, stuck with a decrepit old man. Do you think it's her choice to marry him? Of course not. Her family just thinks it will be a step up for her. That's the only reason they agreed to it.'

'I know he's getting old and pudgy.' Sofiah started to cry again. 'But he's still my husband. I love him. How do you think I feel picturing him with that girl? You're so lucky to have married an Englishman, Mama.'

'Do you think Englishmen are any different?' her mother spat. 'Just because their government won't let them marry more than one woman at a time? Men are all the same. The sooner you realize that, the better.'

Anna fumed the whole ride home. As the thickly settled shophouses gave way to rows of trees and wooden shacks, her anger only intensified. How dare her brother-in-law remarry and leave Sofiah to suffer the humiliation of an abandoned first wife? Sofiah had doted on her husband. She had put up with his nagging mother, endured the painful birth of his five children, cooked, cleaned and catered to his every need. And how does he reward her? By taking up with some girl half his age. Worse still, Sofiah, as the first wife, would be stuck living with her in-laws, taking care of their petty needs, while this new bride would be installed in a house of her own and treated like a pampered princess by her doddering old suitor.

Poor Sofiah, she always took upon herself the role of a martyr. As a child, she was the family pleaser, working herself into knots in order to gain some small hint of approval from their mother. Then she caved in to the pressure to marry this worthless man who never loved or appreciated her.

Anna couldn't wait for Rizal to come home so that she could unburden this horrible news onto him. He would be outraged. Wouldn't he? What if he wasn't? What if he clapped his hands and shouted, 'Good for him.'

Rizal was late as usual returning from the office. For such a brilliant man, he seemed unable to grasp the basic concept of time. He constantly lost track of the hour. They arrived late to every function because he overscheduled himself or forgot to take into account the distance from their home.

No one else seemed to mind his tardiness. To arrive past the hour, huffing and puffing with apologies only enhanced one's status as a much-in-demand guest of honour. Rizal was not trying to put on airs, though. He simply couldn't keep his eye on the clock. Tonight, he was over an hour late. Anna stared out the window searching for his headlights in the darkness.

'Rosanna,' she called to the maid who was setting the table in the dining room, 'there's still no sign of him. Just keep our dinner warm. I'll try to get the baby to bed.'

She occupied herself bathing her son. The little boy splashed his limbs in the water, blissfully ignorant of his mother's growing trepidation. When he was sufficiently clean, Anna tucked his tiny body into a pale blue nightgown and then settled him into bed. She stood over his crib breathing in the soothing smells of soap and talcum powder, willing her husband to return home.

'Sorry, I'm late.' Rizal found his wife standing over the baby's crib, her face scrunched up in some private rumination. He could never tell what to expect when he came home. Sometimes, he found her pacing the floors, fuming over some misconstrued comment. Other times, she flung her arms around his neck as though he had been gone for months.

'How is Kamil today?' he asked, rubbing the baby's back. The topic of their son could be counted on to soften any animosity.

'He was very good. I think he enjoyed all the attention from his auntie and cousins.'

'How's everyone at home?' He had forgotten that she had gone to see her mother.

'Sofiah's not feeling well,' she signed. 'She's heartbroken, actually. She just found out that Zainal is taking another wife.'

'Really? Who?'

Her face transformed from distress to fury. 'Who cares who he's marrying?!' she spat out. 'He's replacing my sister with some girl half his age. Sofiah's completely devastated.'

'Why should she be so upset?' Rizal said. He felt the need to defend himself but couldn't quite figure out his offense.

'Because he's remarrying. Can you imagine? After all that she's done for him?'

'There's nothing unusual about a man in his position taking another wife.'

'How can you say that? How can you sit there and defend such a dishonourable act?'

Rizal took her hand and pulled her out of the baby's room before their argument woke the sleeping infant. Why was she so angry? What had he done?

'I'm not defending him. But I'd hardly call it dishonourable. I'm sure he'll continue to take care of Sofiah. She is, after all, the mother of his children. He'd be a fool to turn his back on her. And anyway, the family would never allow it.'

'But he did turn his back on her. Didn't you hear me? He's getting married.'

'Anna, don't be so emotional. These arranged marriages are like business contracts, so what's the difference if he's entered into another contract? He'll continue to fulfill his obligations to Sofiah.'

Her hands flew to her head, as if to cover her ears from the violation of his voice.

'A business contract, how can you refer to a marriage like that?'

'But it is a contract, mutually agreed upon.' Rizal continued to explain his position. 'He promised to take care of her for the rest of his life and she promised to attend to his needs and to raise his children. So long as they both hold up their end of the bargain, the contract is valid.'

'How can you talk so coldly about a marriage? A contract, you call it. It's a sacred bond between a man and a woman. How can you say these things to your own wife? Do you think of our union in such calculating terms?'

Finally, he recognized the emotion behind her stance. Here he had been enjoying a spirited philosophical debate and she had been measuring their whole relationship by his response. Even after a year and a half of marriage, she completely mystified him. Were other men as confused by their wives or was it just his shortcoming? Now he would have to figure out how to recover.

'I wasn't talking about marriage in general,' he explained. 'I was talking about arranged marriages that aren't based on affection or mutual respect. I only meant that I wasn't surprised by Zainal. Not every man is like your brother-in-law. And you're nothing like your sister. If you were, we wouldn't be having this conversation.'

He could see her shoulders soften, her defensive posture subsiding.

'Believe me. I'd never look at another girl. Why should I want another wife when I have the most intriguing woman right here at home?'

She wasn't sure that she liked the word 'intriguing', but she recognized the sincerity in his voice. He did love her.

Anna tried to make up for their argument. She fixed him a drink and laid out his pajamas. She even massaged his feet while he read in bed. He really was a good man. She must learn to be more accommodating. Of course, he would never remarry. If he ever did contemplate another spouse, it would be her fault for being such a quarrelsome and difficult wife.

5

August 1939

Ibrahim had moved Rizal from his hovel on Market Street to the second floor of an Art Deco commercial complex on Beach Street, near the docks. His office, two doors down from Ibrahim's, now contained the theatrical trappings of an acknowledged executive—velvet curtains, sumptuous leather chairs, and a colossal desk of imported cherry.

'I'd like you to have another look at the trading company.' Ibrahim drummed his fingers on Rizal's glossy desktop.

'Why? Aren't the recommendations working?' He really didn't want to go back through Hafis's department and endure his cousin's simmering outrage.

'Things have improved, but I'm looking for a much bigger payoff. I'm sure the fault lies with my imbecilic son, but his incompetence notwithstanding, I feel certain there's more money to be made in this economy. I could forgive the paltry earnings during the downturn. But there's a war on and business should be booming.'

Ibrahim rose from his chair and stood by the picture window, looking out at the unobstructed view of the harbour below. The evening light accentuated the lines on his forehead and the dark circles under his eyes. Only in the glare of such harsh rays did Rizal remember his energetic uncle's advanced age.

'Look at that port down there,' Ibrahim gestured to the window, 'all that activity. The English are desperate for our rubber and tin to feed

their war. We should be making a killing and I want to understand why
we're not.'

'Have you asked Hafis?'

'He mumbles about higher insurance and storage costs. Claims the
uncertainty of war is causing expenses to rise.'

'You don't think that might be true?'

'I own the insurance and storage companies, so I ought to know
if there's any gouging going on. I can assure you that I offer my own
trading company the best possible rates.'

'I'm not sure how I can help? I already looked at the books.'

'Go a level below the balance sheets,' Ibrahim instructed him.
'Several levels, if you have to. I want to understand the cash flows,
what's coming in and going out.'

'That would take a tremendous amount of cooperation from Hafis.
He probably doesn't know those details either.'

'I want you to work with his operations manager. I'll ask Hafis to
assign him to you full-time. Hafis will be grateful not to have to dirty
his hands with all of those nasty numbers. He's much better at wrestling
with the big picture, like who to entertain and how much to spend.'

'I'll do my best, but I can't promise anything.'

'I have the utmost confidence in your abilities. If there's an extra
dollar to be had, you'll find it.'

6

Anna woke well past daybreak. She heard the clattering of dishes in the kitchen and the babble of her baby with the servants. Rizal would already be at work. She had forgotten to mention the invitation from Hafis. She dressed quickly and then scribbled a note on her stationery, sealed it with a monogrammed stamp, and ran downstairs to hand it to the driver.

She hesitated in the doorway of the kitchen, watching unnoticed as Arun danced with Kamil dangled above his head. The infant giggled in delight as the driver kissed each of his chubby toes. She was pleased by the driver's affection for her son, but suspected he was exaggerating his performance for the benefit of Rosanna, who was sitting at the kitchen table eyeing his antics from over the top of a steaming cup of tea. She had an unmistakable glint in her eye.

Well, why shouldn't she fancy him? The poor girl was probably desperately lonely, stuck in the house all day, tending someone else's baby. Servants were no different from their masters when it came to their aspirations for love. And Arun, Anna had to admit, was fairly well-groomed for a houseboy. And here he was, dancing around with a cooing infant. How could Rosanna resist?

It might be acceptable if they married, but in the meantime, Anna would have to consider the inappropriateness of the situation. True, Arun had his own quarters in the back of the garage and Rosanna slept in the baby's room. But who knew what they might be getting up to when no one was around? Servants were not raised with the same sense of propriety as their educated counterparts. And nothing could be worse than a jilted pregnant girl weeping around the house. Nariza had dismissed a maid last year for the same issue. Anna would have to speak with Rizal about the problem.

She strode into the room and took the baby from Arun's arms.

'Thank you. I'll get him dressed now.'

Arun obediently turned to leave the kitchen.

'Wait,' she said. 'I have a note for my husband. Could you give it to him and tell him I need a response?'

He took the envelope from her hand and sauntered out the door. He did have an arrogant swagger about him. Perhaps she should speak to Rizal about that as well.

'Did you give him the note?' she asked when Arun returned later in the day. 'What did he say?'

'I didn't give it to him yet. Tuan was very busy today. But I'm sure that he would want you to decline the invitation. He does not care for Hafis and besides, he has another engagement that night.'

'Arun, did you read my note?'

'Well, yes,' he said, looking mildly uncertain, 'I didn't want to disturb Tuan unless the matter was urgent. He was in a meeting all day.'

'How dare you read a private message from me to my husband? And who are you to decide what matters are urgent?'

Now he looked frightened, as if his insolence had only just occurred to him. 'I'm sorry, Mem, I meant no harm.'

'The next time I give you a note or anything else for my husband, you are to deliver it as asked. And you are never, ever to open private correspondence again or I will fire you on the spot. Do you understand me?'

'Yes, Mem.' He stared at the floor in an unusually humble pose.

Perhaps, it was not all his fault. Rizal was overly indulgent with this driver. Maybe Rizal's family accepted an unusual level of familiarity with their staff. But this behaviour was unacceptable. She would have to speak with her husband.

7

September 1939

Rizal rubbed his stinging eyes with the back of his hands. Cigarette smoke filled the office of the obsequious operations manager, Isaac, a squat Indian who attempted to compensate for his size with a massive pompadour. Isaac's office overflowed with cigarette butts smashed into a half dozen ashtrays lying on all surfaces within reach of his chair. The ineffective little man required his employees to copy him on every financial report, receipt, tax record, customs form, or other transaction performed by the enormous trading company. He never read the documents, assuming that the mere existence of these bits of paper would keep his staff on their toes. His office assistant meticulously filed each of the reports. One had only to provide the assistant with a description of any document and he could produce it in less than three minutes, unless the requested report was over two years old, in which case he would have to retrieve it from the columns of dead files that occupied three of the outer offices. This could take him up to eight minutes.

When Rizal arrived at the office several weeks ago, he tried to review their financials at the most aggregate level, requesting whatever standard reports the dutiful accountants had prepared each quarter. The broad categories of the sparse line items on these reports were meaningless to everyone except the clerks themselves. After several meetings with these obliging pencil pushers, he gave up pursuing any systematic approach. He started plucking files randomly out of drawers, searching for a needle in a haystack, or more aptly, a nugget in a pile of manure.

After days of wading through the endless stacks of useless documents, Rizal began having nightmares in which he was literally drowning in paper. Today, he was staring at an accounts payable report of a subsidiary, when his mind latched onto a recurring line item.

'What's this company, McCormick Timbers? I've never heard of them. We don't work with any loggers, do we?'

Isaac looked up from his morning tea. He was in the process of consuming his third pastry and eighth cigarette of the morning. Rizal could barely make out the operations manager's figure through the haze of smoke in the room.

'We handle some from time to time, I believe,' Issac pulled out a handkerchief from his breast pocket to wipe the grease from his lips. He pressed the cloth into perfect thirds by running the long nail of his little finger along each fold before placing it next to his emptied plate.

'I don't see any corresponding deliveries or receipts for this company,' Rizal said. 'Who handles them?'

'I'm not sure. Pitchay,' Isaac shouted toward the door, 'could you come in here for a moment?'

Pitchay appeared in the office, pen and pad in hand, eager to conquer his next challenge.

'Ah, Pitchay, could you please provide us with the accounts report for the last year? I would like to know which manager handles the McCormick Timbers Company.'

'Yes, sir.' The assistant stepped to the third bank of file cabinets, pulled out the top door, plucked a manila folder from the drawer, and handed it to Isaac.

'It says right here, ah, yes, well . . . ' Isaac's lips curled in an obliging smile. 'It seems that Mr Hafis handles that account directly. So I'm sure that everything is in order, nothing to worry about there.'

'I see. I think I'd like to see the debit reports for this subsidiary for the last year.'

'That would be quite a lot of paper,' Isaac squawked. 'We produce debit reports daily, I'm not even sure I could locate all of them.'

'I'm quite confident that Pitchay could have them here within the hour,' Rizal said. 'Couldn't you, Pitchay?'

Pitchay practically quivered with the possibility of being so useful.

8

Anna had been meaning to bring up the subject of the servants for some time. She had happened upon several more encounters with Arun and Rosanna, and she was more convinced than ever that an infatuation was brewing. The poor thing could hardly look at Arun without blushing. It was unclear whether he returned her affection, but he couldn't have failed to notice, and there was always the risk that he might take advantage of the situation.

It was only the urgency of this mission that made Anna realize how little time she and her husband spent alone. When they were in the house, Rosanna was always about. If they went out together, Arun would be driving, and once they arrived at their destination, they were always in the company of others. Only when they returned home at night to collapse in their beds, could they manage a few words together. But Rizal usually looked too exhausted to launch into a debate about the household staff.

Finally, one night, they experienced an unexpected furlough. A torrential downpour threatened to flood the roads, and everyone at the dinner party raced home as soon as the meal was over. Anna and Rizal found themselves preparing for bed before ten o'clock.

'I've been meaning to speak with you about the servants,' Anna said as they changed into their nightclothes.

'What about them?'

'It's occurred to me that it's rather inappropriate for us to have two unmarried servants living under the same roof. I think that Rosanna has developed an attachment to Arun and—'

'I wouldn't worry about it,' Rizal cut her off. 'Their personal feelings are none of our business.'

'I consider them both our responsibility, especially Rosanna, who's so young and inexperienced.'

'I'm quite sure that Arun doesn't share her feelings.'

'How do you know?'

'I've known Arun for a long time. You have nothing to worry about.'

'Well, maybe we should consider the larger question. Perhaps Rosanna's infatuation is a sign that she is ready for a suitor. And Arun is not getting any younger. It's always been my impression that employing an unmarried houseboy is like keeping a loaded gun around the house.'

'That's quite a metaphor, Anna. Sometimes I wonder about that household you grew up in.'

'I'm just trying to speak plainly.'

'Well, even if your metaphor is apt, I'm not interested in playing matchmaker for my servants. They'll have to find their own targets, so to speak.'

'Fine,' she said. 'If you won't help me, I'll see to it myself.'

'I'm sure you will.'

He pulled back the covers and climbed into bed. She joined him but was not quite ready to go to sleep.

'There's something else that's been bothering me about Arun,' she said before he could put out the bedside light.

'I can't imagine that you don't have more important things to worry about,' he yawned.

'These are important things. Servants contribute substantially to the smooth running of a household and managing them can be every bit as complicated as overseeing those people in your office.'

'Alright then.' He gave up on the light and rolled back to face her. 'What else has been troubling you?'

'I gave Arun a message for you. It was written on my personal stationery and sealed. I was informing you that Hafis had invited us for dinner but I forgot to mention it to you before you left for work. This was over a week ago now.'

'I don't remember getting a note about a dinner with Hafis.'

'That's because Arun took it upon himself to open the note and decide that it was not sufficiently important to warrant your attention. He informed me that you were busy and that you didn't actually care for Hafis—which I hope is not true as he is your cousin and Ibrahim's eldest—and I don't need to remind you how indebted we are to Uncle.'

'Well, truth be told, I don't care for Hafis and I'm sure that I was busy. What day was that?'

'You miss the point. Arun is a driver, he has no business opening personal messages from me to you and determining how you would respond. This really has to be addressed. I've been meaning to mention it for some time but we're never alone these days.'

'Perhaps he overstepped his bounds. He's been with me for a while and probably doesn't quite know how to conduct himself around you.'

'How could he not know? He grew up as a servant in your parents' house. I can't imagine your mother tolerated her staff opening personal correspondence. I know my mother would have dismissed him immediately. Really, you give him far too much leeway. I would speak to him myself but he hardly listens to me. He acts as if you're the only member of this household.'

'I'll talk to him. I'm sure he won't repeat the mistake. Based on your reaction, I'm sure he's fully aware of the seriousness of his offence even without my involvement.'

'I'd like you to back me up, all the same.'

'I said I'll talk to him. Now can we get some sleep? I have to get up early for another annoying day of wading through bank statements.'

'I thought you were a lawyer.'

'Apparently, I'm a hired gun.'

9

Over 50,000 dollars had been transferred from this tiny subsidiary to five different companies in the last year, with no record of shipments or products. All the companies carried the same office address on Light Street, and all deposits were made into the same branch office of the East West United Bank.

Rizal instructed Arun to take him to 47 Light Street, knowing full well what he would find. The car slowed in front of an empty alley wedged between two boarded-up shop houses numbered 45 and 49.

'Damn.'

'Is something the matter?' Arun asked.

'That alley stinks of a festering rat,' Rizal said.

Arun peered down it to inspect the disturbing infestation but all he could see was an old man peeing on a wall.

'You better take me to the East West Bank,' Rizal said.

Arun still confused by the connection between an empty ally and a financial institution, obediently drove his boss to the stately bank headquarters in town.

Rizal walked into the plush offices of the East West United Bank. His eyes took several minutes to adjust from the blinding afternoon sunlight to the cavernous interior dimly lit by opulent chandeliers hung from arched ceilings. He followed the red carpet to the bank of tellers positioned behind a granite counter.

'Good afternoon,' Rizal greeted a skinny youth blinking behind a pair of glasses, 'I would like to speak with the branch manager, please.'

'I'm sorry, the manager is with another customer at the moment,' the young man said. 'Could I give him a message?'

'Yes, this is Rizal Mansour, I dined with him the other day, at Ibrahim Hamid's house. I have a business matter I would like to discuss with him.'

'Yes, of course.' The man practically jumped at Ibrahim's name.

Within minutes, the teller returned, followed by the obliging bank manager.

'Encik Mansour, wonderful to see you again. I'm honoured by your visit. Please come in and have some tea, won't you?'

Rizal followed the manager into his office, where an Indian woman served tea sweetened with condensed milk and two lumps of sugar. After a few minutes of pleasantries, during which Rizal pretended to sip the lukewarm liquid, the bank manager finally asked how he could help.

'I'm working on a project for Ibrahim Hamid. I've come across several customers whose payments are deposited into this branch. I wondered if you could give me the name of the signatures on these accounts.'

The manager placed his fingertips together in earnest contemplation of the request.

'I would love to assist you. Encik Hamid has been very good to this bank and we would be pleased, that is to say, privileged, to see even more of his business come our way. But, as you must know, the identity of signatures on an account would be private information that I could not possibly divulge. I would require written permission from the signatures themselves.'

'How could I obtain their permission if I don't know who they are?'

'Quite. It is a dilemma. I'm perfectly distraught at not being able to help with such a simple question, the answer to which would only require a brief search on my part through those drawers behind me.'

'I understand your predicament. As you say, the information is quite private. I apologize for the awkward position I've put you in. I know you would help if you could.' Rizal slid an envelope filled with bills across the desk toward the manager's waiting hands.

The manager patted the envelope to determine the size of the stack.

'You are more than welcome to leave the list of companies with me, but as I said, I could not possibly *tell* you the signatures. That would be unethical.'

'I understand. Thank you for your help, all the same.'

Rizal shook the manager's hand and walked out of the office, leaving the list next to the stack of bills on the desk.

The next day, a courier appeared with an envelope from the East West United Bank. Rizal tore open the seal and pulled out a note scrawled on plain stationery.

'Damn.'

Now what was he supposed to do? Ibrahim would be devastated to know that his own son was embezzling from the family chest. Rizal had suspected all along where the trail would lead. At each turn, he kept hoping that he would find a more palatable explanation. Even as he gathered his evidence, he postponed contemplating what he would do with the information. He pursued the answer scientifically, without debating the inevitable conclusion. And now in his hand was irrefutable proof. He didn't bother to go back through the files for other companies or previous years. The message indicated that Hafis opened the bank accounts five years ago. Who knows how many other shell companies existed?

He couldn't tell Ibrahim. It would break his heart. He would have to confront Hafis and hope that the fear of exposure would be enough to stop or at least slow the outflow.

With this confrontation in mind, he wandered into the Blue Moon, an exceptionally dull jazz bar that Hafis owned and frequented. He found his cousin seated at a circular booth next to the piano, where a tuxedoed player hammered out a Duke Ellington tune.

'Rizal, I didn't expect to see you here. Have you met Queenie?' he motioned to the plump woman seated next to him. 'She's the star of the show, aren't you, Queenie? She's up next. Why don't you take a seat and prepare to be transported?' He squeezed her thigh enthusiastically.

The diamonds dripping off the singer went a long way toward explaining Hafis's need for cash. All the more reason to keep his unsavoury transactions from Ibrahim, and by extension, Hafis's long-suffering wife.

The fleshy starlet wiggled out of their booth and climbed onto the piano, stretching her ample body across the top. She belted out a hoarse version of 'Give My Regards to Broadway' in broken English. Hafis stared adoringly at the unsightly figure before turning his attention to his cousin.

'So, what brings you to the Blue Moon? I've been open for three years and I've never seen you here before. Have you finally decided to come and support your cousin's lowly establishment?'

'Actually, I came to find you.' He pushed a manila envelope across the table. Hafis opened the clasp and took a quick glance at the pages inside.

'You bastard. How dare you come in here and threaten me!'

'I'm not threatening you. I'm letting you know what I know in the hopes that you will mend your ways. I have no desire to go to your father with this. But he hired me to find ways to turn your company around, and this seems as good a way as any. I'm only asking that you tone it down. It is your family's business. I'm sure you feel entitled to a larger chunk of the profits than your salary. But really, the sums are outrageous. You run the risk of running your own company into the ground.'

'I don't see how it is any of your business,' Hafis hissed.

'Well, Ibrahim made it my business. I didn't ask for this assignment, but if I say nothing and you keep doing what you're doing, your father will figure it out before too long and he will know that I covered for you. I can't risk that.'

'Well, I can appreciate your predicament,' Hafis pushed the envelope back toward Rizal. 'But I don't see how it's any of my concern. You'll have to do whatever your conscience dictates. In the meantime, I would like to hear Queenie sing.'

Hafis turned his head back toward his starlet.

10

Tong had been working late trying to catch up on his paperwork. Dr Loh's wife kept her husband's accounts, filed his notes and stocked his dispensary. She had offered to do the same for Tong but he couldn't ask her to work extra hours on his behalf while his own wife lazed at home. He hired a clerk to perform these tasks. The well-intentioned moron misfiled everything, so Tong still had to spend hours every evening straightening the mess.

Tong turned the key in his office door and waited in the dark for the driver to pull up the car. He was so immersed in his thoughts that he didn't notice the silent shadow approaching from behind. He jumped at the sound of a voice over his shoulder. His hands clenched his office keys as he turned, expecting to find a petty thief. Instead, he discovered the figure of a young girl, maybe twelve or thirteen, in a cheap cheongsam, her shoulders wrapped in a tattered beaded shawl.

'Can I help you?' he asked.

The girl looked as though she couldn't decide whether to speak or flee.

'You doctor, yes?' she whispered.

'Yes, I'm a doctor. Can I help you? Are you hurt?'

She pointed to her right arm, which hung limply at her side.

He took her functioning hand and led her to the office door. She tried to pull away as he turned the key, afraid, perhaps, that he intended to lock her inside. But he held on tight and explained in as many dialects as he knew that he had medicine inside to help her. She nodded in response when he tried the explanation in Hakka, though his Hakka was so poor, he was not sure what he had actually communicated.

She climbed onto the examination table and stared mutely at the wall while he studied her arm. He tried to engage her in conversation, but her English was not up to the task and his Hakka was even worse. He was pretty sure that he knew her story anyway. In addition to the broken arm, she had bruises on her neck and deep lacerations that wrapped her wrists like fiery red bracelets.

She didn't flinch as he doused the wounds with antiseptic and wrapped her arm in a sling.

'Do you have anywhere to go?' he asked.

Her eyes didn't move from the wall.

'You have house, room, family?' he tried again in Hakka.

This time, she acknowledged his question with a shrug of her small shoulders.

Obviously she didn't have a home, or at least not one she wanted to go back to, so he led her out into the street and motioned her into his waiting car. She climbed into the seat, accepting whatever fate he had in mind for her.

He told the driver to take them to one of the charitable institutions maintained by the Chinese community that provided housing for escaped prostitutes. He would happily have brought her home. They had so many servants, what would one more matter? But his father had absolutely forbidden any of his 'misguided charitable work' to spill over into the domestic tranquility of their castle.

The car pulled into the driveway and past the six foot high wall that surrounded the girls' dormitory. The manicured compound could have belonged to a school, a convent, a genteel prison or a lunatic asylum. The house was dark except for a flickering light in the office window. Tong left the girl in the car and went to the front door. A wizened Chinese lady dressed in black peeked through the window as he knocked. The matron recognized Tong's face. He was a member of the board of trustees and one of the few males allowed to enter the shelter when he made his monthly visits to tend to the residents' medical needs. In the last few years, he had brought a number of girls here who had wandered into his office, just as this one had done tonight.

'Oh, doctor, it's you,' she said as she peered through the latched front door. 'You gave me quite a fright. I thought you might be a burglar.'

'I'm sorry to frighten you, but I have a young girl who needs a place to stay. I was hoping you might take her in.'

'I see.' She undid the chain latch and stared toward the car. 'We might have some room. I'd need to talk to her first, though. We are particular about the kind of girls we accept here. We try to distinguish between the unfortunate girls and the troublemakers.'

'I'm afraid she only speaks Hakka,' he explained.

'That's not a problem,' she said.

Tong returned to the car and fetched the girl, who walked mutely by his side back to the house. The woman appraised the shivering specimen before her. Then she asked the girl her name in Hakka. At the sound of her native tongue, the girl threw her head in her hands and began weeping.

'I think we can take her,' the matron whispered.

Silence greeted Tong as he slipped through the front door of the darkened house. He removed his shoes and tiptoed up the stairs, checking his watch for the first time that evening. It was almost midnight. He should have called Sze-yin and informed her that he was going to be late. For some reason, his good intentions never translated into action when it came to his wife.

The light from her bedroom triggered an involuntary sigh. She was still awake. He stood in the doorway and watched her as she sat facing the mirror on her dressing table, her porcelain back visible through the sheer fabric of her negligee. The straps slipped unconsciously off her shoulder as she applied a cream to her cheeks from one of the silver jars cluttering her table. There was beauty in the fragility of her features, like an exquisite glass ornament, designed for admiration but too delicate to be touched.

Her eyes narrowed when she saw him in the mirror.

'The Tans send their regards,' she said.

He paused, trying to remember the significance of that name in her reproach. Finally, it came to him. 'Tonight was their dinner. I'm sorry. I was called away. I should have let you know.'

Apologies flowed so often from him these days.

'I telephoned them to explain that you had an emergency.' She swiveled in her chair and settled her accusing eyes on him. 'You know that I've been trying to get an invitation to the Tans' for months. I thought he might talk to you about a position on his board. But perhaps you did have an emergency, after all?'

'Of course I had an emergency. Otherwise I wouldn't have left you in such an awkward position. I meant to send word to you, but there just wasn't time.'

Even as he said the words, he could hear the hollowness of his excuse.

'I hope that it was a client this time,' she said.

'Well, no . . . '

'Another girl then.'

He nodded.

'What is your obsession with these girls? You must know what people say about you?'

It took all of Tong's patience to restrain his disgust at her accusations. He was bone-tired after a sixteen-hour day. All he wanted to do was go to his room and fall asleep.

'I'm a doctor. It's my responsibility to treat people. This girl couldn't have been more than thirteen. I can't even imagine what she must have been through. How can I just walk away when someone like that comes to me for help?'

She stared at him with total lack of comprehension. They inhabited different worlds. She could never imagine the life these girls had been forced to live. How they were sold like cattle by uncaring parents to brutal men. He could have tried to explain to her about the bruises and the scars but that experience was so far removed from anything in Sze-yin's life, she could never have understood. Nor did he want her to. Let her live in her innocent and protected world, where the size of one's baubles dictated one's happiness. Contentment was easier in a sheltered existence.

Sze-yin turned back toward the mirror. 'The next time I am required to cancel an engagement on your behalf,' she said, 'I would prefer it was for a client.'

Tong mumbled his promises and left the room.

Sze-yin patted her stomach and apologized to her child for the rise in her voice. She was doing her best to control her temper, but her sheep of a husband continued to try her patience. As a wife, it was her duty to ensure that her family prospered. She did her best to look after their spiritual health, fulfilling all the rituals of their religion. And she used all the powers at her disposal—her good looks, her charm and her gifts of persuasion—to assist her husband in his career. But her efforts were stifled at every turn by his lack of ambition.

Several prominent doctors in Penang served on the Municipal Council but her husband did not seem interested in positioning himself for such an appointment. He chose not to join the Rotary Club, where he could mingle with colonial leaders, and he refused to take an active role in the Khoo Kongsi, whose connections could help him with business and politics. He spent all his time working with useless charities.

She finished her toilette and went to bed. She must get more sleep. Her first duty was to protect her child and ensure the safe delivery of the son who would be the just compensation for her many disappointments.

11

November 1939

Rizal allowed the month of Ramadan to go by without making any further decisions about Hafis. Ramadan presented the perfect opportunity to repent for one's sins and ask for forgiveness from those you had wronged. Now that Hafis knew he was being watched, perhaps he would confess on his own.

If Hafis refused to mend his ways, Rizal would have to do something. If he kept quiet, he would be guilty of abetting the crime. When Ibrahim discovered the truth, his trust in Rizal would be irrevocably damaged. Rizal had little to offer his mentor, except his integrity. Without it, he was no more useful than a common clerk.

Hafis was a selfish fool who deserved whatever punishment he received. But Rizal's compassion for his uncle caused him to hesitate. Though Ibrahim had no illusions about his son's deficiencies, he still believed in Hafis's character. This betrayal would break his heart.

Rizal fasted and attended mosque throughout the month for the sake of custom and propriety. He did not expect any divine guidance, though a tiny part of him remained open to the possibility. The silence did not shake his faith. If anything, it rendered Allah a more realistic being, consistent with his own father, an obscure figure who loved his creations with cold indifference.

Rizal showed up at the office during Ramadan with the same sense of futility with which he attended mosque, half-heartedly scanning financial reports, buying time until the end of the month. He tried to put in a half day on Saturdays to make up for Friday afternoon, which he lost to the mosque. But this Saturday, as Arun pulled up to the office doors, he could not bring himself to enter.

'Let's go for a swim,' he suggested.

Arun was always willing to support his boss's truancy. He parked the car in the usual spot, at the edge of the trail that led to the swimming hole they had discovered on their first bike ride around the island. The road had been improved so that the area was now only a few minutes' drive from the city. Fortunately, the dense jungle still concealed their pool, allowing them the privacy they craved. Someday these trees would be cut and their natural fortress removed. But for now, it remained their private paradise.

Songbirds greeted them as they followed the creek down the ravine to the hidden pond. The forest floor, always wet from the dense covering, was especially damp after the morning showers. The bright foliage sparkled from its morning bath. Arun peeled off his clothes and jumped into the cool, clear water.

They relaxed all morning, revelling in the freedom to enjoy each other's company, if only for a few hours. Sometimes he imagined that this was his life. These stolen hours were his real existence, the rest just a long, weary dream. He made up stories in his head to pepper this reality. He and Arun shared a house, a little cottage, on this far side of the island. They fished and swam all day. When they were hungry, they would ride their bikes to town and have a meal at one of the stalls. But when he reached into his wallet to pay for the food, he would find it empty. Swimming all day couldn't put food on the table. And would he really want an existence that didn't include Anna and Kamil? That might have been his dream once. But now he couldn't imagine it. He loved his life, all of it, however incongruous his two worlds might seem.

They dried themselves on a rock and then reluctantly pulled on their clothes. As they emerged from the path, Rizal noticed a car parked across the road. What could anyone be doing there? Nobody ever used this road. He didn't recognize the black sedan, nor could he make out the driver's face, which was obscured by a newspaper.

There was no point in running away. Rizal's car was too recognizable. Instead, he walked toward the sedan to learn the driver's intentions. But just as he started across the street, the car sped away.

12

January 1940

The family sent Sze-yin to their house on Penang Hill for a month of confinement. She had almost made it to the third trimester this time. The herbalist assumed full credit for the progress, as if a late-term miscarriage was something to celebrate. He informed them that the loss of blood was so significant that her body required the same replenishment as a term pregnancy. The family wholeheartedly supported the prescription. Sze-yin could tell Tong disagreed with the medical basis for the confinement, but he seemed happy to be rid of her for a whole month.

The herbalist forbade Sze-yin to eat or drink anything cold, to wash her body, to brush her teeth, or even to walk outside. Rather than enjoying the cool air in the hills, she was confined to a sick bed in a tiny room behind the kitchen, her sweaty body wrapped in cotton blankets to conserve her heat. A nurse prepared special meals to flush out the dirty blood and supplement the loss of qi. She remained in the cramped, stifling room with only the silent nurse and a docile maid to keep her company, watching the immobile ceiling fan mock her from above, while a taunting breeze beat against the locked shutters. The long hours of solitary inactivity left her with nothing to do but dwell on her failures. The reality of her situation rattled in her mind all day.

If she continued to have miscarriages, her in-laws would insist that Tong take another wife. She didn't object to Tong remarrying after she had children. She was not raised to expect passion or fidelity from a husband. She may have longed for love once. She may have cried the first time her mother slapped her tiny hand away. But she had learned to make do without affection. By the time of her mother's funeral, when Sze-yin was only six, she had learned to suppress her tears. She had stood impassively by the coffin, next to her stone-faced father, while they listened to the professional wailers moan. No, she did not need love. The yearning she dared to hold in her heart was not the desire for tenderness, but a desperate need for respect. She nursed this hope like the glowing embers of the fire that had warmed her lonely childhood nights.

If she could not have children, she would never have respect. She would be as useless as a pebble on the beach. There were times when Sze-yin lost confidence, when she curled up into a ball in her bed and almost gave up. She would rather die than lead a worthless life. It was not in her nature to admit defeat, but she sometimes wondered if this pitiful fate was her only destiny. Ah Ma must have sensed her despair from afar, because she arrived one day at the door of the sickroom with a basket of eggs.

Ah Ma never left Seascape except to attend a funeral or wedding. For these required outings, she travelled as few miles as possible and stayed as few hours as necessary. She used to visit the Pembroke House—as they called their hillside retreat—when it used to belong to her husband, in the days when the journey could be taken in the safety and seclusion of a sedan chair. But now, one had to pack oneself into a public funicular to be transported up the jungle hillside by mechanical wires. Ah Ma would have never braved the trip if she hadn't sensed that her granddaughter was close to a breaking-point.

She entered the sickroom with her attendant. Despite the old woman's bound feet and frail frame, it was her servant who appeared winded after the walk from the funicular station. The ageing maid had worked for Ah Ma for twenty years and had grown soft from attending to such a self-contained and self-sufficient mistress. She placed Ah Ma on a chair next to the bed and then sat down in the corner armchair and proceeded to fan her streaming face.

Sze-yin couldn't help but be buoyed by the unexpected fidelity of her grandmother. The fact that this wise woman took an interest in her well-being was enough to make her want to overcome her melancholy. Ah Ma pulled her chair close to the bedside and placed a basket of boiled eggs on the nightstand. She was dressed as always, in black Chinese robes draped over embroidered slippers on her tiny feet, her gray hair tied on the top of her head, the ends plaited into a long swallowtail, the style she had worn since the day she was married. Though her face had the sunken quality of an opium addict, her black eyes still danced with life when she spoke.

'It is important to eat three eggs a day. I was worried that you didn't have enough chickens at Pembroke.'

'Thank you for your thoughtfulness,' Sze-yin said. She had too much pent-up sorrow to continue with pleasantries. 'Everyone blames me for the miscarriages,' she confessed her fears. 'They think I'm being punished for some past impropriety.'

'I don't think they harbour any conspiracies about your conduct,' Ah Ma assured her. 'The herbalist seems to blame your temperament.'

Sze-yin was so tired of hearing this accusation that the rebuttal poured out of her like a raging river toppling a weighty dam. 'I'm a rooster so of course, I am quick-minded and ambitious. Naturally, I can be impatient and critical. But I don't believe my frustration spills over into the kind of anger that might harm my child.'

'I agree. That's why I came here. I have thought about this for some time. I believe that girl souls are entering your body and that Zhusheng Niangniang is causing the miscarriages to honour your request for a baby boy.'

Sze-yin had not thought of this possibility. What a wise and insightful woman Ah Ma was. Of course, that must be the problem. 'But what should I do? Should I go back to the temple and tell Zhusheng Niangniang I would accept a girl? I can't risk another miscarriage.'

Ah Ma placed a reassuring hand on Sze-yin's matted hair. 'I think you should return to the temple to learn what the gods have in mind for you. You need to speak to a fortune-teller.'

'But you told me they could not be trusted.'

'When I was a little girl, I went with my grandmother to an oracle in the hills above my village. Though I was quite small, I could feel the fortune-teller's power just by looking in her eyes. It has been many years, but I think I would be able to detect an honest and true seer. I will go with you to the temple to find a fortune-teller who speaks the truth.'

Sze-yin understood what an extraordinary gesture this was for her reclusive grandmother to make. 'Ah Ma, I would be honoured if you would accompany me.' She felt the flicker of hope for the first time in over a week. 'Can we go as soon as I am released from confinement?'

'We should wait until the birthday of Zhusheng Niangniang. That will be the most auspicious time to visit the temple.'

'But that is still several months away.' She had waited so long and endured so many disappointments, she wanted a resolution sooner.

'These things must be done at the proper time,' Ah Ma assured her. 'Whatever we learn will not change fate. Your footprints are already etched on the path you must take. The fortune-teller will only help us see the route more clearly, to prevent you from stumbling on the way.'

13

Rizal and Anna entered the garden of Ibrahim's compound. Family and friends had gathered to celebrate Hari Raya. Guests lined up around buffet tables while children scampered on the grounds, tugging on sleeves and smiling their best smiles, as they wished the adults 'Selamat Hari Raya.'

Rizal carried Kamil through the crowd. The boy's aunties and uncles pinched his cheek and shoved crisp bills of cash into his chubby fists. Anna left her husband and son to soak up the admiration of their family while she ran to find her mother and aunts, who were probably elbow-deep in food preparation in the kitchen.

'My husband says that we should start stocking up on canned foods just in case war comes to Penang,' Zaharah's youngest sister was warning.

'Penang is a peaceful island,' Fareeda, the eldest and a know-it-all said. 'The war in Europe has nothing to do with us. Abdul was in a briefing this week. The governor assured our business leaders that the war would have no impact on us. The governor should know what he is talking about. He's privy to all the military updates.'

'Maybe he was lying?' Aisha suggested.

'Why should he lie to us?' Fareeda said. 'He has nothing to gain by misleading the population.'

'But I heard a Chinaman say that the Japanese were planning to attack the peninsula,' the youngest sister whispered. 'He said they won't stop until they take all of Asia from the Europeans.'

'So what if the Japanese come?' Aunt Fareeda said. 'They have no quarrel with us. What do we care who runs the country, as long as we are left in peace to raise our families and earn a decent living?'

'I'm going to start stocking up anyway,' the fourth sister insisted. 'If the British were to leave, they would take their imported goods with them. Noordin would be so grumpy if he didn't get his tinned milk and marmalade with his tea.'

'This is a day for family and prayer,' Zaharah reminded her sisters. 'Enough of this talk about war.'

'Zaharah's right,' Fareeda replied, never one to be out-pioused by a younger sister. 'Marmalade and tinned milk, indeed. We should be focussing on the many blessings in our lives, not contemplating the hoarding of imports.'

'Anna, there you are,' Zaharah used the approach of her daughter to bypass the sisterly confrontation. 'Come, greet your aunties.' Anna went around the room greeting her mother and her aunties in ritual succession, 'Selamat Hari Raya. Maaf zahir dan batin', bowing to each, extending both hands to touch their right hand, then touching her heart with her own right hand.

When she had finished, her mother asked, 'Where's Kamil? I want to give my grandson his duit Raya.'

'Rizal's carrying him in the garden.'

'Tell them to come in here so that I can have a look at them.'

Anna stepped back outside and scanned the yard for her little family. She spotted Rizal in a crowd surrounded by Faisal, Ibrahim, Hafis and Ibrahim's sons-in-law. Ibrahim towered over the other men, his regal features and thick silver hair enhanced by a pale blue tunic and pants. Faisal stood next to his uncle, tapping his foot with boyish energy, his ever-present grin on his face. Hafis slumped beside his father. Poor Hafis had none of his father's stature or charm. But what he lacked in posture, he made up for in flash. He wore a baju pantsuit like the others but his neck held a gold chain that could rival any of the women's for bulk. On his wrist, he displayed several small chains and a shiny Dunhill watch. His shoes of soft, fragile leather gleamed with glossy polish.

But the most handsome figure on the lawn was her husband. Rizal stood with the others, smartly attired in a maroon baju wrapped with a plaid songket, a black songkok on his head. He was holding his mirror image, little Kamil, dressed in a new silver baju. Anna wasn't disappointed that their son showed no traces of her own features. She loved to look at Kamil next to his father, with their matching chestnut skin, rich brown eyes, and their majestic smiles.

Anna ran to her husband and kissed his cheek, an impetuous gesture in this stiff circle of men. Another man might have scolded his wife for embarrassing him in public, but Rizal just laughed and shook his head as he always did when she failed to restrain her little impulses.

'Selamat Hari Raya,' the men greeted Anna in unison. She went around the circle touching each of their hands in greeting.

'I was just telling everyone,' Hafis said, 'how delightful it is to see Rizal settling down into married life. You're a very good influence on him, Anna. He finally seems to be curbing his workaholic tendencies. Who could blame him for leaving the office early when he has such a lovely family waiting at home?'

'I wish what you were saying was true,' Anna said. 'Rizal seems to be working as hard as ever. I can never get him home in time for a warm dinner.'

'At least he's stopped spending his Saturdays at work,' Hafis said. 'I swung by last weekend to give him some documents and was surprised to find his office dark.'

'Rizal was in the office last Saturday, weren't you?' Anna turned to her husband.

'I stepped out for a while to watch a little cricket,' Rizal explained.

'Yes, well, sports and hobbies are important,' Hafis said. 'I love my music, couldn't live without it. It's important to have outside interests like music or cricket or a vigorous afternoon swimming session, wouldn't you say, Rizal?'

'If you say so.' Rizal handed Kamil to Anna. 'I haven't seen your mother yet. Is she in the kitchen?'

'I just left her. She wants you to bring Kamil in to get his duit Raya.'

Anna walked with her husband and baby across the lawn, absorbing the approving nods of their relatives, who couldn't fail to admire the handsome threesome.

14

Rizal left for work at the crack of dawn after another sleepless night. Ibrahim was expecting him for lunch and anticipating a briefing. What could he possibly tell him? He had turned up nothing except Hafis's unsavoury dealings. Those were off-limits for discussion. Hafis had made that perfectly clear.

What could he do? He didn't have the independent means of other men who could flaunt society and live as they chose. He depended on the trust and goodwill of others for his livelihood. Nor did he have the character of some men who turned their defects into strengths, the theatrical performers who earned their keep providing comic relief to the masses. It was too late anyway. He had made his bed, so to speak. Anna, Kamil and Arun were everything to him. He refused to choose between them.

He reread the message in his hand, a squiggly note attached to a few sheets of paper.

Dear Cousin,

While you were busy chasing false leads, I took it upon myself to do some of my own research. I have identified a few areas where our company might be able to improve profits by changing a few terms with suppliers and synchronizing delivery times to reduce the cost of holding inventory. You are welcome to present these findings as your own. I require no thanks or praise for my hard work. The knowledge that I have been useful is reward

enough. I have enclosed a few notes with my findings. Feel free
to come to me with any questions you might have concerning the
attached reports.

Yours affectionately,
Hafis

Piddly savings but it would have to do. He had worked hard for
everything he had attained. He wasn't about to risk any of it for a
bastard like Hafis.

Part V

1

April 1940

Ah Ma tied her shawl under her chin. She stepped out of the car and gripped her granddaughter's hand. Ah Ma was never comfortable venturing beyond the walls of her house. After spending most of her life cloistered in the back rooms of her parents' and then her marital home, she had continued to harbour an abiding suspicion of the outside world. House spirits were one thing. She knew all the amulets and offerings necessary to keep those mischief-makers at bay. But the demons and ghosts that roamed the earth were too numerous for her to cope with.

Monkeys chattered from the swinging branches, showering nuts down on the ladies below. Yellow vipers slithered in the brush, keeping their watchful eyes on the patrons. Ah Ma placed a tiny foot on the first stone step, transferred her weight onto her granddaughter's side, and swung her second foot up to meet the first. In this way, she climbed the steps to the hazy Snake Temple. What she lacked in physical strength, she made up for in determination. She would help her granddaughter find an oracle to read her fate.

It had been many years since Ah Ma had felt useful. She had been the happiest when her children had been young and her hours occupied. Though confined to only a few rooms, her world had been full of joyous activity. She woke with the first rooster, before the servants, to roll out the dumplings and prepare the morning meal. She served her husband first, if he was in town. When he was in a good mood, he would ask her to sit and engage him in a conversation about the children. After he left for work, she would enter the children's room and wake them up one by one with a palm to their cheek. They looked up at her with sleepy eyes filled with gratitude to her for keeping them safe through the night. They trusted her to use her charms and amulets to protect them from the dangers that could befall small children.

But as they grew older and left the house for school and parties, they no longer had use for her knowledge. She could not advise her boys on their schoolwork or careers or help her daughters choose their outfits or navigate their friendships. Her husband died, her daughters married and moved away, and the boys took on haughty wives who had no use for her old-fashioned ways. She waited patiently for grandchildren to arrive so that she might be productive again. But her grandchildren never learned to speak Hokkien and the language barrier proved too great to transcend. She had survived beyond her utility.

An English doctor had prescribed opium to Ah Ma years ago, after a bout of tuberculosis left her lungs permanently damaged. She had started smoking to prolong her life but now depended on her pipe to shorten each day. The drug helped quiet her mind so she could fit more comfortably into a passive role. She often wondered why the gods had allowed her to remain so long without a purpose. And then this granddaughter came into her life and she realized that she had been kept alive to help this special girl fulfill her destiny.

They entered the smoky temple cluttered with women praying. Beggars and pickpockets silently weaved through the worshippers while monks manned the entrances with paper money and joss sticks for purchase. A bald man in saffron robes approached them, shaking a red cylinder of bamboo sticks.

'Would you like to know your future?' he asked.

Sze-yin looked to Ah Ma for confirmation. Yes, Ah Ma nodded, this oracle appeared to be legitimate. Sze-yin allowed the man to take her arm and guide her to the altar of Zhusheng Niangniang.

She placed her hands together and bowed before the statue of the goddess. Her knees felt weak. Did she really want to know the answer to her question? What would she do if she learned that she would never have a son? How would she cope? And what would Ah Ma think?

Would her only ally abandon her? Sze-yin couldn't bear to think of the possibility. But there was no turning back now. The oracle was waiting.

'Zhusheng Niangniang, please tell me if I will have a baby boy?' Sze-yin whispered.

The fortune-teller shook the cylinder of bamboo sticks and allowed her to select among them.

'Number nine. Is this a good fortune?' she asked the man.

The fortune-teller pulled a piece of paper from his robes and read from the script. 'Number nine. Yield not to greed and hate; cast them aside. Let your conscience be your only guide. Your heart will be open, pure, sublime and bright. Just like the full moon that shines high in the sky.'

'What does it mean? Will I have a son?' Sze-yin asked, impatient with these ancient riddles.

The fortune-teller smiled, revealing his deep red gums. 'This lot depicts a full moon lighting up the sky,' he laughed. 'Everywhere is lit up with the brightness of hope. It means that a boy will be born.'

Sze-yin turned to Ah Ma for confirmation. Was this fortune true? Could this oracle be trusted? Ah Ma clasped her withered hands around Sze-yin's fingers. Yes, she nodded. This seer spoke the truth. Tears streamed down Sze-yin's face. The two women locked eyes in shared joy.

They left the temple arm in arm, filled with excitement about the future. They had just entered the sunny courtyard when the blind oracle with the milky eyes appeared from nowhere. She stepped in their path and turned her face to meet them. Ah Ma could feel the cosmic energy emanating from her hazy pupils. This was indeed a woman of true power.

'Daughter, you have come back to seek your fortune,' the woman said.

'Yes, wise one, I have just received a chim,' said Sze-yin.

'A chim can only answer a single question but I can look into your future and see your fate. Give me your palm,' the oracle commanded.

Ah Ma nodded and Sze-yin obediently reached out her hand. The oracle took her wrist and turned it over, running her fingers across Sze-yin's palm.

'Water is not kind to you,' the woman began. 'A ship sails but does not blow. You must not take that voyage.' And then she stopped and held Sze-yin's gaze. 'How much do you want to know?'

Sze-yin snatched her hand away and placed it on Ah Ma's shoulder for support. This was not what she had come to hear. 'I only wanted a chim,' she stammered. 'I came for a chim to see if I will have a baby boy.'

Ah Ma handed the oracle a few coins and steered Sze-yin out of the courtyard with newfound strength. 'Thank you, wise one, for your warning, but we have already heard all that we need.'

Sze-yin didn't dare ask Ah Ma about the encounter. It was obvious from Ah Ma's reaction that she was taking this pronouncement seriously. But Sze-yin didn't have any journeys planned. The danger could be years away. The only fortune she cared about was the one that promised her a son.

2

Ibrahim and Rizal sipped their drinks on a bench beside the empty tennis courts. Rizal still panted from the exertion of their friendly game. He would have liked to pretend that he had allowed the old man to win, a noble gesture from the courteous youth to his elder. But they both knew he had fought for every point and still managed to lose to his uncle's exceptional serve.

'That only puts you up one match,' Rizal reminded him. 'I'm sure the winds will blow in my direction next week.'

Ibrahim motioned for another lime juice from the waiter who stood in the corner of the lawn waiting for his last guests to finish. The server disappeared into the club to retrieve the drinks, his impatience carefully concealed behind years of assiduous training. The sun dipped behind the clubhouse, leaving the men to talk alone in the evening shadows.

'You seemed distracted,' his uncle said. 'Is something on your mind?'

'No, I don't think so.'

'In that case, I'll ask you a question.' Ibrahim considered the unlit cigarette between his fingers then turned the tip expectantly toward Rizal. 'Why didn't you tell me about Hafis?'

'What about Hafis?' Rizal fumbled with his lighter as he held it to his uncle's outstretched cigarette.

'I'm not as ignorant as you presume. Your report wasn't up to your usual standard.' He paused, giving his nephew a chance to confess. When his offering was met with silence, he continued. 'I had lunch with an acquaintance, the other day, who happens to be a manager at the East West United Bank. He alluded to a favour he had performed for you, something to do with Hafis's accounts. It didn't take me long to retrace your steps. So I ask you again, why didn't you tell me?'

Rizal had known for months that this moment might come and yet he found himself completely unprepared. He couldn't come up with a satisfactory explanation.

'I'm sorry. I guess I hoped he would stop when I confronted him.'

'I suppose you were trying to protect me,' the old man sighed. 'But how can I expect the rest of my managers to resist temptation when my own son is blatantly pilfering?'

'I'm sorry.'

Ibrahim nodded to accept the belated apology. The waiter reappeared with two short glasses of juice.

'We can lock up on our way out, thank you, Musa.'

They sipped their drinks in silence while Rizal waited to hear his fate. The last rays of light disappeared and left them in darkness. Nature in the tropics moved at a dizzying speed. Dense vegetation sprung up in a season, peaceful clouds turned to angry storms in moments, and the evening sky changed from brilliant to black in thirty minutes. If you allowed yourself to get distracted, it was possible to miss the whole performance.

'Hafis will no longer be involved in any of my businesses,' Ibrahim said to his glass. 'He's my son and he'll receive his share when I die, but in the meantime, he'll have to fend for himself. I've made him soft. I see that now. He's never known a hard day's work. Perhaps he'll learn some responsibility when he's forced to earn an honest living. He won't suffer too much. There are plenty of suckers out there willing to offer him a job in the hopes of currying favour with me.'

Rizal couldn't feel sorry for his cousin any more than he could pity himself. Ibrahim was justified in his outrage at both of them. Hafis had disappointed his father, but Rizal hadn't done much better. He deserved whatever punishment the old man had in mind.

'I've considered my response for some time and I've decided to make you the head of the trading company,' his uncle continued.

'And to provide you with added incentive, I'm prepared to offer you Hafis's share in the company.'

'I don't understand. Why should you reward me for my dishonesty?'

'Everyone is allowed one mistake,' Ibrahim said. 'Just see that it doesn't happen again.'

3

February 1941

Sze-yin fastened the ivory buttons of her lace jacket. She motioned for Tong to clasp the pearl choker. She had the narrowest neck, like the delicate cranes on the antique carving above their bed.

He watched his wife as she applied her powder. In less than five years, she had transformed from a frightened girl into a self-possessed socialite. The tropical climate had given her sallow skin a healthy hue, and the rich Penang food had encouraged a little weight gain. With her fine bones and delicate features, she was considered by many, including herself, to be quite a beauty. Tong was often congratulated for his exceptional catch, as if he had anything to do with the selection.

Her beauty, it seemed to Tong, had become her raison d'être. She was, in fact, obsessed with aesthetics. In another life, she might have been a successful artist. But as a wealthy society matron, the only canvas she was permitted was her toilette. So she became instead a connoisseur of fashion. She could recount the details of every handbag, shoe and bauble on any of the other women. Did he notice the new ring on Madame Bee? Her husband purchased it in Italy. The stones were well-cut but the bulky setting made her fingers look stubby.

Over time, Tong noticed, the student had become the guide. Other young Penangites now looked to Sze-yin to set the fashion trends. One day, he had walked in on a session with her tailor as she was instructing the man on where to insert tucks and how to taper the waist to best suit her figure. The awed tailor had been taking copious notes on her suggestions to pass on to his other clients. Tong paid the tailors and haberdasheries, knowing that his wife had no conception of the enormous sums she had been spending. His salary was insufficient to meet these outlays. But he had a substantial inheritance to pull from to keep her content.

Most astounding were Sze-yin's remarkable social instincts, her ability to translate other people's subtle body language. She had a keen sense for false praise, inconspicuous snubs and concealed attractions.

Noting his wife's obvious intelligence, Tong thought perhaps she might be a latent intellect whose potential had been denied by the lack of a formal education. He tried to engage her in conversations about history and some elementary political topics. But she cared little for the world outside of her immediate social circle. She understood vaguely that there was a war on in Europe and in China. She had accepted his assurances that her parents were safe. There was no point in alarming her until he received irrefutable evidence to the contrary. Instead, the family would focus on finding increasingly elaborate distractions, such as this evening's festivities.

Tonight was to be an engagement party for Tong's youngest sister. Noting the younger set's fondness for modern Western music, his father had suggested dusting the ballroom and hiring a popular swing band. Tong's father was growing soft and indulgent in his old age, at least toward his daughters, and had allowed the girls a free hand with the guest list. Not surprisingly, the invitations favoured the younger generation. All of the up-and-comers were invited, Chinese, European and Malay. Anna would be attending with her brother and sister-in-law and, of course, her husband. The four were on every aspiring hostess's shortlist.

Sze-yin made a few last-minute adjustments to her hair and then turned to assess her husband. Her eyes narrowed into disapproving slits.

'You're not planning on wearing that shirt, are you?' she asked.

'What's wrong with it?'

'The cuffs are a bit long.' She glanced at the clock. 'Never mind, we've got to get down there. You'll keep your jacket on, won't you?'

The central hall overflowed with guests, a swirl of multicoloured skin tones in suits, bajus, sarongs, saris and ball gowns, all dripping with gemstones. Tong spotted Anna in the doorway, the crook of her elbow locked around her husband's arm. Why did the sight of her growing belly bother him so much? It wasn't jealousy on behalf of his wife's flat stomach, but a different kind of envy, the nature of which was better left unanalysed.

Anna's jade gown hugged her body, accentuating her growing curves. The dazzling dress, accessorized only by her long wavy hair, exposed the tips of her exquisite collarbone and dipped tantalizingly toward her healthy bosom. He couldn't help noticing how anemic his own wife looked as she pecked Anna's rosy cheeks.

Before Tong had a chance to offer Anna a proper greeting, Sze-yin, her instincts sharp as ever, grabbed Anna's hand, whispered conspiratorially and led her away toward a group of women gathered in the ballroom.

Tong was left to escort Rizal to the drinks in the game room.

'I haven't had a chance to congratulate you in person.' Tong hoped his tone sounded sincere enough. 'Anna looks well.'

'Thank you. She's doing great. She was a little under the weather for a while but nothing compared to the first time. Her mother insists that an easier pregnancy means it will be a girl.'

'It's better not to speculate. Women have their superstitions, but in my experience, they're wrong as often as they're right.'

They entered the game room where a group of men were gathered around the billiards table. A waiter in black-tie offered them a glass from his tray of assorted beverages.

'As long as Anna stays well and the baby's healthy, that's enough, I guess.' Rizal tipped his champagne glass to toast the air. 'And what about you? I heard that Sze-yin was expecting.'

'No,' Tong shook his head, 'she's not.'

'I must have heard wrong. I'm usually the last person to know these things.'

Faisal rescued them from their awkward pause by sauntering up behind Tong and grabbing his arm.

'Some host you are. Why don't I have a drink in my hand?'

The waiter handed Faisal a glass of champagne, which he rejected in favour of a whisky.

'Your parents have outdone themselves again.' Faisal saluted in the direction of the ballroom with his raised glass. 'I hope the band's not going to play all that modern jerky stuff. I prefer the slower tunes. You can get a tighter grip on the ladies.'

'I think they're going to play a mix,' Tong said. 'Unfortunately, my wife loves the new steps. She even dragged me to a few lessons.'

'An expert,' Faisal laughed. 'I'll be sure to watch you when the music starts.'

'Please don't. I said my wife loves the steps. I'm a reluctant fool.'

'A fool for love,' Faisal teased, 'my favourite kind.'

'Speaking of love,' Rizal nudged his friend, 'where's Mina? You didn't leave her at home did you?'

'No, I lost her somewhere on the way in, but don't worry, she'll find me again, she always does.'

Tong left the two in the capable hands of the waiter while he went to greet a few of the other guests. Sze-yin kept close tabs on her husband all evening. She sucked him into small talk with people she deemed important and pulled him onto the floor for a few dance numbers. During the dinner service, he was forced to entertain the new municipal councillor and his wife, whom Sze-yin had contrived to be seated at their table. The Oxford-educated Chinese lawyer was an eloquent orator who enjoyed nothing more than the sound of his own voice. At the moment, he was going on and on about traffic patterns and road signs.

'We must have consistency of road signs with the rest of the peninsula. Our lorry drivers, who traverse the roads from Singapore to Penang, require the education of international translators in order to discern the many ways in which we direct them to stop at an intersection. You see, in general, we use the "Stop" sign here, but recently we have started using "Stop at Major Road Ahead" sign, while in Ipoh and Kuala Lumpur they have been employing the "Stop, Look, Go" signs which are infinitely more precise, don't you agree?'

Tong nodded as required while trying to glance past the councillor's head toward the other tables. She probably left early. Her condition made a ready excuse for an early evening. He couldn't blame her. He would have slipped away himself if his mingling skills were not being so closely monitored by his vigilant wife.

The councillor continued to drone on. Somehow, the able politician had segued from stop signs to war.

'I hear your father has started a fund to collect money for China.' The councillor happened upon the controversial subject as if by chance. 'He must know that the British are less than thrilled by his campaign. They're very concerned about our loyalties. They consider us to be colonial subjects, not Chinese citizens.'

Tong wasn't going to get sucked into this conversation. His father's activities were annoying, but surely not the stuff to be whispered about at dinner parties.

'I thought we were all on the same side,' he said.

'For now, but the British are thinking about the future, after the war.'

'They should concentrate on getting through the war first. From what I read, things aren't going so well. Anyway, you're talking to the wrong person. I have nothing to do with my father's activities.'

'You must have some influence.'

'I'm his son. I have less influence than a housefly.'

The councillor looked around the room, as if scanning for spies, before lowering his voice conspiratorially.

'At least he should be concerned for your family's safety. If the Japanese came to Penang, your wife's ties would be dangerous enough. Now, because of your father's fund, your family would surely be targeted for repercussions. You know what they did in Nanking.'

'The Japanese would never invade Penang.' He refused to match the councillor's melodramatic tone.

'Don't believe everything the governor says. The Japanese must have some aspirations about Malaya, they've been sending their agents here. You remember the photographer, Mr Yomikoto? Well, I hear that the British were keeping a file on him and several others.'

'The British keep thousands of files. They love paperwork.'

'Apparently, Mr Yomikoto slipped out of the country last month, just ahead of his arrest.'

Didn't these city councillors have anything better to do than to spread rumours?

'The Japanese soldiers are a bunch of peasants with primitive weapons. They're no match for the European forces. They've made headway in China only because the country is in the midst of a civil war.'

'I wouldn't underestimate them. They're dangerous fanatics with no sense of the civilized laws of war. The British have their hands full in Europe. They'll have to make some sacrifices abroad.'

'England would never tolerate the loss of a vital colony like Penang. They might allow a few spots to fall but they'll defend India, Singapore and Penang. They need our resources.'

'So do the Japanese.'

Sze-yin, sensing the heated tone of the conversation to her right, tilted her head toward the councillor and inquired about his soup. Didn't he like it? Could she get him something else?

The diversion succeeded. The councillor didn't try to resume the conversation. Instead, he allowed Sze-yin to flatter him into a long-winded discourse on his student travels to Paris. She listened with rapt attention to his rambling descriptions of the fashion capital of the world.

When dinner was finished, the band reassembled for their second set. They kept to a more traditional repertoire as couples leaned closer, taking advantage of the late hour and dimmed lights.

Tong broke free from his wife and circled the ballroom, scanning for Anna's green gown. He spotted her sitting on a chair against the wall, her cheeks burning with colour.

'You looked flushed. Are you alright?' He sat in the empty chair beside her.

'I felt a little warm for a moment. I think I just needed some water.'

'You should come in for a check-up sometime, prenatal care can be just as important as the delivery.' Tong suggested, knowing full well that women never consulted a doctor during their pregnancy unless there was a problem.

'Really, I've never felt better. Mama thinks that means it's a girl. I know Rizal's hoping she's right, but I feel so big, I think it must be a boy.'

'The second pregnancy always feels a little bigger at first,' he told her. 'I came to ask you for a dance, but I guess you're not feeling up to it.'

'I'm feeling better. I just needed rest.'

She placed her gloved hand in his and allowed him to lead her to the dance floor. He rested one arm on her shoulder and wrapped the other gently around her expectant waist. He held her a little closer, trying to imagine what it would be like to spend every day like this. He envisioned their passionate conversations about books, poetry and love. Their discussions would be even better now than the letters they had written then, because they were older and had more experiences to draw from. Did she ever think about those letters?

'What are you reading?' he asked, hoping to draw her back to those days.

'It's so hard to find the time to read anything,' she sighed. 'And it's getting difficult to get any new book shipments from Europe. I've started collecting a few American authors. What about you?'

'I read *War and Peace*.'

'No kidding.' She punched him on the shoulder. So she did remember.

'I thought it was an appropriate choice, given the state of the world.'

'How was it?'

'Long, but worth every minute.'

'I'll have to give it a try.'

He started to offer to send her a copy when the music stopped. In the brief pause, Sze-yin caught his eye. She made her way toward them with some pretext about a broken ceramic.

Their moment was over. It would have to be enough to carry him through.

Anna searched the darkened corners of the ballroom for her husband. The weariness that had plagued her all evening had now spread to her limbs. Her exhausted legs ached with the extra weight of her heavy belly.

Despite her fatigue, she'd been happy to dance with Tong. She was still angry with him for leading her on, so many years ago. And she cringed when she thought about what a foolish girl she had been to let herself be so humiliated. But at the same time, she couldn't help but take pride in the knowledge that he was still infatuated with her. She hoped he was still pining for her, regretting the decision to toss her aside for that feeble, social climber of a wife. Of course, things had worked out for the best. She loved her handsome, earnest husband

and their beautiful growing brood. She knew that people watched and admired her family. How could they not? She was careful not to dwell too long on these thoughts, as vanity was a sin. But every now and then, she couldn't help but feel a little self-satisfied.

Where was her husband? She really needed to be getting home. Her feet weren't going to last much longer. She spotted Hafis' hunched frame sitting alone in a corner with an empty beer glass.

Poor Hafis, while she couldn't condone the crime he had committed, she still felt sorry for him. How could he possibly compete with her brilliant husband? Even as a child, Hafis had suffered from the knowledge of his inferiority to his imposing father. And now he had his exceptional cousin to contend with. He wasn't a bad person—misguided, perhaps, obnoxious at times, and certainly, he had acted dishonestly and deserved to be punished. But Anna couldn't help pitying him.

She walked up and settled in the chair beside him, to show that she harboured no malice. As soon as she saw his bloodshot eyes and the crazed look on his face, she knew she had made a mistake. She got up to leave but he grabbed her arm and pulled her back down beside him.

'How are you, dear Anna?' he slurred. 'I've been looking for you everywhere. I came to this insufferable party especially to find you.'

She glanced around for Rizal or Faisal to help escort Hafis out before he made a scene.

'You've been drinking, Hafis. I think you should go home. Why don't you come with me and we'll find your driver.'

'I'm having a wonderful time watching the festivities. That was a lovely turn you took on the dance floor with our able host. Good thing Rizal didn't see you. He might not have approved of the look in your partner's eyes.'

'I don't know what you are talking about.' She tried again to rise but he held her arm.

'Of course, how could Rizal possibly object? Why should you be the only faithful spouse?'

'You're hurting me, Hafis.' She tried to pull away but he squeezed her arm so tight, she could see the white indentations of his fingers pressing into her flesh.

'I'm only trying to warn you. You've always been my favourite cousin. You're far too lovely to end up with a beast like that.'

'I am not listening to you, Hafis, you're drunk. Let me go.' For some reason, she felt a tremor in her voice. She didn't want him to continue with his tirade. There was something in his tone that terrified her.

'Keep a close eye on that husband of yours. I'm warning you for your own good.' And then he let go of her arm.

When she tried to flee the ballroom, her knees threatened to give way.

'Anna, are you alright?' Mina found her leaning against the wall for support. She led her trembling sister-in-law to Rizal and Faisal, who were seated at an abandoned dining table smoking cigars with a group of men. They immediately helped her into the car. Rizal sat next to her, holding her hand, while the driver sped them home.

'I didn't realize you weren't feeling well,' he said. 'You should have said something earlier.'

4

Anna would not give her cousin's words any credence. She took every opportunity over the next few days to prove this to herself. She did watch Rizal closely, but only for signs of his continued adoration. Hafis was a liar and a cheat, while her husband didn't have a dishonest bone in his body.

She looked forward to Rizal's arrival every evening. On the nights that he went back out after dinner, she usually tried to stay up until he returned home, in case he wanted something to eat or a drink before he went to bed. He protested that she shouldn't risk the health of the baby by tiring herself, but she did not want her duty as a mother to interfere with her responsibility as a wife.

Tonight, though, he was later than usual. She tried to sleep but an unwelcome jangle of energy kept her tossing and turning until she gave up and threw off the oppressive covers. She crept down the hallway into the sitting room and plucked a book off the shelves. Her mind tried to concentrate but the letters kept jumping around on the page.

Finally, Rizal's car pulled into the driveway. She sat in the chair, waiting for the sound of his approaching steps. Where was he?

She threw down her book and ran across the lawn, the wet grass tickling her bare feet. Her eyes took their time adjusting to the darkened garage as she peaked through the opened doorway.

Her husband climbed out of the backseat, laughing with an impish grin, probably remembering some joke from the evening. He reached into the front of the car for his briefcase and then lowered his head toward Arun. His mouth touched the driver's waiting lips.

Anna felt the air escape her body. She scrambled back to the house, stumbling down the dark hallway to the safety of her covers, only remembering to breathe when her husband entered the room, a few minutes later.

She lay in bed all night listening to the sound of his breathing. The image replayed in her mind over and over like a broken phonograph record. Her husband's lips settling on the horrid driver's mouth. It had been dark. Maybe her eyes had deceived her. If she could just close her eyes and sleep, maybe she would wake and realize it was just a dream.

But she couldn't sleep because she couldn't turn off her mind, so she willed herself to gather her thoughts. She could not reconcile what she saw with the reality of her life. And she would not address her pain, the mere edge of which felt so sharp, she winced each time it approached. All she needed to figure out was what to do. How to make everything as it was before. She must focus her energies on a solution. What was to be done? When a solution presented itself, she was finally able to banish the images in her head and fall asleep.

She occupied herself the next morning, rehearsing her words, martialling her resources for the confrontation. She bathed Kamil, chopped the onions and garlic, and rearranged her wardrobe. What had her music teacher said? 'The devil finds work for idle hands.' But no, she didn't believe in the devil. She believed in Allah's grace. God is great.

'When a man committeth adultery, faith leaveth him; but when he leaveth such evil ways, faith will return to him.' She would save her husband.

Rizal came home for lunch before returning to the office for a long afternoon of meetings. He was triumphant from the success of his recent acquisition. He had just signed the deed for a rubber estate that he had secured for a song. The uncertainty of war was causing the Europeans to abandon their plantations to anyone willing to hand them a few dollars. The estate was in abysmal shape—mismanaged and overdeveloped. But he felt certain that he could eke out a small profit. And in the long term, the value of the land, positioned as it was close to the new highway, was sure to increase at least threefold.

He was disappointed to discover that Kamil had already been put down for his nap. But at least he would be able to enjoy a pleasant meal with Anna before plunging back into work.

Anna sat at the dining table, her small hands curled in her lap, fingering a strand of pearls. She didn't greet him at the door or even look up when he kissed her cheek. He hated trying to guess her moods, which seemed to swing even more frequently with this pregnancy. He waited for the maid to serve their rice and return to the kitchen.

'Is everything alright?'

'No,' she said. 'Everything is not alright. I'm afraid that we have a very serious problem.' Now she placed the pearl necklace on the table between them. 'I found this in Arun's room.'

He glanced at the glossy white stones without comprehending their meaning.

'I don't understand.'

'I've been missing a few pieces recently. I didn't want to alert you until I had solid evidence.'

'Evidence of what?'

'Arun. He's been stealing my jewellery, probably selling it, for who knows what paltry sums.'

He shouldn't have laughed, he realized, as soon as the sound escaped him, but the ridiculousness of her accusation drove him to it. Her face twisted as if he had just slapped her. His mind began to spin, frantically looking for ways to change the direction of this discussion. 'Anna,' he tried for a reasonable approach, 'Arun would never steal anything.'

'Are you saying that I'm lying?' She stood, the full weight of her bulging belly pressed against the table.

'No, of course not. There must be some misunderstanding. I'll talk to him. I'm sure that there's an explanation.'

'There's no point in talking to him. There's only one explanation for pearls in a servant's quarters. Either he is stealing or I'm lying. You are going to have to choose.'

The intent of her stance did not escape him. There would be no rationalizing or compromising. She was forcing him to choose between his life and his reason for living. He would have liked to believe that he was thinking only of the baby, of Anna's wild eyes and trembling body. In reality, he was only thinking of himself. His instincts for self-preservation overrode any other option. He realized in that moment, the depths of his cowardice.

'Alright.' He said the words he would regret for the rest of his life. 'Dismiss him. I have to get back to the office. I'll send Arun back home after he drops me and you can talk to him.'

Rizal stared out of the car window, thinking of everything possible other than the matter weighing heaviest on his mind. When he arrived at the office, his eyes lingered one last time on Arun's trusting smile.

'Anna would like you to return to the house,' he told him. 'She wants to speak with you about something.' Before Arun could answer, he grabbed his briefcase and escaped from the car and through the double doors of the entrance without a single glance back.

Rizal filled his afternoon with meetings, paperwork and important decisions. His calendar was crammed with people hoping for a favour or seeking his advice. With his promotion had come a new set of expectations based on his presumed influence. Friends and relatives crawled like ants out of the woodwork to seek his patronage. The commissioner asked him to join the Rotary Club and Legislative Council. His name was even circulated as a potential Justice of the Peace. Rizal didn't mind helping when he could, but he didn't welcome the additional demands on his time or the added spotlight on his affairs. Today, he was in no mood to be useful. He listened to each request and offered assurances, though at the conclusion of each meeting, he could not recall what had been discussed or decided.

Around three o'clock, the manager of his newly acquired rubber plantation appeared in his office, nervously fingering the tips of his mustache. The little man in a cheap suit and scuffed shoes accepted a spot of tea but seemed too fidgety to bring the cup to his lip. He was clearly worried about the security of his job with this new owner. He answered each question with the defensive posture of a cornered animal, until the nature of the discussion convinced him that his new boss was only interested in facts.

Yes, everyone agreed that oversupply was a temporary problem, sure to be rectified as the war expanded. They could introduce new automation that would reduce production costs in the long run. As the manager prepared to rise, confident in the success of the interview and the security of his position, Rizal posed one more question.

'I have a servant who has been working with my family since he was a boy. He speaks English well and can read and write and perform complicated sums. Unfortunately, he's fallen into some trouble with our maid, you know how these things go, and I'm afraid I have to let him go. I wonder if you could make use of his skills on the plantation.'

'We're always looking for labourers with some ability. It's hard to find coolies who can rise to the challenge of even a basic level of responsibilities.'

'Wonderful, I'll have him contact you.'

Rizal's secretary poked his head into the office. The young man had transformed himself since Rizal's promotion. He wore a new songkok and leather shoes, and answered the phone in the haughty tone of someone who now worked for a big boss.

'Sir, the driver wishes to talk to you regarding some matter at home.'

'I don't have time to see him right now. Could you give him this note for me?' His hands shook as he scribbled the name and address of the plantation manager as well as the number of an account at Standard Chartered bank.

5

Anna's belly grew large and cumbersome until she lacked the energy for even basic household chores. The oppressive heat weighed on her heavy frame and forced her to seek the seclusion of her bedroom for much of the day. Rizal came and went from work, arriving late at night to eat his cold dinner alone. If she forced herself to be awake when he returned, he would join her in the bedroom and talk about the goings-on in the office. She smiled when the story contained humour or commiserated when he expressed his frustrations.

She wanted to communicate more but she lacked the strength. She hoped that he understood he had been forgiven. What had she actually seen in that dark garage anyway? They may have kissed or simply embraced. Either way, Rizal had dismissed the driver without hesitation. And since then, he had been exceptionally solicitous of her. The hussy driver had been placed in their lives as a trial, an evil temptation tossed in their path. Rizal may have been temporarily waylaid, but he had passed the test and would receive the benefit of Allah's grace. Her husband was not one of those men, or he wouldn't have married her. Their relationship would return to normal after the delivery, when she had time and energy to devote to him.

She found herself drawn to the mosque. She visited every week, despite her fatigue because the trip renewed her strength. She found great comfort in prayer and the recitations of the Quran. Allah was merciful. He understood the weaknesses of men and the frailties of women. He alone would be their judge.

6

April 1941

Mina walked through the clinic door with Anna following behind.

'Her water broke,' Mina announced. 'I shouldn't have dragged her out. I only wanted to take her to the market. I thought the fresh air might help.'

Tong had not seen Anna since the party but had replayed their dance many times in his head. So it took him a moment to shake off his lingering feelings and put on his professional face.

'Come in.' He rose from his desk to help the girls. 'Are you having any contractions?'

'It's too early,' she cried.

'It's not an exact science,' he said. 'Each baby has its own timetable. Have a seat on the table and let me have a look,' he said.

Anna climbed up with Mina's help. Tong pressed her abdomen to see if the baby was positioned for delivery.

'It feels like the baby might be breech. I think we better take you to the hospital. They'll be better equipped to deal with any complications.'

'Complications?' Mina echoed.

'I don't want to go to the hospital,' Anna cried. 'Hospitals are for sick people.'

'It's better to be safe,' Tong said. 'They have a wonderful obstetrician there. He'll take excellent care of you.'

The girls followed Tong to his car, Anna leaning on her sister-in-law for support.

'We have to get a message to Rizal,' Anna remembered.

Right, the husband. For a moment, Tong had managed to forget about him.

'I'll send my clerk.' Tong ran back inside to relay the message.

* * *

A petite Chinese nurse with agile hands poured Anna into a wheelchair and whisked her away. Tong found a perch on the windowsill of the reception room. Mina paced the floors, asking every few minutes if everything was okay, as if Tong had clairvoyant insight into the proceedings on the other side of the doors. He assured her in his best professional voice that Anna would be fine. He hoped that he was telling the truth.

The halls echoed with the sounds of boisterous visitors. The occasion for a hospital visit was momentous enough to draw out entire extended families. A puffy white nurse appeared in the doorway. The buttons of her uniform threatened to pop over her doughy waist.

'Dr Khoo,' she called in a thick Scottish accent. 'The doctor wanted to let you know that the delivery is not progressing well. He will need to perform a cesarean. Is the father here?'

'No, not yet.'

'Well, perhaps you can inform him when he arrives.'

Not progressing well, then he was probably right about the position. She'll be fine, he told himself. Just then, Rizal raced into the hall.

'Where's Anna?'

Tong rose to greet him. 'She's in the delivery room,' he said in the practiced voice of a steadying physician. 'They're preparing her for surgery.'

'Surgery? Why?'

'I suspect that the baby is not correctly positioned. A cesarean is usually the safest option for the baby and the mother. I'm sure they'll be fine.'

'I want to see her,' Rizal said.

'You can't go into the operating room. They need to keep the area sterile.'

Rizal slumped in a chair and fiddled with his watch. Then he followed Mina in her purposeless march up and down the hallway. Faisal and Zaharah joined them. The whole family paced the corridor, their heads bent, arms swaying by their sides. Tong sat at his seat on the open windowsill, a silent bystander, unable to join but unwilling to leave.

He watched white-clad hospital workers tromp through the lush hospital grounds. The pristine gardens lent a comforting sense of order to the hospital. As if the capricious nature of one's mortality could be contained by trimmed hedges.

'What's taking so long?!' Rizal snapped. 'Why don't they tell us anything?'

'It takes time,' Tong assured him. 'I'm sure they'll let us know as soon as they're finished.'

Tong was not an expert at cesarean deliveries but he did think they should have heard something by now. After what seemed like a lifetime, Dr McAllister strode down the corridor, still dressed in his operating clothes and introduced himself to the family.

'There were some complications,' he explained to the assembled family. 'But everyone's okay. The mother is recovering and the babies have been taken to the nursery.'

'Babies?' Rizal asked.

'Yes, little girls, a matching pair, cute as buttons. They're a little on the small side, but they have strong lungs. I expect they'll be just fine.'

'Congratulations!' he said and shook Rizal's hand and chuckled. 'I always love announcing twins—some dads turn white as a sheet, but you did okay.'

'Can I see them? And Anna?'

'Give them a while to get the babies cleaned up and do a quick examination, and then you can hold them. The mother is going to need some time to recover. The operation was not a complete success. We had to perform an emergency hysterectomy. I'm sorry.'

'What's that?' Zaharah asked in alarm.

'She'll be fine. She just won't be able to have any more children.'

'As long as she's going to be okay.' Rizal said.

'Women sometimes take the news quite hard,' the doctor warned him. 'You'll need to be patient with her.'

Shortly after speaking to the doctor, an attendant led the family, with Tong trailing behind, to the observation window of the nursery. She took Rizal to the sink to wash his hands and put on a smock. Then she placed him in the chair near the window and handed him two pink bundles. Tong had to peer over the heads of Mina, Faisal and Zaharah to see the tiny faces, two identical cocoa beans with fuzzy black hair, blue-gray eyes and a smattering of freckles across their noses.

'No wonder she was so huge,' Faisal said. 'I didn't want to say anything, but she was as big as a house.'

Mina punched her husband in the arm.

Rizal swivelled his chair so that the family could get a better look at the girls. Tong allowed himself a momentary pinch of jealousy as he watched the proud father cuddle his tiny infants.

7

August 1941

Rizal's sedan sped down the bumpy highway that connected Butterworth to the rural plantations in Kedah. He had endured the slow ferry ride and sweltering journey, mired by a mid-afternoon downpour and the foul stench of the doddering new driver. Neither the humidity nor the driver's pungent odour could quash his excitement.

The encounter played over and over in his mind. He would draw Arun away on the pretext of requiring assistance. The new driver had a family located conveniently near the plantation. Rizal would allow the old man a few days' leave. In the meantime, he would require a driver. The plantation manager would be obliged to lend him his old servant.

He took the precaution of checking into a guesthouse before proceeding to the estate, lest the manager expect him to remain on the plantation as a guest. The rest house for locals appeared a sad stepson compared to the grand one for Europeans across the road. But Rizal found the interior of the rural accommodations to be surprisingly spacious and clean.

A wispy old man with a bent spine wrestled with the driver for Rizal's bags. The attendant showed Rizal to his room, furnished with a solid double-bed strung with mosquito netting, starched sheets, and lacy linen curtains blowing in the breeze. The house boasted a shared, indoor bathroom with hot water, and a small but immaculate dining area for guests' meals.

Rizal unpacked his valise, sent the driver on his way, and then climbed back into the car, his heart pounding in anticipation of the long-awaited reunion. He would explain everything to Arun—his fears, his cowardly behaviour and his misery. He had suffered over the last few months, waiting for an opportunity to visit. He had endured the difficult pregnancy and then the babies' fussy first weeks. Now that things had settled down, it might be possible to arrange a monthly trip to check on the progress of his estate. Someday, he might find the excuse and the courage to bring Arun back to Penang.

He drove past the gated entrance to his new plantation with its wooden signboard declaring his name in bold black letters. Labourers in dingy sarongs tied around bony legs stared at the big car floating down the drive. He passed two miles of rubber trees filled with a small army of Tamil workers, emptying clay cups of sap into large pails suspended on poles on their backs. The bright pastel towers of a Hindu temple peeked over the tops of the trees. He drove up to the manager's bungalow, a whitewashed house with a pitched roof and a large wraparound verandah.

The man scampered down the steps to greet his boss.

'Encik Mansour, we weren't expecting you until this evening.' He practically tripped over himself to offer his apologies. 'You must have made excellent time on your drive. Please come in. Boy, some tea for the boss. Come in, come in.'

They sat on cane chairs in the darkened parlour, black-and-white chick blinds shielding the interior from the afternoon sun while the fawning manager filled Rizal with glowing reports of improved efficiencies and modernized tapping techniques.

The estate's finances had improved. But this had more to do with the booming international market than spectacular managerial feats. Still, Rizal allowed the manager his moment of glory. He was in too good a mood to dampen the man's enthusiasm.

The manager pressed him for details of his visit. How long was he staying? Was there anything else he would like to see? Wouldn't he stay as their guest? They had plenty of room.

No, no, he couldn't stay. His impatience with the groveling man was growing by the minute. He waited for a pause in the manager's chatter to ask his question.

'I wonder,' he said as if the thought had only just occurred, 'is the servant that I sent still around? I hope he's working out.'

The manager's face scrunched as he tried to remember which servant his boss was referring to.

'Oh yes, the young man with exceptional English—an excellent worker, very useful. I made him a foreman, in charge of several tappers. There was some resentment at first, but he gained their respect over time. Unfortunately, we lost him in the fire. Dreadful business. The barracks went up like a box of matches. I lost twelve of my best men that night. Just awful. I can assure you that such a thing will not happen again. I have instituted the strictest punishments to anyone caught smoking near the sleeping quarters in the future.'

Rizal's mind blurred, jumbling images and impressions, a handshake, an opened car door, and the jagged ride to the rest house. He found himself in a darkened room with an empty whisky bottle, the smell of vomit on wood. The room spun, shards of glass scattered across the floor as a bottle flew into the wall. An anxious knock on the door, hands helping him to bed, big knotty hands, not Anna's, not Arun's. Blissful oblivion, a deep sleep interrupted by smoke, fire and the sounds of voices screaming in the night.

Where was he? Starched linens, lace curtains, the guest house. No sign of disorder in the room. Had it all been a dream? A steaming pot of tea rested on the bedside table.

Yes, it was all a dream, a nightmare to be rectified by the cleansing sunlight. Rizal dressed with care, restoring order to his dishevelled appearance. He splashed his face with cool water from the washbasin. Over tea, he scribbled a note to the manager explaining his abrupt departure, and another to the driver, calling him back early.

He stayed in his room for the rest of the day, rather than bothering the housekeeper with his petty needs. She had had enough to handle with that difficult guest from last night. Well, no matter, he would be checking out soon anyway. He stretched out on the bed and closed his eyes, waiting for the driver to arrive.

Finally, Arun came. What had taken him so long? He slipped into bed, resting his head on Rizal's shoulder. Rizal begged his forgiveness. He had not meant to be away so long. Arun held him while he cried, his body convulsing with sobs. There was no need for tears, Arun whispered. He was here now and he would never leave again. Now they could be together forever.

Part VI

1

November 1941

The garden had lost all semblance of order in the last few months but Rizal could still feel Arun's presence there. He liked to sit on the bench, under a rambutan tree, and watch Kamil play in the yard. He could hear Arun laughing at the boy's little antics. When the maid bundled the girls and brought them outside to enjoy the fresh air, Rizal explained to Arun how to tell the babies apart; Selima had a little mark on her heel while Nura had a dimple on the left side when she smiled.

When he was not visiting Arun in the garden or the jungle, Rizal buried himself in his office with urgent matters that occupied the vacant spaces in his mind. Work provided an anaesthetizing balm for his pain. Each morning, he rose from his bed to honour his responsibility to his family. He could no longer bring himself to fulfill his obligations at night. The thought of that distasteful playacting now turned his stomach.

His behaviour disappointed and confused Anna, but he felt powerless to help her. When her frustration turned to anger, he was actually grateful. Her accusing stare filled him with excruciating relief, like lashes on his wounds. After two months of unspoken animosity, Anna seemed to give up. She abandoned him to his solitary misery. She came and went in silence. He attended to his functions and she to hers. When their activities overlapped, they behaved like indifferent strangers placed together for the sake of propriety.

Rizal tried to minimize his social obligations, using the mounds of paperwork as an excuse, even when it cost him the indignation of people he used to like. But he couldn't refuse Faisal's invitation to an afternoon of fishing, not without risking a permanent breach in their friendship.

Faisal rowed the battered boat to one of the islands. They dropped their fishing hooks in the water. The shared silence calmed Rizal's mind. When it became obvious they weren't going to catch anything, they propped their poles in the dirt and retreated to the shade. Faisal opened two packets of fried rice and a packet of cigarettes.

They ate with their fingers, in peaceful quiet until they were finished.

'My father used to take us here when I was a boy, before Adi died,' Faisal finally said. 'We rarely caught anything. We skipped stones and hunted for treasure. I found a shark's tooth once, or what I thought was a shark's tooth.'

Rizal didn't mind a conversation, as long as Faisal was going to offer himself as the topic.

'How old were you when your brother died?' Rizal asked.

'I was only eight. You don't really understand anything when you're that age. You just accept what people say about them going to a better place. I almost envied him, I pictured a paradise where he ate candy every day and never had to go to school or do chores. But I suppose every experience leaves its mark. I learned that you can be alive and healthy one day and in the ground the next. I'm not taking chances on the promises of paradise. I want to enjoy myself right here.'

'I think many people feel that way,' Rizal said. 'It's the execution that's the challenge.'

Faisal lit his cigarette and then offered his lighter to Rizal. 'You should take it easy. You're working too hard. A man can only handle so much pressure, and with all those babies in your house, it's natural to want to seek a little release outside the home. But you can't let it interfere with your home life. That's the key. If there's no peace at home, there's no peace anywhere. Take it from me. I've been there.'

This was the closest Faisal would get to a heart-to-heart and Rizal was eternally grateful for his discretion. He had no idea what Anna might have divulged to her brother, probably nothing too detailed. But regardless, Faisal was letting him know that he would not take sides. He was probably the one person Rizal could count on never to pass judgment. Rizal could tell him everything right here, right now, and Faisal would probably pat him on the back and tell him not to take life too seriously. 'Home's fine,' he said. 'I've been working hard, but Anna understands. There's no problem.'

The two finished off their cigarettes and rowed back to shore. Faisal was relieved to be spared a confession. All couples quarrelled on occasion, especially bull-headed personalities like Rizal and Anna. He should have anticipated these complications before he introduced them. But despite the current unpleasantness, he couldn't regret the part he had played in their match. They were well-suited and would be happy again. He was sure of it.

At least Rizal had the good sense not to drag Faisal into their quarrel. Faisal really didn't want to get involved. Of course, there were rumours that would explain the dispute, vindictive rumours, most likely started by their brooding cousin Hafis. Penang was full of malicious talk. A person would have to shove cotton in his ears to avoid hearing it. Faisal never liked gossip. He preferred to accept people at face value, as they chose to present themselves. Everyone had a few secrets. If not, they led boring lives.

This particular piece of gossip had little merit because of its source and the ridiculousness of the accusation. Anyone could see that Rizal was not one of those guys who walked around town swaying his hips like a woman. Still, there was an element of truth to every rumour. Rizal had probably dallied with someone inappropriate. But so what? He was a good guy. He loved his wife. Faisal wouldn't hold it against him. Why should Anna?

His sister could be impossibly childish. She should do like most women did—extract some painful price which would make her husband think twice before straying again. Mina had refused Faisal's attention for months after she had learned about one innocent tryst of his with a dancer. He had learned his lesson and would certainly more careful in the future. Mina had been furious, but she had never allowed their disharmony to spill into their public life. And now, they were as happy as ever.

He thought of sending Mina to talk to Anna, but he didn't want to dig up any smouldering resentment in his wife. So, he cooked up a scheme to get Sofiah back in town.

Birthdays were not celebrated with much fanfare in the Parker family. One had to reach a more impressive age, like sixty or seventy, before festivities could be expected. But Faisal couldn't think of any other excuse for a get-together. So he announced his desire for a family dinner to celebrate his thirty-fifth birthday.

Sofiah couldn't refuse even the most ridiculous request from her brother. She braved the flooded roads, with all her five children, in her advanced condition, to attend. Mina, who loved to entertain but was rarely allowed the opportunity, prepared the menu for the feast and decorated the house with greenery from the garden. Zaharah didn't protest. She understood the masquerade.

Five minutes into the meal, a worried furrow crossed Sofiah's brow as her eyes scurried between her mute sister and brother-in-law. She had not been informed of the reason behind her summons but it didn't take her long to deduce the problem. The next day, she grabbed her driver and set off to get to the bottom of the quarrel.

Anna had returned from the dinner party as despondent as ever with her husband's behaviour. Mostly, she hated the bitterness that his inattention provoked in her. Lately, she had found it easier to ignore him, avoiding the pain of each failed encounter while still hoping this condition might disappear as quickly as it came.

She decided that her appearance had something to do with his lack of interest. She had regained her old dress size but her skin hung around her waist like a sagging pouch. Her wavy hair lacked its former lustre. Dark circles surrounded her eyes from the late nights with crying babies. One sister would wake the other and the two would wail. Even one night nurse was not enough for two babies who refused to sleep through the night. She could accept that her husband no longer found her attractive; if only, he showed her some sign of his former tenderness.

Sofiah appeared at Anna's door the next morning.

'I came to talk to you,' Sofiah said, getting right down to business as soon as Rosanna left the room. 'I couldn't help but notice that you and Rizal were behaving oddly last night.'

'What are you talking about?' she asked. She thought they had behaved quite normally, but maybe she had forgotten what normal behaviour felt like.

'You barely looked at each other. You were rolling your eyes at everything he was saying. And Rizal did not stop fidgeting the whole night. Faisal said you two have been quarrelling for months.'

'I'm surprised Faisal even noticed.'

'So you have been quarrelling.' Sofiah removed her scarf, ready to settle in and solve her sister's woes. As if a simple chat could make her difficulties float away.

'We would have to be speaking to be quarrelling.'

'Well, why aren't you speaking?'

'You'd have to ask Rizal. I really have no idea.'

'It takes two to quarrel. You must have some inkling as to the issue.'

Anna finally allowed herself to confide her misery. If anyone could understand her heartache, it would be her sister.

'Rizal doesn't find me attractive anymore. He has no interest in the children or me. He goes to work, comes home, goes to bed, without a word to any of us.'

'Is that what this is about?' Sofiah sighed, as if relieved to have such a minor difficulty before her. She reached over and patted Anna's knee like a mother consoling her infant. 'It's natural for men to lose a little interest after a few years of marriage. At first, they're like boys with a new toy but then—'

'Then what? Then they treat their wife and family like worn-out undergarments? They toss them aside in favour of fresh ones?'

'I'm sure that hasn't happened,' Sofiah cajoled her.

Anna was furious that Sofiah would dismiss her distress so nonchalantly. She acted like Anna was a child crying over a lost doll.

'I'm not like you.' Anna stared at her sister's swollen belly. 'How can you share a bed with your husband, knowing that he spends his nights with someone else?'

Sofiah withdrew her hand from Anna's knee and placed it on her stomach.

'We're not talking about me. Rizal hasn't taken another wife. He's just grown distracted.'

'Well, the way you talk, it's just a matter of time, a natural progression, boys with toys, a little diversion, and then another wife and a new set of children. That may be acceptable to you, but I would be too humiliated to watch my husband chase after someone else.'

Now tears began to fall in earnest from Sofiah's eyes. Her face contorted from the pent-up pain.

'You are too cruel. Why are you so contemptuous of me?'

Now it was Anna's turn to cry. She threw her arms around her sister and begged for forgiveness. Why had she said such a hateful thing? She was turning into a bitter, spiteful person. She had to find a better way to cope. She refused to become her mother.

2

7 December 1941
Sunday

Anna wrapped herself in her children, her faith and her charities, trying to lose herself in service to others.

She attended a first-aid course sponsored by the ladies' auxiliary to prepare the women on the off chance war should come to their peaceful island. The women gathered in the community centre adjacent to the central mosque. Even a few of the colonial wives attended, in the spirit of community camaraderie brought about by the threat of war. They sat on rattan chairs in their sarongs and skirts, a colourful collection of future Nightingales ready to absorb the practical wisdom of their instructors.

Tong lectured the women on the proper technique for applying a tourniquet, bandaging a wound and splinting a broken limb, as well as on how to identify the first signs of shock. Anna had never before noticed his commanding presence. He communicated these skills with an easy authority that caused the tittering admiration of all the women, or so Anna sensed.

He demonstrated how to take a pulse by grasping Anna's wrist and placing his fingers on her veins. He leaned over her shoulder as she practiced bandaging a wound. Somehow, at the end of class, she found herself standing next to him, drawn to his side by some invisible force. He offered her a ride home.

They walked in silence down the street. But rather than turning left in the direction of his car, she took his hand and led him to the water, down an abandoned pier to a bench that seemed to be waiting for their arrival.

She told him everything. The words poured out of her, the emotions flowing in a desperate search for understanding. The dinner hour came and went as she revealed the depths of her disappointment at her husband's indifference to her. Tong, in turn, confessed his feelings for her. They spoke with all of the earnest emotion of their early letters, but their physical proximity added an intimacy that their written words had lacked.

He rested his hand on her thigh and stared into her eyes with an innocent expression of tender sympathy. His lips grazed her cheek on the way to her ears. 'I've always loved you,' he whispered.

Love, yes, that's what had been missing. How had she not noticed? Love, of course! It was so obvious now. A sense of urgency grew as night fell. She put her arms around his shoulders and he embraced her waist. Their lips met. She felt a desperation in his kiss that she had never noticed with Rizal.

And yet, she pulled away. She ran up the pier to the street without turning around. When she found herself on the sidewalk under the glare of the streetlight, she regretted her childish behaviour. Why had she run away? She wanted to go back and explain. But how could she explain what she couldn't understand herself?

Rizal had never looked at her with such longing or touched her with such tenderness. Nor had he ever, in all this time, spoken of love. She had assumed it. But it was obvious to her now that she had been duped.

Anna hailed a rickshaw. The long ride gave her time to focus her fury. When she arrived home, she threw open the front door as if she might actually catch Rizal dallying with a maid. Rosanna was asleep in the babies' room and her husband was nowhere to be found. She ran through the house searching for him, an inexplicable fear constricting her breath. She entered the garden to look under the rambutan tree. She found him on the bench, his silhouette barely visible in the moonlight, his hands in his lap, his head bent as if he might be asleep.

'Where is Arun?' she shouted.

He looked up, his eyes searching the darkness in a confused half slumber.

'What?'

'Where is Arun?' she shouted again. 'Are you still seeing that man?' His eyes focussed on her for the first time in months.

'Arun is dead.' He uttered the words with a despair that should have been reserved for her. Then he picked up his hat and walked away in the direction of the stream.

She woke the startled driver and insisted he take her to her mother's house. He discreetly searched for his boss to sanction the orders of his hysterical mistress. Only when Anna put on a mask of calm and uttered some excuse about her mother being ill, did he help her into the car. She would send word in the morning to the maids to bring the children. Her mother would have to let them stay once she understood the extent of Anna's humiliation.

It had been that horrid driver all along. How had she been so blind? Her husband had never loved her, could never love her. He was one of those men who lusted after other men, a sinner and a sodomite. Why had he married her? Why trick her into falling in love with him when all along, their marriage had been a hideous farce? Did they laugh at her when they lay together?

Zaharah showed no surprise when Anna arrived at Rumah Merah with her overnight bag and bloodshot eyes. She led Anna to her father's library, which had been converted into a guest room.

'We'll talk about this in the morning,' her mother whispered so as not to disturb Faisal and his family, who were sleeping, as any sane person would be at that hour.

Anna spent the night running her fingers along the spines on the bookshelves, wishing for her father. If only he were alive. He would understand her misery. Nobody would ever understand her like her father had.

The next morning, she waited for Faisal to leave for work and Mina to disappear on errands before she left her room. Zaharah stood on the verandah, supervising the restoration of a rotten pillar, scolding the bare-chested coolies and their sloppy workmanship with her acid tongue. She stopped her lecture when she saw her bedraggled daughter approach.

'Who is watching the children?' Zaharah asked.

'I didn't want to wake them last night. I'll send for them this morning.'

'You'll do no such thing. You and I will have a pleasant breakfast together and then you'll return to your family.'

'But Mama, you don't understand. I can't go back to that house. It's too awful for me to explain.'

'I don't want an explanation. You've quarrelled with your husband and now you must return and make up with him.'

'No, Mama, there's no point in making up with him. Rizal doesn't care about me. He doesn't love me. He can never love me.'

The full depth of her sorrow forced itself on her as she uttered this heinous truth. She had promised herself not to cry. Her tears always destroyed any shred of sympathy from her mother. Zaharah met her sobs with a sigh of annoyance.

'I know all about Rizal. It doesn't change anything.'

'You know?' Was it so obvious to everyone else?

'Ibrahim and I discussed the issue at length before introducing you two. It was your uncle who suggested the marriage. He was concerned that Rizal had become overly fond of his houseboy. He wanted to see his protégé confirmed in a safer union.'

'You knew about him!' Her face flushed with rage. 'And Faisal, did he know too?'

'No, Faisal could never see the unsavoury side of people. He was thrilled with the idea of his best friend marrying his sister. All I had to do was drop a few hints and make him think the match was his idea.'

'How could you do that? How could you marry me to a man who could never love me?'

'What is this love which you keep talking about? Love doesn't put food on the table. It doesn't save your children from harm. It doesn't even keep a husband faithful. Love is a foolish and impractical notion found in children's fairytales and those silly books of yours. It is not the basis of a lasting marriage.'

The coolies had stopped tinkering with the post and had inched their way closer to the morning's entertainment.

'May you never know the pain of losing a child,' her mother continued, undaunted by her audience. 'If you did, you'd realize how foolish all your other concerns are, the fancy parties and pretty dresses, even your husband's attention means nothing compared to the health and well-being of your children. A woman's first responsibility is to raise her children in a stable family, to help them grow up healthy and strong, and see them married to a worthy spouse.'

'How can you call Rizal a worthy spouse?' Anna asked incredulously.

'Allah gives us our flaws to try us. Rizal is a good man and a loyal husband. I've studied each of my children since their birth. I know you better than you know yourselves, which is why the selection of a marriage partner has always been a parent's prerogative. I shudder to think of the spouses you children would have chosen. Sofiah required a man who wouldn't take advantage of her servile tendencies. Her grovelling behaviour would incite most men to violence. Zainal is not the most intelligent creature but he has a gentle nature and he understands his duties as a husband. Faisal, unfortunately, takes after his father—he required a patient, practical woman who wouldn't leave him when he followed his fancy. The girl he initially selected was completely unsuitable, so I convinced the father to offer the eldest girl. Faisal saw the wisdom in the match.'

'What about me, Mama? How could you possibly think that Rizal was suitable for me?'

'You were the biggest challenge. I blame your father. He raised you with unrealistic expectations. You've never shown the kind of restraint that comes naturally to most girls. You required a husband who would look the other way, no matter what your impetuous nature tempted you to do. Men like that are hard to find. Rizal's the perfect husband for you. You've just been too foolish to recognize it.'

'If I had been allowed to choose a man who loved me,' Anna said, the fury rising in her throat, 'you wouldn't have to worry about my impetuous nature.'

'And who would you have chosen? That spineless doctor? I know all about him, too. You think your illiterate mother can't recognize her own daughter's name on an envelope? All I had to do was leave one of his letters for your father to find. We wouldn't have prevented the match. Your father couldn't deny you anything. But your prince went running at the first sign of displeasure, like a dog with his tail between his legs. You need a man with more backbone.'

'You're wrong about Tong,' Anna cried. 'He loves me.'

'There's that word again. He lusts after you. It's a different thing entirely and no basis for a relationship either. Besides, he made his choice. He's married and so are you. Things were working out just fine until you dismissed the houseboy. Your foolish pride got in the way of reason. Now you'll have to suffer the consequences. But this will blow over eventually and everything will return to the way it was before.'

'You're wrong. It can never be the same. I'll never go back to him.'

'Well,' her mother placed her hands on her hips, 'you can't stay here.'

They heard the sound of an approaching car. The front door opened and heavy feet thudded up the stairs. Faisal appeared on the verandah.

Anna stepped into the shadows of the pillars to hide her tear-streaked face.

'Where's Mina and Rozi?' he asked with an odd tremor in his voice.

'They went to the market,' Zaharah said.

'I'm going to find them. Anna, you better get back home.'

'What's going on?' Anna asked.

'We're at war. The Japanese bombed Singapore, Hong Kong, Manila and Honolulu last night. They've landed in Thailand.'

Anna didn't need to be told what the news meant. The Japanese meant to take the continent.

'Go back home and stay there,' Faisal commanded with unusual authority. 'You're far enough out of the city, you should be safe.'

Anna stepped into the car. An eerie sense of calm filled her. She wouldn't have to think about her mother's hateful words or fret over her next move. War had made her responsibilities clear. She needed to go home and take care of her children.

As they passed through the centre of town, a low hum like a swarm of mosquitoes crept through the air. The driver stopped the car and pulled to the side of the street. Anna got out of the car and put her hand on her brow to shield her eyes from the sun. Dark shadows appeared in the distance, growing larger with each second. All necks were craned toward the sky as the crowds on the sidewalks watched the spectacle.

The planes glided overhead, close enough for Anna to make out the letters on the underside of their silver bodies.

A white cloud billowed from their metallic bellies as streams of paper rained on the crowds below. Anna caught one as it drifted past her. The message, typed out in English, warned the public to evacuate the town. The Japanese were waging war against the white devils.

Anna searched the sky for signs of British fighters or anti-aircraft explosions, but the Japanese planes flew over the island in perfect formation, undeterred by any visible resistance. The silver birds turned to tiny specks as the planes disappeared in the direction of Butterworth. A distant rumble, like the concussion of heavy fireworks, woke the crowd from their trance and left them scampering for their vehicles.

When Anna got home, she hugged her little ones so tightly, the maid had to pry her arms loose and beg their mistress to explain her tears. They had not heard the planes in the city and nobody had thought of listening to the radio. She explained the news in the simplest terms possible to the uneducated maids. The girls tore through the house, bumping into each other as they looked for a place to hide. Even unschooled maids had heard of the atrocities of the Japanese soldiers against captured women.

Anna calmed them down and then soothed the children, who sensed the adults' agitation. She marvelled at her composure as she issued level-headed instructions regarding appropriate preparations. The maids scurried to the market to stock up on supplies in case they needed to stay home for a few days while the British defended the city. Anna sent word to her mother and sister-in-law to join them in the country. They refused to come. They were more concerned about looters than invaders.

Rizal stayed at the office that night. He sent the driver to check on the family. The Japanese had bombed the air force base in Butterworth. No one had been hurt but it was best to remain inside until further notice.

3

Tong had stopped himself from running after Anna. She would return to him once she had had time to absorb the change in their relationship. He had told her that he loved her and she had shown him how she felt. They couldn't hide their feelings for each other any longer.

He experienced no guilt on behalf of his wife or Rizal. He felt nothing but contempt for the man who had squandered the love of such an extraordinary woman. And Sze-yin had attained what she required of Tong. She was entering her eighth month and felt secure enough in a term delivery to disregard his presence.

When the Khoo family woke Monday morning to news of war over the radio, Tong became anxious, not at the thought of the destruction that might come, but at the horrible possibility that he and Anna might be separated. Though the warplanes had left Penang unscathed, his father insisted they go to Pembroke. The hillside retreat was far enough from the town to be safe from bombing raids and would provide a secluded perch from which to watch the sea and skies.

The family arrived at their Penang Hill house on Monday evening, just as the sun was setting. It had taken them most of the day to arrange the transport of Ah Ma by stretcher, who was not feeling well and Sze-yin, who was under strict orders of bed rest. The family had to wait in line for thirty minutes for the funicular. They were not the only people who sought the safety of the hills that day.

The Tudor-style house had been built by Tong's grandfather on a prime spot with views surpassed only by the English homes at the summit. Until the funicular was built, the homes on the hill could only be accessed by steep footpaths, which residents traversed on horseback or in a sedan chair. As a child, Tong had made the 1,500-foot climb on foot many times, as his father didn't believe healthy boys should be transported like women on the backs of beasts or men.

Once the family had settled in Pembroke, Tong had returned to his office for a few hours, in case there were any emergencies. But the clinic had been unusually quiet. The population appeared to be facing the possibility of war with robust health. He locked up at six o'clock and returned to Pembroke House, his head filled with Anna and ideas for getting a message to her.

He found his father sitting alone in his study, anchored to his desk, his body leaned into the radio, trying to decipher the latest broadcast for clues. No updates were forthcoming, only assurances of the British defense. A deep furrow burned into his father's brow, the stress of war and the responsibility for his large family drawn on his face like an etching in rough sand. In addition to his immediate family, Tong's father had a duty to his daughters' extended families, his three sisters and their families, as well as fifteen servants, not to mention his many employees and their families, who were begging for his help. Sze-yin's advanced condition only added to his worries.

'We need to be prepared to leave on Friday.' The sun filtered through the windowpanes and draped his father's face in heavy shadows. 'I've diverted a boat. Kian has found a house in Singapore big enough for all of us. There's no use waiting here to be ambushed.'

'Don't you want to wait a few more days? Maybe everything will blow over if the British scare them off.'

'The British will likely consolidate their forces in Singapore. They may let the rest of Malaya go, but they will never let Singapore fall.'

'I heard that the British were reinforcing their northern defenses.'

'It may not be enough. We can't take any chances.' His father closed the topic for further discussion. 'We will leave on Friday. All of us. You need to talk to Sze-yin. I understand that she doesn't want to make the journey, and under normal circumstances, I would agree. But we must all leave before it's too late.'

'I'll talk to her,' he promised.

Tong had his own reasons for not wanting to leave for Singapore but he couldn't add to his father's troubles. Hopefully, they wouldn't be gone long.

* * *

Tong knocked on the ground-floor guest room, where Sze-yin lay sequestered after making the perilous journey up the hill. Two oscillating fans hummed on either side of her bed. She rested under the covers, a billowy mass of silk and cotton lumped in the middle of the mattress, propped up by a collection of pillows behind her back. Her fingers deftly manoeuvred a sewing needle through an infant's frock.

'How are you feeling today?' Tong asked with the polite demeanour of an attentive husband.

'Hot, tired, as usual,' Sze-yin sighed.

'Only a few more weeks to go.'

'I'm well aware of how many weeks remain,' Sze-yin snapped. 'And I'll gladly suffer the penance for a healthy child.'

'Of course.' Tong pointed at the gown she held in her hands. 'Is that for the baby?'

'I'm adding a few details at the neckline and embroidering his initials on the hem.'

'You'll have to undo all of your stitching if it's a girl.'

Sze-yin rolled her eyes at the stupidity of his remark. 'You doctors think you know everything. I've told you that it's a boy.'

'Perhaps we could at least discuss the name before you embroider it.'

'We've discussed it. The generational name is Teng, and as this is our first child, we'll name him Chaun. Khoo Teng Chaun. I've already started on the monogram.'

'Well, at least you're keeping busy.'

Tong moved toward the bed to sit down, but the flicker of displeasure in her eyes discouraged him. He grabbed a chair and pulled it beside her.

'Sze-yin,' he began, 'we must discuss the necessity of an evacuation. There have been planes flying over the city.'

'I know about the planes. But they haven't hurt anyone.'

'We don't know their intentions.'

'Why should they want to harm us?'

'There's no answer to that question. Why do countries go to war? We don't need to understand their reasons. We just need to take steps to protect ourselves.'

'By running like cowards with our backs to the enemy? What happened to your pride? Aren't you men supposed to try to defend your homes?'

'I plan to leave the defense to the British Military. It's our job to get out of their way. This is serious business, not the purview of untrained civilian men. It's my responsibility to make sure that you and the baby are safe.'

'Which is precisely why I intend to remain here, in my bed, where I have been ordered to stay by my doctor.'

'You won't be safe here. None of us will. The Japanese have sent their spies. They know about our family and they'll come after us if they take the island.'

'They won't take the island if it's properly defended.'

'We can't take that chance. Father has ordered that we leave for Singapore on Friday. I'll make sure that we have all the medical supplies we need if something should happen en route.'

'Nothing is going to happen en route, because I'm not getting on that boat.'

She turned back to her stitching and left him to ponder his next move.

'Alright,' he gave up. 'We'll talk about it later.'

4

Rizal didn't return home on Monday or Tuesday night. The office, he explained via the driver, was in chaos as international speculators attempted to hoard raw materials in expectation of an expanded war. But nobody could find any ships willing to risk the dangerous waters.

The planes had returned to the city. Again, they dropped leaflets and bombed military targets in Butterworth. Again, the local citizens searched in vain for a response. They received assurances in the form of posted signs declaring that the British defenses were strong and their weapons efficient.

The lack of activity almost reassured the population. No air-raid shelters were built. No drills were performed. Administrative personnel remained at their usual posts as if nothing had happened. If the British were not concerned, why should the rest of the population be?

Anna's solitude, trapped like a prisoner for two days in their rural home, left her with time to smoulder over her husband's behaviour and her mother's words. By Wednesday, she couldn't be alone with her thoughts anymore. She decided that something needed to be done to break this stalemate. She would get her husband's attention.

* * *

Tong closed the office at five o'clock, as there were no more patients to see. He dismissed his clerk and spent a few hours sorting through his papers and checking his dispensary. He wanted to leave things in order while he was away in Singapore. A light knock jostled him from his work. Perhaps the clerk had returned; the nitwit was always forgetting something. He slid the bolt aside and opened the door. Anna's eyes peeked through the doorway.

'Come in.' He took her arm and led her inside. They walked in silence to the examination room. He should say something. The moment called for delicacy or tender phrases but his mind couldn't form a coherent sentence.

She didn't appear to expect words. She kissed him boldly on the lips, as if to begin exactly where they had left off. Random thoughts raced through his mind as his body came alive. A bed, he should find her a bed. She deserved a soft pillow, silk sheets, a mattress filled with rose petals. If not a bed, at least a comfortable place to lie down.

Finally, his mind gave way to the urgency of his body. His hands took over. He unravelled Anna's sarong and dropped it on the floor, then he reached his palm around her back to grasp her exposed flesh. He fumbled with his belt buckle, refusing to remove his lips from her mouth or his hand from her skin. He managed to undo the stubborn buckle and his trousers joined the sarong in a mad heap on the floor. Anna grasped the edge of a chair with one hand to steady herself as he leaned her against the wall.

Tong had made love to Anna a thousand times. Every time he had lain with his wife, he had pictured Anna's beautiful face, had touched her sensuous curves. Now he realized how foolishly tepid those fantasies had been. Nothing could have prepared him for the heady aroma of the perspiration on her neck, or the penetrating caress of her sigh as it reverberated in his ears. He abandoned all thoughts and experienced the flood of release from all those years of pent-up desire. She must have felt it, too. When they finished, she crumpled to the floor crying. He tried to soothe her, to hold her to him. But she wouldn't stop sobbing. She crawled on the floor to her skirt and dabbed her eyes with it before wrapping it around her waist.

'I have to go,' she said.

'No, stay.'

'I can't. I'm sorry.' She wouldn't look at him.

He shouldn't have let her go but there was conviction in her voice that he didn't dare challenge.

'I'll be here,' he said. 'I'm not going anywhere.'

She grabbed her purse and ran out the door.

'I love you,' he called, but she had already disappeared down the hall.

5

Anna felt the sneers of her fellow passengers boring into the back of her head. *What must they think of me?* Her hand moved to smooth a lock of hair from her mangled tresses, but she stopped herself. She gave up caring about what they thought.

It was her mother's fault. If her mother had left things alone and not tricked her father into scaring Tong away, she would be married to the man she loved, the man who had always loved her. If they had had more time to get to know each other, Tong would have given up his arranged marriage. They could have run off to Singapore together and lived happily. She could have learned nursing and helped him with his profession. They could have worked together, tirelessly, selflessly, in the same charities. And when they would collapse in bed together after a long day of caring for the sick, he would have held her and told her how much he loved her. Their lives could have been wonderful together, if only her mother hadn't pulled them apart and then pushed her into a marriage with a man who could never love her. But she would show her mother, and she would show her husband, what had become of the life they had chosen for her.

Anna stumbled off the bus and marched the remaining miles home. She kicked her shoes into a ditch when the callus on her heel slowed her down. Mud clung to the hem of her skirt as it dragged on the ground.

The driver, resting against the garage door, turned to greet her as she tromped down the drive. He raised his eyebrows at her unusual appearance.

'Selamat malam, Mem. Is everything alright? Are you hurt? Tuan has been looking for you.'

He's home. Good, let him see. She passed the driver without response, quickening her steps to the front door.

Rizal sat alone at the dining table in front of his plate of rice. He turned toward her when she walked through the doorway.

'Where have you been?' he asked. 'I came home hours ago. Nobody knew where you were.' He sounded genuinely concerned. *Well, good, let him fret.* She hoped that he had worried all evening over her.

He saw her bare feet. 'Where are your shoes?'

She ignored his question. 'I was with Tong,' she announced.

He looked confused.

'Dr Khoo? Are you sick?'

'No, I'm not sick. Don't act so concerned about my well-being. You don't care about me.'

He stood up from the table, prepared for the oncoming confrontation. 'Keep your voice down, Anna. The children are sleeping.'

'What do you care about the children? You scorned us and our love but I've found another man who does love me. He's a good man and he thinks I'm beautiful and I was with him this evening in his office and we laid together as lovers.'

Rizal's eyes widened as they took in the implication of her dishevelled appearance. This was not the confrontation he had been expecting. He leaned his hand on the table as if it might provide him with some support. Anna waited for his reaction. She hadn't realized until this minute how much she had counted on his grief. Her future teetered. She prayed he would give her something, some demonstrative response, anything that showed he cared what happened to her.

'Tong?'

'Yes, Tong. He loves me.' She aimed the words like darts at his chest. 'What do you think of that?'

'Do you love him?' he asked.

'Yes.' She felt a triumphant shudder as she noted the anguished look on his face. But rather than tears, remorse, or even anger, he simply lowered his head.

'I see. Then I won't stand in your way.' He turned his back to her and walked down the hall.

He might still turn around before he reached the bedroom. He might grab her arm, pull her to him, and beg for her forgiveness. His hand touched the doorknob. He might still call back to her and tell her that he loved her, that it was all a terrible misunderstanding. But he didn't turn around. His shrinking figure disappeared into the darkened room.

Anna fled back outside. She ran the whole way back to the bus station. Her feet bled from the rocks she trampled. But she was oblivious to the pain. No bus, just a lone puller sleeping in the seat of his carriage. She rapped on the top and jerked him awake.

'Can you take me to town?'

She had no idea where to go. Her mind searched the possibilities but each time it came up blank. He dropped her at the gates of Rumah Merah but she didn't dare enter. She couldn't face her mother's rejection again. For the better part of an hour, she wandered in the direction of the financial district, until she reached the esplanade.

She had never realized how the city transformed at night into a public resting place. Night watchmen snored in camp beds in front of their offices. Pullers slept in the carriages of their rickshaws. Old men with sunken cheeks lay in front of a closed toddy shop. Entire families lay stretched out in rows on the grass of the esplanade, five or six half-naked children next to their fathers and mothers, their families' possessions nestled between them in drawstring bags.

Anna found an empty bench in one corner of the lawn and put her handbag under her head as a pillow and spread her skirt across her legs, stretching her body along the wooden planks. She had never felt so tired. Her body felt heavy against the wooden slats. She closed her eyes and wondered for a moment what it would be like never to open them again.

6

Rizal crept through the dark hallway, his hands feeling the wall for guidance, to the back door. The brilliant moon illuminated the sky, draping the house in a bright halo. He staggered into the yard, intending to seek comfort under the rambutan tree. Instead, he found himself in the garage, switching on the bare bulb dangling from the centre of the ceiling. What was he doing here?

His eyes scanned the room for an explanation. The garage reeked of the sour stench of mold and rotting wood mixed with the pungent tang of spilled gasoline. The new driver kept everything in disarray. Their belongings were tossed haphazardly all over the place: a pair of dulled clipping shears, a fishing pole with no string, two tennis rackets, a rusty bike, his old hunting rifle.

His hands gripped the rifle. Why had he purchased that silly thing? Faisal had talked him into bird-hunting. What a joke. He couldn't shoot a water buffalo if it was standing in front of him. He was lucky he hadn't killed himself.

His fingers stroked the slender barrel. What if he had killed himself on one of those senseless hunting excursions? None of this would have happened. Anna would have been free to marry the man she loved. She wouldn't have had to feel the pain of furtive love, the hurtful lies and stinging recriminations. None of this was her fault. He had killed his lover and ruined his wife. His lies had destroyed everything he cared about. Maybe this was Allah's punishment.

But it wasn't too late. He could still save her. He pictured Arun's beautiful face smiling down on him. Maybe they could still be together.

Maybe Arun was waiting patiently for him on the other side; he would not be nestled in the Prophet's bosom. Faggots were not welcome in Paradise. His love would be relegated to Hell. Well, so be it. If that's where Arun was waiting, that's where he wanted to be. His fingers gripped the trigger, testing the resistance of its spring.

'Bang,' a little voice called from the doorway. 'Papa, is that your gun? Can I hold it?' Kamil walked toward him, his outstretched hands reaching for the barrel.

Rizal jerked the rifle away. 'No, don't touch it. Guns aren't for playing. They're very dangerous.'

He opened the latch, pulled out the bullets and shoved them in his pocket. He took his sleepy son's hand and led him back to bed, tucking his body under the covers. He kissed Kamil's forehead and tiptoed out of the room.

He would get rid of the gun in the morning. He couldn't risk the children finding it and harming themselves. They were so fragile. They needed his protection.

7

11 December 1941

The first rays of the sun splayed across the horizon. For a delirious moment, Anna imagined she was waking in her own bed, the smell of fried rice warming the air. Her stomach stirred at the possibility. She opened her eyes to the reality of her situation and her aching neck. She sat on the edge of the bench, watching the sun rise over the city, postponing the moment when she would have to stir from her stupor and figure out what to do.

The city grumbled to life. Cars and rickshaws jammed the road that lined the park. Hawkers dotted the sidewalks with their enticing offerings. She reached into her purse to determine her financial situation. Only a few coins. Her ankles cracked as she pulled herself to standing. A few vagrants took notice of the movement on the bench, perhaps hoping to snatch the coveted seat.

Workers and coolies surrounded the food stalls, their tin cups steaming with frothy tea. The women would be jostling each other at the market down the road, haggling over fresh fish, vegetables and fruit for their afternoon meal. Anna approached a cart operated by a toothless woman with raisin eyes and a sparse white bun. The woman filled six open banana leaves with portions of coconut rice, egg and dried fish. Then she ladled a generous helping of chili sauce over the top. Her veiny hands wrapped the leaf around each portion with rapid precision. A little girl handed the packets out to the line of men, collected the money and counted the change.

The men stepped back to make room for Anna, as if the misfortune of such a bedraggled gentlewoman might be contagious. The little girl eyed Anna suspiciously and held out her hand for payment. Anna pulled off a gold bracelet and placed it in the grubby paw. The girl held the sparkly bangle up for her mother to see. The old woman took it from her and held it to the sunlight, eyeing the piece like an experienced jeweller. Then she bit into the metal with her gums.

'How many do you want?' she asked, mentally calculating the worth of her stock versus the golden bangle.

Anna picked up one packet. The woman slipped the bracelet into her pocket, shrugged her shoulders, and returned to work.

The purchase attracted the attention of one of the men, who followed behind as Anna made her way back to the bench. 'Leave her be,' the old woman yelled and indicated with a spiraling finger at her temple that the lady was not okay in the head. A few of the other men made threatening noises to chase the stalker off. Anna returned to her bench, picked up the rice with her fingertips and began shovelling the food into her mouth.

She tried on the image of the resident lunatic. She could wander the park worrying only about her next meal. She could play the part well. She felt herself to be halfway there already. A few more nights in the park and there would be no going back.

A man and boy were walking in her direction. The man balanced a long pole on his shoulder with rattan baskets hanging from either end. He walked with a slight limp that caused the baskets to sway back and forth, toward and away from the boy. The little boy was smiling at something. His round cheeks puffed out like an angelic cherub. He had a twinkle in his eye that reminded her of Kamil. The man noticed her and slowed his steps, perhaps wondering if he should walk in a wider circle around the bench.

All three sensed the buzzing at the same time. They turned their heads in the direction of the sound, where a dark spot hovered in the sky. The planes glided in formation like a flock of seagulls scanning for prey. The mechanical whine grew in intensity as the awesome array of fighters, nine in all, passed overhead in the direction of the market. The little boy covered his ears to muffle the disagreeable sound.

The gleaming bellies of the planes opened, releasing whistling shadows. Anna felt the first explosion as the shadows dropped somewhere near the market. Her eyes fixed on the puffs of smoke rising over the rooftops. She didn't notice the plane that had veered off toward the esplanade until she heard the rat-tat-tat of a machine gun.

'Run,' the man shouted. He dropped his pole and grabbed the boy's hand. 'Get to the cars.' The man pulled her with the force of his voice.

She ran behind them to the line of parked cars at the edge of the lawn. She could feel the rattle of shattered glass as the spray of fire advanced behind her. The man shoved the boy under a car and then grabbed her wrist and pulled her down. Her head hit the sharp edge of the side mirror. She lost sight of his pant leg as a fuzzy film covered her eyes.

8

Rizal lingered with the children a little longer than usual that morning. The maid seemed satisfied with his excuse for Anna's absence, an illness at the Parker's. Something in her expression led him to understand she knew more than she was letting on. Well, of course, she probably heard everything last night.

What did he care if she knew? By now, Anna's entire family probably knew. What would she do? Would she leave him? Would she take the children away? He had every right to demand his children. But he would never do that to her. None of this was her fault, after all.

He felt a horrible stab of jealousy when he thought of Anna with someone else. Remarkable to realize after all this time that he did love her, not as a lover, but as a friend, companion and the mother of his children. He loved his life with her, their private moments spent laughing together, the beauty of watching her with the children, and even the times when they fought. He remembered the exact moment, early on in their marriage, that he realized, not without some delight, that he had actually married his sparring equal. No, to be fair, in the debating sphere, he had found his better. She had a unique way of looking at the world. Her view was enticing.

He had no right to be jealous. He was a horrible man who deserved to suffer. But he had never meant to hurt anyone. It was all Allah's fault. Why had he made him this way? Why give him Arun and then take him away? Why tempt him with the promise of this life with Anna and the children, and then pull it out from under him?

Jealousy, guilt and anger swirled within him. And yet, mixed with these emotions, he noticed an odd sense of relief, as if he had been holding his breath all these years and now the air was slowly flowing out of him. Maybe it was better this way. No more lies. He had no idea what would happen. He might lose his wife, his children, his job, and most certainly, his reputation. But if he lost everything else, he might regain a little integrity.

After assuring himself that the children were well, he left the house and headed to Rumah Merah to check on Anna. He didn't expect her to talk to him. But he felt he had a right to ask after her. The thought crossed his mind that perhaps she had not fled to her mother's last night. It was possible that she had run to her lover. If necessary, he would swallow his pride and go to Tong's office. He had to make sure that she was all right.

The bitter scent of burning rubber reached him before he saw the smoke rising over the city. A few men and women passed his car, trailing carts and baggage behind them. The trickle turned into a steady flow of pedestrians, cars and carts, all heading away from town.

'What happened? What's going on?'

Most passed without answering him. A few stopped and pointed toward the city. They opened their mouths to speak but only fragments came out.

'Planes . . . fire . . . '

The driver continued like a fish swimming upstream, slowing as the rush of refugees blocked his path, until they couldn't move anymore. They left the car and continued on foot to Rumah Merah. At some point, the driver wandered off.

Slowly, a picture formed of the morning's drama. The planes had returned. They had dropped their bombs on the innocent citizens who had stood gaping up at the sky. Then just to drive home their point, they circled around and gunned down anyone who dared remain standing. Why? Of what use could such malicious instruction be? The Japanese had claimed that they wanted to liberate their Asian brothers from the imperialist white devils. Was this liberation? They hadn't aimed their guns at military targets this time, but at the very population they claimed to be emancipating.

Rizal could see the same confused stupor written on everyone's face. He pushed out thoughts of the intangible future and focussed on his immediate mission. Zaharah and Mina opened the door. Little Rozi's face peered out from behind her mother's sarong.

'Is Anna here?' he asked, embarrassed by the need to ask for his wife.

'Anna?' The women looked at each other. 'Isn't she at home?'

'No, she left last night. I thought she came here.' He stared at the ground rather than meet their inquisitive eyes. Did he really need to explain?

'I think I know where she is,' he said. 'I'll go look for her. Is everyone here all right?'

'Faisal's out there,' Mina gestured in the direction of the street. 'He left for work this morning. We haven't heard from him.'

'I'll find them. Stay and wait for us to come back.'

He had to pass through the market on the way to Tong's office. The unmistakable smell of burning rubber now mixed with another more ominous scent, the foul stench of human sweat, feces and congealed blood. His nose tried to prepare him for the horrific sight as he turned the corner toward the market. Bodies and limbs were strewn across the street among overturned carts and the remnants of charred produce. Blood was splattered on every surface. A severed arm still clutching a rolled-up pamphlet lay across his path. Red water flowed through the open sewers, flushing charred bits of masonry, wood and flesh. He plucked a child's teddy bear from a puddle and wiped it clean.

The dead and dying lay together wherever they fell. Those who had given up hope lay crumpled in moaning heaps. Others called for help. Healthy people squatted over the injured. Doctors, nurses and other citizens tried to provide assistance. His brain took in the sights as if they were images on a screen. He couldn't allow himself to become immersed in the scene. He had to find Anna and Faisal.

He spotted Tong bent over a young woman. Rizal stepped over the broken bodies.

'Where is Anna?' he asked.

Tong looked up from his patient.

'Anna? Isn't she with you?'

'No.'

Tong gave him the same puzzled look as Mina and Zaharah.

'Is she with her mother?'

'No.'

Tong cast his eyes across the sea of waiting bodies as if seeking permission to leave and search for her. He seemed paralysed with indecision, neither continuing with his case nor abandoning the desperate patient. Rizal felt no dilemma. He had only one responsibility right now. He turned and walked off.

'Check my office,' Tong called after him, 'or the hospital, or the police station. Let me know when you find her.'

Rizal took off without responding. He propelled his legs forward in purposeful motion, mouthing all sorts of promises. If he found her, then he would . . . what? Anything? God would not be so cruel as to take both Arun and Anna from him. But of course, he would. Rizal only had to look around at the decimated bodies to convince himself of Allah's indifference.

A line of people stood outside Tong's clinic but Anna was not among them. He checked Faisal's office, or the location where Faisal's office had once stood, which now lay in a heap of rubble. He ran toward the mound of debris and began clawing through the pile, tossing clumps of rocks and dirt in every direction. A crowd of onlookers stood around watching him.

'Where are the people?' he asked. 'Was anyone inside?'

'They took them to the hospital,' a little boy answered. 'In a cart. They dug them out and took them in a cart.' The boy pointed toward the General Hospital.

9

The smell and sights at the hospital mirrored those of the market. Bodies lay on stretchers waiting for attention. Occasionally, a wail went up from the crowd when help came too late. Rizal stared into the faces of the injured. He didn't dare check under the sheets draped over lifeless forms. He stepped through ward after overflowing ward, where doctors and nurses buzzed with efficiency, triaging, washing and bandaging.

'Check the morgue,' a helpful nurse with a stack of blood-soaked towels suggested.

'Rizal,' a voice called as he stepped into a small ward at the back of the hospital. He turned in the direction of the sound. Where was she?

'Rizal,' she called again and then he saw her, a dark brown gash on her forehead. She was sitting up in a chair, alert, her eyes as clear as ever. A little boy clung to her side and a man lying in the adjacent bed rested his hand in her palm.

'He saved my life,' Anna indicated the man whose hand she clutched. 'He's going to be okay. He only has a superficial wound and I'm waiting to get stitches.'

The man turned his glazed eyes in the direction of Rizal as if to acknowledge the truth of this pronouncement.

'His wife's here. She's talking to the doctor. I promised to stay with the boy.'

'Faisal's missing,' he said.

'Faisal?' She shook her head to dismiss his concern. What was it about Faisal that convinced everyone of his invincibility? 'He's probably out helping people.'

'I'm sure you're right.' He didn't mention the state of the office building.

A nurse finally appeared to sew Anna's forehead back together. Anna turned the little boy over to his mother and kissed the man's hand. They headed to Rumah Merah, Anna stumbled on her bare feet. She instinctively grasped Rizal's arm for assistance.

The women hugged each other in the doorway. Zaharah led Anna to the kitchen, where she examined her wound and fed her rice and tea. Faisal hadn't returned. The women seemed determined to suppress their worry. They exchanged hopeful scenarios, assisting others, maybe stuck in traffic. At the very worst, he could be injured and waiting for treatment somewhere.

Rizal left the women and went to fetch his car. The colonial offices were eerily quiet. With nobody in charge, the town had disintegrated into chaos. No one gave out orders or directed traffic. The masses still moved with instinctive drive toward the countryside, away from the death and destruction of the city. Rizal made his way slowly through the traffic to the hospital for another look.

The hospital, by comparison, functioned with surreal efficiency. The wards thinned as doctors and nurses treated the injured while the custodian staff cleared the dead. The corridors filled with people looking for loved ones. Rizal encountered a few people he knew. They compared notes. Had he seen their sister, mother, brother, cousin, or whomever they were looking for? He was able to tell a father that his missing son waited outside on the curb.

Nobody had seen Faisal. As evening approached, he reluctantly entered the darkest corridor in the hospital. A sense of order prevailed even in the morgue. The smell of disinfectant failed to mask the unpleasant stench of mutilated bodies. Rizal gave a description to a clerk positioned behind a desk. Medium height, medium build, tan skin, dark hair and eyes. What distinguishing characteristic could he offer, other than his cousin's boyish grin, which would not be present on a corpse? The clerk led Rizal to the rows of unclaimed bodies. A few others searched the rows but no one made conversation or eye contact. They moved down the line, intent on their gruesome task.

He lifted a blanket that covered a form whose size and shape appeared about right. The man's skull had been blown in half, revealing parts of his brain that should never be visible. Rizal felt an acidic liquid rise in his throat but he swallowed it down and continued his search.

He couldn't lift another sheet and risk a second image like the one he'd just seen. Instead, he focussed on the shoes and feet that poked out from under the blankets. In this way, he could eliminate the women with their anklets and toe rings. He could distinguish the hard, callused soles of coolies and vagrants. A few corpses wore shoes; brogues, work boots, sandals or slippers. Henna stains covered the feet of a new bride.

Something shiny caught his eye, lying on top of one of the blankets, an antique pocket watch with a silver and tortoise shell. He didn't want to peel back the blanket but the clerk required a formal identification. Despite the chaos, or maybe because of it, the fastidious man insisted on protocol.

The clerk lifted the blanket. The swollen face seemed familiar but the colour was all wrong. And the expression, the odd contortion on his lips, like an angry smirk, it was not an expression Faisal would ever make. The body, though mercifully intact, was coated in bruises and caked blood.

Again Rizal felt the vomit rise in his throat. He fled the room, searching for fresh air. The clerk ran after him with a makeshift mortuary form. The department had long since run out of proper documents. He collected himself and somehow managed to fill out the required paperwork and then return to the room, where the sheet again concealed the ghastly sight. Another worker helped him carry the stretcher to his car. The man motioned toward the trunk. Rizal refused to think of this lifeless mound as Faisal. It was only a pile of broken bones that bore no resemblance to his dashing cousin. But he couldn't bring himself to shove it in the trunk. They laid the corpse, still wrapped in the hospital's white sheet, across the backseat.

The rains descended in angry streams as if Allah was so disgusted by the blood, he was determined to wash the streets clean himself. Rizal's wipers flapped back and forth in a furious effort against the downpour. The streets were cleared in a self-imposed curfew, as everyone had long since found some shelter. The city was as black as an ink spill. The power had been knocked out and heavy clouds blocked any celestial lights from reaching the deserted roads. Rizal couldn't think about the bloody corpse in the backseat. He focussed on the treacherous drive, peering into the darkness, unable to see more than a few feet ahead. He had to get Faisal home safely.

Candles kept watch behind the closed shutters at Rumah Merah. The family hovered in the doorway watching Rizal climb out of his car, alone. Their faces looked hopeful, expectant. As his expression emerged into the light of their candles, the hope fled from their eyes.

'Did you find him?' Zaharah asked. There was solidity to her voice, so he ignored the other women and addressed his mother-in-law.

'Yes.' He bowed his head. 'I'm sorry.'

Mina dissolved into the ground and had to be helped into a chair by a maid. Anna's eyes were wide with disbelief. Only Zaharah continued functioning competently, much like the nurses he had observed in the hospital. She motioned for the maid to take Mina to her room and watched Anna for any sign of instability before addressing Rizal.

'Where is he?' she asked.

Rizal pictured the crumpled body lying in the back of his car. Why had he brought it home? They couldn't see Faisal looking like this. But Zaharah would see through any lie. She wanted only facts.

'He's in the back of my car.'

'Please, bring him in and then go to the mosque and find Imam Abdullah.'

Rizal went back into the storm. He pulled Faisal's bruised form out of the car and placed it on the lawn, allowing the rain to wash away the dried blood. The bitter liquid rose in his throat again and this time he couldn't stop it. He doubled over and vomited at his friend's side. Their fluids, blackened blood and pink vomit, mingled and flowed down the drive.

His stomach threatened to rebel again but he got control of himself. How would he carry Faisal to the house? He placed one arm under his neck and the other under his knees and tried to cradle the limp body like a sleeping child. He held his breath and staggered a few feet and then bent his legs to rest the body on his knees before continuing. In this way, he made it to the house. Zaharah met him at the door. Anna hovered in the back of the room.

Rizal carried the body into the sitting room and placed it on the blankets Zaharah had laid out on the floor. His mother-in-law dropped next to her son and gently closed his eyes with her fingertips. The maid rushed in with a cotton blanket and a cooking pot filled with water. Zaharah draped the corpse with the blanket and began uncovering him piece by piece as she washed his face and limbs. She touched her son with the tenderness of a mother bathing her baby. Zaharah's peaceful demeanour triggered some hidden strength in Anna. She knelt to help her mother. The maid rushed back and forth between the kitchen and the sitting room, carrying buckets of water and washcloths that arrived clear and clean but left fouled with colours so disturbing, their source could not be contemplated.

Rizal sat helplessly on the couch, marvelling at the women, his own energy and emotions drained. Zaharah turned to him, not without sympathy.

'Rizal, could you please go and find Imam Abdullah. I would like him to say the prayers.'

Her voice infused him with enough power to rise from the couch and return to the car to search for the imam. The rains had stopped. Their clatter had been replaced with the sounds of mourning. Behind every closed curtain, in every house, Rizal imagined people crying.

What would happen tomorrow? Would the planes return? How many more would die? What the hell were the British doing? Where were their defenses? What are we supposed to do now?

The island didn't contain enough holy people to attend to the dead. The priests, imam and ministers did their best, but they couldn't get to every house. Imam Abdullah Halim, a long-time family friend, came to Zaharah's assistance to help her bury her son. He performed the ritual cleansing, removing all earthly impurities. Then Rizal and the imam lifted Faisal's body and placed him on three muslin sheets on the floor. Zaharah kissed her son's bruised lips goodbye and stepped back to allow the men to cover him. 'Sleep well, my son.'

Rizal envied them their religious convictions. He couldn't cry or pray. Where Zaharah envisioned the beauty of Allah's impenetrable wisdom, he saw only the cruelty and wanton destruction of brutal men. He was frustrated by his helplessness and his frustration made him angry. Hell on earth, he thought. *Perhaps it's good preparation.*

Part VII

1

News of the breach of the Jitra Line spread quickly. Japanese soldiers had trooped through jungle paths in the middle of the night and surrounded the Indian battalion that was providing the only defense. The remaining British forces were in retreat toward Singapore, marching in the monsoon rains, harassed at every step by bombers. At this pace, the Japanese would reach Penang in a few days. To locals like Rizal, who had been raised to believe in the superiority of the British Empire, the defeat was scandalous.

The Japanese bombers returned to Penang, the next day. This time, two single-seater fighter planes met them, the sole defense for the island offered by the British. The planes rose when the bombers came into sight, trying desperately to reach an adequate firing altitude. The bombers knocked off the first effortlessly, sending it plummeting to the ground. The second pilot turned tail and fled before he could be struck down as well.

The city collapsed into chaos with the news of these bewildering defeats. Police, civil administrators and military personnel disappeared. First-aid and air-raid posts were deserted. Emboldened thugs openly looted abandoned shops and houses. Telephone and electric wires remained broken. Water and sewer mains leaked their contents into the ravaged town.

Zaharah, Mina and Rozi joined Rizal and Anna in the countryside. Other relatives followed. Rizal counted about forty people sleeping in every available crevice of their tiny bungalow. The women and children took over the bedrooms, while Rizal slept in the sitting room with the other men.

The family provided a tight net of mourning around the Parkers. The women huddled around Mina, covering her in a blanket of concern. In the company of her sisters, Zaharah allowed herself a few tears. Rizal never actually saw her cry; he noticed her reddened eyes when she came downstairs to prepare breakfast.

The volume of relatives in the house provided a convenient buffer for Rizal and Anna. The couple skirted each other with no confrontations and no resolutions. They became skilled at carrying on conversations through unsuspecting intermediaries.

'I'll be back in a few hours,' Rizal would say to the crowd in his kitchen, 'I'm going to the market.'

'We're out of rice,' Anna might say to no one in particular as her husband headed out the door.

Rizal no longer felt the numbing sorrow he had experienced after Arun's death or the hurt and frustration he had suffered at Anna's revelations. He thought of these catastrophes often, along with the loss of his cousin, but he remained resolutely stoic except for the nightmares that jolted him from his sleep, usually involving a raging fire and the need to drag someone to safety. The victim of the fire might be Arun, Anna, Faisal, one of the children, or a random relative. The presence of so many women and children in his house filled him with an anxious sense of responsibility.

The emotion that threatened to overwhelm him during his waking hours was rage. He found a concrete target for his anger in the British colonialists. His fury fastened onto these irresponsible, incompetent buffoons. The British were paralysed. No word came from the colonial offices, no calls for evacuation, no preparations for defense or surrender, nothing. The governor couldn't be reached as he was theoretically trapped in meetings. As it turned out, the only preparations being made by the British were for their own evacuation.

The European women and children fled on a secret evacuation ferry on Saturday night, two days after the terror bombing. Volunteers with loaded rifles manned the dock to repulse any locals who had the nerve to try to join them. On Monday, the men slipped away—all except the medical superintendent of the General Hospital, who refused to abandon his post. The highest-ranking official left behind, a Singaporean excluded from the 'whites only' evacuation ferry, was given no instructions for surrender.

When the Japanese planes returned on Monday, they dropped more pamphlets, taunting an enemy that had already fled. They released a single bomb near the funicular of Penang Hill that ignited the engine room. Rizal gathered with other angry men in an impromptu town meeting that evening. What could be done to prevent more bloodshed?

The chaos required leadership and several men stepped up to assume the role. Saravanamuthu, the editor of the *Straits Echo*, offered to climb the flagpole at Fort Cornwallis and raise a white flag. Another man, a Eurasian horse trainer, volunteered to cycle the twenty-one miles to the Japanese frontline to inform the enemy of the British departure.

What next? Prepare for the arrival of the Japanese troops. But how would these soldiers descend upon the city—as conquering hoards determined to rape, murder and loot as they had in Nanking, or as triumphant liberators? The population had to be prepared for the worst.

The group decided to form a volunteer force to step into the vacuum left by the British. They organized an emergency communication system, medical response teams, twenty-four-hour street patrol, and a registration process for rationing. Rizal offered to take the night patrol, anything to avoid more nightmares. His job was to drive his car back and forth along a commercial thoroughfare near the docks to protect the area from vandals.

During his first shift, he heard a distant clang echoing down one of the streets. He turned down the road and pulled into the driveway of an abandoned British storehouse. A bare-chested teen stood outside the storehouse, pounding the padlock with a metal stick until the old lock gave way. He should probably have stopped the kid. But was robbing from the absentee British really a crime? Why should these possessions be allowed to fall into the hands of the Japanese? The two wordlessly ransacked the shed. Rizal packed his car with canned goods, gasoline and automobile parts, while the young man filled a handcart.

When the boy had stuffed his cart, he walked to a wooden desk in a corner of the warehouse, grabbed a portrait of King George from the wall, and slammed it onto the ground. A jubilant grin crept across his face. Rizal was seized with the need to break something, anything. One piece of glass would feel so good. He grabbed a photo of a blond woman and smashed it on the desk. The sound, like the popping of violin strings, released a pent-up force within him.

They began pulling papers from the drawer and throwing them in all directions. But the destruction failed to quell the blood pumping through his veins. The young man, as if reading his mind, tore up a wooden crate and placed the broken slats in a pile outside. Rizal joined him and the two tore up more crates, until they deemed the stack sufficient. The boy doused the wood with gasoline while Rizal produced a box of matches from his pocket, lit several at once and threw them onto the pile. The flames burst with the force of an explosion. The heat caused the nerves on his skin to tingle to life. They opened a crate of whisky and tossed the contents one by one into the fire. The bottles flew from his hands in graceful floating arcs and erupted like Chinese firecrackers.

Their activities attracted the attention of others, who wandered out of the shadows into the warehouse. They carted off anything they could carry. Each added a memento to the blaze: a stack of colonial stamps, a handful of military fatigues. Someone produced a British flag and threw it on the flames to the roaring approval of the gathering crowd. A few, who could not bear to waste any of the loot, added a wad of spit. As the fire reached its apex, as many as fifteen men stood around, each fanning the flames with his own silent fury as the smoke curled to the sky. Rizal waited until the sparks had died down and his heart had stopped pounding, then he unclenched his fists and returned to the car.

As he drove through the silent, sleepy streets, a motorcycle overtook the car and sped out of sight, down the winding two-lane road. The slender motorbike looked homely and fragile, nothing like the metallic beauty Faisal used to ride. But there was something about the way it skimmed along, as if the owner might actually be out for a morning joyride. His mind jumped to the memory of the day when he and Faisal had skipped work and ridden through the city streets. He would give anything to return to that other lifetime—when he was truly happy, when the world seemed willing to give him everything he wanted. He had to pull the car to the side to keep from swerving off the road. He bent over the steering wheel and allowed the waves of tears to wash over him.

2

On 20 December, a cluster of Japanese soldiers landed in the harbour to occupy Penang. Instead of a triumphal entry, the soldiers trooped through town in ill-fitting uniforms, cloth sun caps, stolen British rifles, bayonets and rubber boots. Nothing like the crisp regimentals and polished leather shoes the colonial officers wore on parade days. These peasants looked like coolies. They had compact bodies and sunburned necks, and spoke with rough guttural voices as they pointed and shouted to each other.

This description reached Anna from the men who had ventured out to see the arrival. The women had kept to their houses. Despite precautions, a few girls still fell victim to the soldiers' clutches. Some husbands might have preferred to keep the more unpleasant details from their wives, but Rizal was unaccustomed to sheltering Anna from news. He spoke openly of the atrocities with Ibrahim and the other men within earshot of anyone who cared to listen.

Through their conversations, Anna learned that the military police had arrived with a list of enemy citizens provided by the spies sent before the war. The police went straight to the homes of the people on their list and carted the offenders off, mostly Chinese, who had supported the Aid to China campaign, as well as students of the Chinese schools known for their anti-Japanese activities. Communists or Nationalists, the Japanese made no distinction. A few on the volunteer committee were detained, questioned and then dismissed from their duties.

The family held their collective breath waiting to see if anyone would be summoned. After two weeks went by, a note arrived demanding that the Parkers open their warehouses for inspection. Rizal agreed to go. Since Faisal's death, he was now in-charge of those warehouses.

Anna approached Rizal as he prepared to return to the city to meet the Japanese at the appointed time. She needed to find out what had happened to Tong. She had hoped to catch her husband alone, but a private conversation was impossible these days with so many relatives around. So she followed him as he walked toward the car.

'Rizal,' she called after him.

He stopped in his tracks, startled to hear her speak to him directly.

'I want to ask you something,' she said.

He didn't look her in the eye but focussed somewhere on the centre of her forehead. He actually looked frightened. What did he think she was going to ask? Surely there were worse possibilities for him than the question she had in mind.

'What do you hear about the Khoos?' she asked. 'You said that some families had been taken. Do you know what has happened to them?'

Now, Rizal met her gaze.

'They got away,' he said. 'They slipped off in one of their ships before the Japanese landed.'

'Good, I'm glad they're safe,' she said. 'Thank you.'

'For what?'

'Thank you for telling me,' she said.

He looked confused. His eyes lingered on her face as if trying to understand an abstract painting.

'Since you asked me,' he said, 'why wouldn't I tell you?'

'I thought the question might make you angry.'

'Anna,' he sighed, 'I don't have any anger left. I'm just trying to figure out how to cope from day to day. I'm doing the best I can.'

He looked so unhappy. She wanted to rub away the lines on his forehead. But it was no longer possible for her to yield to these useless impulses. She couldn't touch him anymore. She hoped that time would help her shake these lingering feelings for her husband, which continued to threaten her composure. If only she could forget what she had seen. If only Allah would grant her this tiny bit of amnesia. But of course, that was impossible. No force of will or God could return things to the way they had once been, or more accurately, to the way they used to be in her mind. The truth had never actually changed, just her perception of it.

At least Tong was safe and far away. She wouldn't have to figure out what to do about him until after the war. And she had spoken to her husband. A barrier had collapsed between them. Perhaps they could continue like this until the end of the war. A decision in the midst of this chaos might be too rash. She needed some calm and an atmosphere of certainty to consider her options.

* * *

Rizal arrived at the warehouse at the appointed time. The commanding officer who met him at the front door looked young but haggard. His shoulders lacked the girth of a full-grown man but his eyes were already etched with lines. An extra belt hole held his pants to his body. Next to him stood another officer, equally youthful, but this man lacked hard lines. He didn't have a sword on his belt. Instead of a weapon, he held a pen and a composition pad.

The officer with the pen spoke first. 'I am Seiko.' He bowed slightly, then remembering himself, stood back up. 'Major Seiko and this is Colonel Imanaka.'

Colonel Imanaka neither bowed nor shook his hand. He grunted to his companion, who translated in perfect English.

'Would you be so kind as to open your warehouses for our inspection?'

Rizal fumbled for his keys. After several attempts, he managed to get the key to turn in the lock. The officers pushed open the doors and stepped inside. Rizal followed and stood placidly by the doorway as they wandered up and down the rows of shelves.

They didn't take anything during this meeting, but as they surveyed the shelves, Seiko made crisp notations in his composition pad. The slender fingers that gripped his pen lacked calluses. The nails were clipped and cleaned. He could have been a student taking notes at a university lecture.

Two filthy foot soldiers, looking like lanky teenagers out on prowl, entered the warehouse and spoke to the officers.

'Please follow these men,' Seiko instructed.

The soldiers escorted him to the esplanade, where a crowd was being forcibly gathered around the colonial bandstand. The young men cleared a path to the front and motioned for him to follow, as if directing him to choice seats for a public concert. Instead of an orchestra, he was offered an unobstructed view of two men on the platform. The men stood with their heads bowed and their hands tied behind their back. Their clothing suggested they were Chinese students, but the blindfolds made it impossible to judge their age.

A sturdy officer stood behind the men, his feet spread apart, his fingers massaging a transparent moustache. He waited like a patient headmaster for his audience to stop fidgeting. When he deemed the crowd sufficiently large, he pushed down on the prisoner's shoulders to make him kneel. His head fell with a single swipe. As soon as Rizal realized what was happening, he turned away. He heard the thud as the head hit the ground. The crowd gasped as if on cue. Seconds later, he heard another swipe and then a thud. Rizal turned back in time to see a leg still jerking on the ground. The man behind him retched onto the back of Rizal's pants. The executioner wiped his blade with a cloth and replaced his sword in its shaft. He turned to face his audience with a benevolent smile.

'You are pleased to go now. Thank you for your time.'

No explanation was offered to the silent crowd, who had never before witnessed such barbaric proceedings. The British could be contemptuous of locals, but under their rule, the population had come to expect a civilized method of charges and litigation. Everyone hesitated to disperse, fearing that any movement might attract the attention of the executioner's sword. Finally, the soldiers shooed them away like naughty children who had stayed too long at a party.

3

February 1942

Fears of rape subsided with the establishment of the comfort houses. Though their existence gnawed at the conscience of the population, the solution seemed an appropriate compromise. As long as these comfort houses were filled with prostitutes, what harm could be done? That coercion might be necessary, at times; well, few people would lose any sleep over the fate of a prostitute. The arguments didn't convince Anna, who had recently gained a new empathy for these fallen women, but she felt, as with so many other things in this war, that the events were beyond her control. At least she could safely leave her house now, though always with a headscarf and her face blackened with charcoal, lest the soldiers mistake her for a European.

The house emptied as their relatives crept back to the city to pick up the threads of their lives. Zaharah and Mina remained with Anna and Rizal. The driver never reappeared, so the maids moved to the room behind the garage. Zaharah and Mina slept in the children's room and Anna and Rizal returned to their awkward marital bed. An odd pattern developed and began to feel almost normal. Anna retired early, after the children were settled. Rizal stayed up late and woke before sunrise, spending the fewest moments possible in the bedroom.

Rizal resumed his work as commerce returned to the island. The Japanese, like the British before them, required traders, merchants and shippers to extract raw materials from the occupied territories. Rizal was now responsible for the trading firm, as well as the Parkers' enterprises. He tried his best to keep these companies afloat for the benefit of his family. He put in long hours at work and spent his spare time engaged in side trips to procure fresh produce, a spot of milk, an extra ration of rice, or a few eggs for the children.

Public transportation resumed. Anna took the bus to the city a few times a week to meet Nariza to go shopping, in search of hidden treasures. A new market had sprung up around the rubble of the old, where hawkers ostensibly sold tapioca and maize. The women haggled for these authorized goods until the soldiers turned their backs and the real trading could take place.

After a successful day at the market—Anna had traded a small bottle of perfume for an entire bag of sugar—the ladies headed back to Nariza's house. They travelled down Northam Road and passed what remained of Millionaires' Row. The Japanese had looted and desecrated most of these houses, taking over the best ones for their high-ranking officers. They had ripped up the iron gates and fences, devouring the raw materials for their war engine. Nariza picked up her pace in front of Seascape. A handful of soldiers clustered in the driveway, eyeing the ladies as they walked by.

'What's happening in that house?' Anna whispered, once they had safely crossed the drive.

'They're using it as some kind of interrogation headquarters. Neighbours say they hear screams coming from the house all the time. And a phonograph. Apparently, the chief interrogator likes Bach.'

This last bit of information seemed too grotesque to be true, the kind of thing that got added in the retelling just to spice up the story. But who knew anymore the difference between fact and fiction? Their lives had begun to resemble a dime-store horror novel. If a legion of vampires descended on their city, Anna wouldn't be surprised.

'Who are they interrogating?' she asked.

'Anyone they feel like. Haven't you seen the round-ups?'

'What round-ups?' Were they living in an American Western now?

'You're so lucky to live in the country!' Nariza exclaimed. 'They come through first thing in the morning and cordon off an area, usually Chinese, and then round up all the residents and make them stand on the street corner. A truck drives by with hooded men in the back. Whomever the men point to, gets thrown in the back of a police van.'

'Who are the hooded men?'

'Who knows? Probably just people who've been promised release if they point their finger at someone else. Or maybe they're neighbours trying to settle old scores. You can't trust anyone these days. There are informers everywhere.' This last part, she whispered for effect.

'It's a good thing the Khoos got out when they did,' Anna thought out loud. She had been thinking of Tong lately, wondering if they had arrived in Singapore safely. Had Sze-yin given birth? She hoped the child had survived. Tong would make a good father. He deserved a healthy child.

'Haven't you heard?'

'What?'

Nariza, always happiest when she was gossiping, beamed with the possibility of sharing a juicy morsel with her friend.

'Tong and his wife didn't leave,' she whispered.

'But Rizal said the Khoos left.'

'The rest of the family got out but apparently Sze-yin refused. They're hiding out in Pembroke. Since the funicular was bombed, the Japanese soldiers are too lazy to hike up the hill.'

'How do you know?'

'Everybody knows. It's the worst-kept secret in Penang.'

'If everybody knows, then it's just a matter of time before the Japanese find out.'

'You're probably right, but what to do? They should have gotten out when they had the chance.'

'Somebody's got to help them,' Anna said.

'The Chinese should take care of their own.'

'And if they don't?'

'Anyone who tries to help puts their own family at risk. Better to keep your head down and hope for the best.'

'Then who'll help us when we're in trouble?'

'If you keep your head down, there won't be any trouble.'

4

'Soldiers!'

A shout went out before the car had even pulled into the driveway. The sound travelled like a wave through the compound. The maids grabbed the children who had been playing in the yard and rushed them toward the stream. Rizal shooed his relatives into the kitchen and then went outside and stood by the front door. He could offer no defense for his family except his own body positioned in front of the door. Two soldiers in cloth caps and heavy black boots emerged from their car. One of the soldiers shouted something, but whether it was a greeting or a command, he had no way of knowing.

'Can I help you?' he asked in as calm a voice as possible. The soldiers were unpredictable, but a non-confrontational stance seemed like the best option. 'I am Rizal Mansour,' he said helpfully.

'Come.' The command was unmistakable.

He followed the men to the car, his heart pounding in his chest. He caught sight of Anna watching from behind a clothesline.

The city went by in a blur. What had he done? Where were they taking him?

The car pulled in front of Rumah Merah. The iron gates had been ripped from the entrance. Bare hinges marked where the front door should have stood.

One of the soldiers pulled him out of the car and marched him to the door. His knees threatened to buckle. It took all the strength in his legs to climb the front steps into the empty house.

Everything of value had already been packed up and moved to his house. But that hadn't stopped vandals from ripping out light fixtures and prying up floor tiles. The denigration of Faisal's home appalled Rizal. They might as well have dug up his corpse and picked at his bones.

The officer with the clean nails and perfect English was sitting on the staircase, looking at a book. He stood when Rizal entered and said something to the soldiers. The men touched their caps and disappeared out the door.

'Thank you for coming,' he smiled warmly. 'I am Tanaka Seiko. We met at your warehouse.'

Rizal nodded mutely.

'I'd offer you a seat but there don't seem to be any,' Seiko continued. He indicated the book in his hand. 'One of my men found this in a box on the second floor. It seems the looters aren't interested in Dickens. I asked around and was told this is your house.'

'It's my in-laws'.'

'Your in-laws are English?' the officer asked.

There didn't seem any point in lying. The Japanese spies seemed to know everything.

'My father-in-law was English. But he's dead.'

'I understand that your brother-in-law died in the air raids. I am very sorry for your loss.'

Was he being baited? He held his breath. He would not let them agitate him.

'Do you like Dickens?' the officer asked.

'I haven't read any since university.'

The officer smiled as if he had mentioned a fellow acquaintance.

'I knew you were a university man. Where did you go to school?'

Had he entered some twisted form of an interrogation? Did they start out friendly and smiling, and then pull out brass knuckles?

'I went to Cambridge.'

'Cambridge. How lovely. I've always wanted to visit the land of Shakespeare.' His fingers stroked the book in his hand. 'Such a beautiful book. Do you have more?'

'I might have a few more at my house.'

'Wonderful. I'd love to see them some time. May I borrow this?'

'Please, help yourself.'

Seiko clapped his hands like a delighted schoolboy. 'I won't take any more of your time. Thank you for coming out. I will return the book when I'm done. Would you like a ride home with my soldiers?'

Was that it? Was he being dismissed? What kind of a soldier would ask to borrow anything? What kind of lunatics were these people?

'No, thank you. I can find my own way back.'

5

The fall of Singapore crushed any hope for a speedy end to the occupation. Instead of attacking by sea as everyone had predicted, the Japanese infantry had pedalled 550 miles across the jungles of the Malayan peninsula, riding stolen bikes, armed with weapons abandoned by retreating troops. The advancing soldiers had been ordered to take no prisoners, lest they be slowed down. Captured Allied troops were doused with petrol and burned to death. Churchill had tried to harden his forces. 'There must be no thought of sparing the troops or population; commanders and senior officers should die with their troops. The honour of the British Empire and the British Army is at stake.'

That honour vanished when the Japanese crossed the causeway into Singapore, 'an impenetrable fortress, the very symbol of British military might', and overwhelmed the larger Allied defenses in a matter of days. 100,000 men were taken prisoner. It was the largest defeat in British history.

Their Asian brothers would have been more impressed if the Japanese hadn't unleashed unspeakable brutality on the population. Locals who had helped the Allies had been tortured before being murdered. A Malay officer had been used for bayonet practice and 2,000 local volunteers had been massacred on the beaches of Changi.

Anna couldn't stop worrying about Tong and Sze-yin. She had a plan to help them but it would require Rizal's assistance. Now with Singapore's defeat and new information that the funicular was being repaired, she knew that she couldn't put off the uncomfortable conversation any longer.

She waited until the others had gone to bed and then entered the sitting room. Rizal was reading by candlelight, stretched out on the couch, a book propped between his hands. She hated to disturb him, especially considering the topic she had in mind, but she couldn't risk waiting another day.

'Rizal,' she spoke into the semi-darkness. 'Did you know that Tong and Sze-yin are still in Penang?'

His hand reached for the light on the end table, forgetting for a moment that the electricity was still out. She couldn't make out the expression on his face in the shadows of the dim candlelight.

'What are you talking about?'

'Nariza told me that the rest of the family had sailed away but Tong and Sze-yin had stayed behind. They're hiding at Pembroke.'

'That's impossible. They'd have been discovered long ago.'

'Nariza says they're still there. She says everybody in Penang knows about it.'

'Well, I didn't know.' He sounded defensive. 'I'm obviously the last to know anything.'

'I'm not accusing you of lying.'

He held the candle up, toward her face.

'Well, what about it then?'

'We need to help them.'

'Do *we*?' he asked incredulously. 'And how would *we* do that?'

'We can bring them here.'

'No, we can't.' He was trying to contain the volume of his voice but the pitch rose perceptibly. 'I won't allow it.' As soon as he had said the words, he knew his mistake.

'What do you mean you won't allow it? Who are you to forbid anything?'

'I didn't mean to say that,' he said quietly. 'I meant that I don't want them in this house.'

'Why not?'

Because you're in love with him, he wanted to say but he knew he didn't have the right.

'Because it's not safe,' he said instead. 'Do you want to put our family at risk? What about the children?'

'The Japanese never come out here.'

'Why should I help him?' he asked.

She had anticipated this question and prepared a response, though his plaintive expression caused her to soften her tone.

'Because you can. Would you stand by and let someone die when you're in a position to prevent it?'

Why was she asking this of him? Was this some kind of test? Even if she wanted to sacrifice his life for Tong, she must realize that they'd probably both be killed. The idea was ludicrous.

'Even if we could get them here, how long are we supposed to keep them? This war could continue for a very long time.'

'Until we can get them out of the country. You have Papa's ships. You'll figure out a way.'

'The Japanese are inspecting every ship in the harbour.'

'So it might take awhile. Until they let their guard down.'

She wasn't going to back down. He would either die trying to get them out, or worse, maybe he *would* get them out. But then what? Would she run off with Tong? Slip away to Sumatra or Australia? No, she would never leave the children. Things would continue unresolved, festering, until the end of the war, when Tong would return and demand his rightful place at her side.

Maybe Rizal could whisper their whereabouts to the Japanese. If everybody knew about them, no one could accuse him of being the snitch. But he could no more send a man to his death than he could strangle him with his own bare hands.

'Anna, I don't want him here.'

'I know you don't. But you will help, won't you?'

He sighed. He was out of rational arguments. This last had been a personal appeal. But it had failed.

'I'll ask around. Maybe they've already left.'

* * *

Once Rizal resigned himself to the rescue, he actually relished the thought of the penitence. He no longer knew what he believed about fate or God, but if there was some ledger book weighing his deeds, perhaps this would put some credit in his bankrupted column. And if he died in the effort, surely that would count for something—if not in Allah's eyes, then maybe in Anna's.

Mina had objected to the plan when he had shared it with the family. She had argued that the Khoos' presence would put the whole family at risk. But Zaharah had been adamant.

'Of course we must help them,' she said. 'To turn our backs would be a sin. They can stay in the driver's quarters; the maids can move back into the house. If the Japanese happen to come this way, we'll tell them he's our gardener. They'd never suspect that the son of a Khoo would be hiding out as a gardener.'

'Malays don't keep Chinese gardeners, Ma,' Mina countered.

'Do you think the Japanese know that? Besides, the soldiers don't patrol out here. It's too far from their comforts.'

A few inquiries led Rizal to the maid who was helping Tong and Sze yin. He would have gladly paid someone else to do his sleuthing but no one could be trusted these days. Anna scribbled a note and he slipped the maid the message as she entered the temple. That the Japanese soldiers didn't even notice a Malay Muslim loitering at the entrance to a Chinese temple, showed the depth of their ignorance of the local population.

6

Tong thought he smelled the faint aroma of Anna's perfume when Elsie entered the kitchen, carrying the tin of milk and wilted greens she had managed to find at the market. What a faithful girl this young servant had turned out to be. She had lived in his household since she was a little girl and yet, Tong had never given her any thought. She wore little tokens of his brother's affection, a silver chain around her neck, and two tiny studs in her ears. But Tong hadn't considered her more than an amiable servant. He could never have imagined the depths of her loyalty. That she considered herself a member of the family, a dutiful sister, had come as quite a shock to him.

Without her, they would have starved. She risked her life to bring them food and information. She was quite an intelligent girl with the eavesdropping skills of a well-trained agent. Through her, they learned the identities of the victims in Seascape. He didn't know the Chinese students or Communist sympathizers, but many of the other names were too familiar.

Two days ago, Elsie had arrived in tears and relayed the horrible news of the fall of Singapore. She understood that his family's fate would be no better than those who had stayed in Penang. Maybe worse, as the occupying troops in Penang seemed almost soft compared to those in Singapore.

His grandmother had made the right choice, drifting off to her final sleep with the aid of her pipe, the night before their departure. Rather than a magnificent wake, the family had paid a caretaker at the Khoo Kongsi to perform the funeral rites. These were pathetic provisions for the matriarch of such a prominent family, but they were better than the send-off the Japanese soldiers would have given her.

The baby continued to thrive. At four weeks, he had put on weight and was holding up his head. Remarkable, considering that he had almost died in utero.

Tong had watched helplessly as Sze-yin faded during the struggles of childbirth, knowing he lacked the tools to perform a successful surgery. The colour had drained from her face, all movement in her pelvic area had stopped. Just at the point when he had given up on her, she had rallied. He had been stunned by the reserve strength in her frail body. Before she had recovered enough to even sit up, she had taken the baby to her breast. She was probably the first woman in her family to feed her own child in generations.

And now, a month later, without the usual postpartum prescriptions, she appeared fully recovered. She seemed to be in good spirits despite their circumstances. It helped that she had no understanding of the geopolitical realities surrounding their confinement. He assured her that their situation was temporary. The British would take back the city any day. They only had to wait, keep quiet, and try not to be discovered. So she devoted all her energy to tending to her new infant and quieting his cries.

He might as well lie to her, rather than burden her with his fears during their last days. He focussed on saving the child. He was determined to get the baby out of their hiding place and to safety. Even an orphanage would be better than the fate that awaited him here.

His reassuring lies about their situation had the unfortunate effect of lulling Sze-yin into complacency. She refused to allow her son to be taken anywhere. He thought of whisking the baby away at night but she kept the infant curled tightly in her arms when she slept.

The sight of Anna's stationery, the jasmine scent of her perfume, and her beautiful sprawling handwriting, filled his senses with joy for the first time in weeks. He had thought of Anna every day since their liaison in his office. Even as his family had departed, while he had gathered supplies in the house and prepared for the worst, he had still fingered the place on his neck where her lips had pressed. He could recall every moment, every turn. He had, in fact, relived their lovemaking a thousand times in the hollow darkness of his prison cell.

He only wished that he had had the opportunity to say goodbye. He would never forgive himself for calling after her too late. She had disappeared down the hall before he had had a chance to tell her how much he loved her.

Follow Elsie down the footpath at midnight tonight.
Please take care and I will see you soon.

Anna

She had not signed it 'with love' but the fact that she would risk her life to help him was proof enough of her feelings.

He explained to Sze-yin that Elsie had come with a message from Anna.

'Anna? How does she know we're here?'

'I don't know, but she says to follow Elsie down the footpath tonight.'

'Maybe it's a trap?' Sze-yin said.

'Anna wouldn't set a trap for us.'

'Maybe someone else wrote the message.'

'Nobody else would know to send a note from Anna.'

'Why would she help us?' Sze-yin asked, her uncanny intuition crackling back to life.

'I don't know,' he lied.

She narrowed her eyes in accusatory slants but chose not to pursue the topic.

'What will we do at the bottom of the hill? Who will meet us? Where will they take us?' She asked.

'I don't know.'

'You don't know much, do you?'

She placed the sleeping baby on a blanket and pulled a cloth bag filled with jewellery out of her backpack and began sewing it inside the lining of her skirt.

'What are you doing?' he asked.

'Who knows where we'll end up? These will work as currency wherever we go. A woman is born with more common sense than a man acquires in a lifetime,' she said as she continued with her needlework.

* * *

At midnight, he collected his wife and child, his medical kit and backpack. Tong had made this trek so many times as a boy, he could have walked the path blindfolded. He tied his son to his back with a sarong and held his wife's arm to help her navigate the roots and branches. They finally emerged at the bottom of the hill.

Tong could make out the silhouette of a puller coming toward them. As he got closer, the puller's features came into view. Rizal? What was he doing here? Maybe it *was* a trap? Anna would never have sent Rizal for them. He looked back up the trail they had just come down. Which fate would he prefer, torture by the soldiers or death at the hands of a jealous husband? At least Rizal wouldn't hurt Sze-yin or the baby.

'A baby?' Rizal whispered. 'Nobody mentioned a baby.'

Was his plan for killing Tong ruined by the existence of a baby?

'My son,' Tong said.

'Alamak,' Rizal exclaimed. 'How are we supposed to travel silently with a screaming baby?'

'He's sleeping,' Sze-yin informed him.

'Where are we going?' Tong asked. If Rizal had wanted to kill him, he would have done it by now.

'Back to our house. You can stay there until we find a way to get you off the island.'

'From one hiding place to another,' Sze-yin said. 'How is that any better?'

'Our house is out of town. The military police never come by. You'll be safe there until we find a ship to transport you off the island.'

'Can't we just wait until the British return?' Sze-yin asked. 'Wouldn't it be easier to just wait?'

'You might be waiting the rest of your life,' Rizal replied.

Sze-yin stared at her husband.

Elsie, who had accompanied them down the path, grabbed Tong's arm. 'Take me with you,' she cried.

Tong turned, startled by desperation in her voice. 'It's not safe. You'll be better off away from us.'

'I have nowhere to go,' she said. 'Take me with you, please.'

Tong turned to Rizal, who shrugged his shoulders as if to say the whole thing had already got out of control with the baby. Tong helped Sze-yin and Elsie into the carriage and then offered to pull the rickshaw.

'You'll look too suspicious in those clothes,' Rizal said.

So Tong sat in the carriage with his wife, maid and son, pulled by the husband of the woman he loved. The baby stirred but didn't cry. Tong watched the sweat collect on Rizal's back as he laboured under their heavy weight. They rolled silently down the village streets.

7

April 1942

Rizal had plenty to worry about: the war, the daily struggle for basic necessities, his wife's lover living under his roof. And now that officer had taken to visiting them weekly, exchanging his books as if Rizal were a lending library. The first time Seiko had arrived at the house, he had set the whole compound into a panic. Everyone had run for the woods, and Tong and his wife had barely made it out of sight before the officer emerged from his car, oblivious to the frenzy he had created.

'Ah, Mr Rizal, so glad to have caught you at home. Good morning, or should I say, Selamat pagi. You see, I'm learning some Malay. Perhaps someday, we can converse in your native tongue. I hope you don't mind my dropping by. I've brought your book back. May I come in?'

His courtesy only served to enrage Rizal further. What was he doing here?

'Of course, please come in. Could I get you some tea?'

And so Seiko had entered the sitting room like an honoured guest. Rizal put on the kettle himself because the servants were crouched in the woods. Seiko surveyed the sitting room with obvious curiosity.

'I can see that your wife didn't exactly marry above her station.' He chuckled at his impropriety. 'I'm sorry. No offense intended. My own wife didn't do so well either. My salary as a lecturer could never compete with my father-in-law's. And my linguistic skills, so heavily prized by the military, haven't done much to raise my esteem in my in-laws' eyes.'

'Do you have any children?' Rizal asked, to change the topic as he handed Seiko a teacup.

'I must have by now,' he said. 'My wife was due this month. But I haven't heard anything.'

Seiko made his way to the bookshelves and surveyed Rizal and Anna's odd assortment of books.

'The Dickens was lovely,' he said. 'Have you read it?'

'No, I haven't.'

'You should. Such a beautiful story. He was a master storyteller.'

'Hmm,' Rizal answered. Where was this conversation going?

'May I borrow another? They give us nothing here. Not even writing paper.'

'Take any that you like.'

Seiko picked up a volume of natural history and began flipping through the pages.

'Do you have any books on the local flora? I consider myself an amateur horticulturist. The plants here are absolutely exquisite. Just the other day, I found a heliconia that must have been at least four feet tall. I keep a notebook with all of my observations. But I don't know the names of many of the plants.'

'I might have something,' Rizal said. 'It's an English publication. I can't remember where I put it.' He searched the shelves desperately. If he could give the man what he wanted, maybe he could get him out without an incident.

'Here it is!' He pulled out the book and handed it to Seiko. Would he go away now?

If only it were that simple. Each week, Seiko returned and sat in the sitting room sipping tea as if on a pleasant social call. In addition to his insatiable appetite for books, he seemed to be using Rizal as a private Malay tutor, trying out different phrases, asking him the meaning of others. He seemed more desperate for company than books. He would talk about his life in Japan, how he had been ripped from his university and sent to this strange country. Not that the island wasn't beautiful—a paradise, in fact—but he missed his wife and wanted to see his child.

Rizal listened and interjected just enough into the conversation to appear polite but not overly friendly. He didn't know what to make of this man.

'Does he want you to be an informant?' Ibrahim asked.

'No, nothing like that. He hasn't asked anything of me.'

'He just borrows books?'

'Yes, and he talks incessantly. He goes on and on about the plants on the island, and language and his homeland.'

Ibrahim looked for a moment at Rizal as if he were considering a question.

'Do you think . . . ?' He shook his head. 'Never mind.'

'What?'

'His intentions seem harmless,' Ibrahim said. 'Who knows, his friendship might come in handy.'

'He's not a friend.'

'Well, enemies don't drink tea and borrow books. Either way, polite cooperation seems like the safest option.'

Of course, his uncle didn't know about Tong and his wife. Each time Seiko visited, the whole household was in danger. But what could he do?

8

It is inappropriate to lust after the wife of your host, especially when that host saved your life. So Tong kept his hands and his thoughts to himself during the weeks in Rizal's home. It was enough to be alive. He was grateful for the opportunity to breathe fresh air, watch his son grow, and stand so close to Anna. He considered each day a gift. He knew with eerie certainty that he would not survive the war and that knowledge gave a certain philosophical detachment to his thoughts.

How beautiful this part of the island was, with its abundant fruit trees and burbling stream, so tranquil compared to the crowded, polluted city where he lived, or had lived before the occupation. And the charming bungalow, so much more reasonable than the monstrosity he had grown up in. Even his humble room behind the garage seemed like a cozy guest cottage, though he felt guilty for displacing the maids.

The accommodating girls, five in all, including Elsie, now slept in rolled-out bedding on the kitchen floor. He made it a point to notice each one and to learn their names. The house could use a few more bedrooms to accommodate all these people, especially once the children grew older. And more servants' quarters were needed, what with all the maids; and eventually, a new driver. They could use a gardener, too. A yard this size required a full-time gardener. Tong could see that great care had been taken with the layout of the garden. Had Anna or Rizal plotted the grounds themselves or had they hired a professional to design this wonder? *Paradise on earth*, he thought, each time he strolled along the footpath.

Never in his life could he remember being so idle. He hated feeling useless. He had spent his life trying to redress the inequalities around him by dedicating himself to the service of others. But now, in this stubbornly healthy household, he lacked the skills to be useful. Everyone else had responsibilities. Rizal shuffled back and forth to the office. When he was not at work, he scoured the island, procuring supplies for his family or searching for transportation for his unwelcome guests. Anna watched the children and managed the household. Sze-yin wrapped herself in the care of her infant. Tong tried to assist the maids by mending his borrowed clothes; he had plenty of experience suturing. But they laughed at his attempts and swatted him away.

So he tended the garden. He weeded the flower beds around the house. He transplanted the overgrown banana tree to the back, where the shrubbery had died from lack of attention. He trailed the bougainvillea back up the arbours. He made remarkable progress in a few weeks. The garden began to blossom in its former glory—or what he assumed was its former glory, as he had not seen the yard before its deterioration.

He was amazed by the pleasure of soil on his fingertips. As a young man, he had watched with pity the sweaty gardeners straining under the hot sun as they struggled to maintain the manicured gardens of his home. The hedges required constant trimming, the fountains daily cleaning. And the lawn! His grandfather had had the audacity to plant three acres of grass in the tropics that had to be cut weekly by an army of mowers.

He no longer pitied the hardworking gardeners now that he realized how fulfilling this physical effort could be. He revelled in the satisfaction of watching new buds sprout, stems spring up where there had been only dirt, vines obediently climb along their intended path. He was grateful to spend his last days humbly tending these magnificent gardens, pulling weeds and watching Anna.

She was everywhere in this house. And now that he could see her in the full light of her rich life, she was even more enchanting. He loved the shape of her pert mouth when she kissed the children. He worshipped her slender fingers as she pushed back the hair that slipped onto her eyes. He admired the outline of her delicate ankles, visible when she lifted her skirt to chase after her son.

Anna had been his one selfish indulgence in life. For years, he had stored up images of her from parties and other social occasions like ethereal snapshots. Every night, when he returned home after a tiring day of caring for the sick, he flipped through the album in his mind.

But now that she was so close, their intimate relationship no longer a farfetched fantasy, his thoughts of her became a bit unsettling. He could accept the role of an adulterous husband. Sze-yin and he had no feelings for each other beyond some vague notion of duty. But he found himself uncomfortable in the role of 'the other man'. That Rizal knew what had transpired was obvious in the wide berth he had given to Tong. Why had Rizal saved him? Perhaps he was also helpless before Anna's entreaties. Anna had said that her husband didn't love her. And yet, Rizal seemed caring and attentive toward her. To an outsider, they would appear to be the perfect couple.

Tong should have had the courage to marry Anna years ago, before Sze-yin, before Rizal. If he had understood the instability of life, he might have taken more risks. As a doctor, he had encountered death countless times. But somehow, his own mortality had remained a vague, hazy notion. He could never have imagined how quickly everything could disappear—in the flash of an exploding bomb. The father he had feared to cross was dead. They learned that the house his family had rented in Singapore had been hit during the air raids. There had been no survivors. His family's position, protected and preserved for generations, had been whisked away in a single day. He should have given it all up long ago, in exchange for a few years with the woman he loved. Perhaps, if the war had not come and ruined his life, he would have thrown himself at her, divorced his wife and begged Anna to leave her husband. But now, it was too late.

His certain death infused him with a generous spirit. He assumed she would stay with her husband. He wished them well. His own future was no longer a consideration. He had only two small requests left. If he could be assured of his son's future, he could die in peace. If he could have one more moment alone with Anna, he could die happy.

9

Sze-yin understood now the danger they were in. She learned more in the few weeks in Anna's house than she had in all her years at the Khoos'. The Japanese had swept through Asia. Her family in China had probably been killed long ago. The British were fighting for their life all over the globe. Tong's entire family had been felled by a single bomb. How could they have not told her? No wonder Tong had wanted to send their baby away. Her poor baby, her beautiful little boy.

The war had deprived her of the joyous celebration that should have accompanied her first son's birth. But even worse, it had deprived Ah Ma of the grand funeral she had deserved. Ah Ma should have been laid to rest in a magnificent mahogany coffin, dressed in her white wedding pajamas, a pearl in her mouth. All of Penang should have turned out to watch the funeral procession wind its way through the city streets. Instead, on the morning of Ah Ma's death, her father-in-law had only been able to locate a rough-hewn pine coffin. He had hastily arranged for the funeral rites with a caretaker. Would this caretaker have overseen all the prayers and rites, or simply pocketed the money and buried the body?

Ah Ma would not have minded missing out on an elaborate funeral. She had lived her life in the shadows and didn't require any public praise. It was Sze-yin who craved accolades. Sze-yin had so desperately wanted a son to earn the approval of her in-laws, who had not even lived long enough to see her accomplishment. But she realized now how little their recognition mattered. Death did not discriminate between the distinguished and the disgraced.

Sze-yin had begged to visit Ah Ma's grave to thank her for the safe delivery of her baby. Everyone had insisted that the journey would be too risky. So she had placed the jade talisman in her son's pudgy hand and whispered her thanks. Ah Ma had led her to the oracle that had warned her not to undertake the journey to Singapore. And Ah Ma's spirit had given Sze-yin the strength to carry on during the delivery when her body had almost failed. She would be joining Ah Ma soon and the two of them would be able to watch over her son together.

Tong intended to leave Teng Chaun with Anna, if and when they found an escape route. Sze-yin would have insisted on staying behind, preferring to spend a few more days with her baby before her death, but their remaining would put him in danger—he was better off without his fugitive parents.

So she watched Anna, not as a rival, but as the potential mother of her child. Sze-yin had never cared for Anna. Others insisted that Anna was easy-going but Sze-yin thought she was pretentious with her books and her education. She dressed in plain gowns with simple jewellery, and hair always flowing in unkempt waves. A tighter crop and hair clips would have given her a neater appearance. Why did people find her beautiful? Her colour might have been considered striking but her features were not fine, her eyes were a bit wide-set, and she had the broad shoulders of a washerwoman.

Sze-yin had observed her husband's surreptitious glances toward her as early as their wedding day. She didn't expect monogamy, but Tong should not have taken up with a woman in his own social circle. It was inappropriate to make his wife socialize with the object of his affection.

Still, Anna might be a decent mother to her child. Anna's children were too young to provide any indication of her skills. The girls seemed well-cared-for, healthy little infants, tentatively toddling on their chubby legs; the little boy, Kamil a boisterous handful, but as well behaved as a three-year-old boy could be. The little niece, Rozi, was a bit clingy, but then the poor girl had just lost her father. Rozi's mother, Mina, seemed soft, emotional, too enamoured by the children to scold them.

Sze-yin was most impressed by Anna's mother. She had heard that the mother had withdrawn from life. But Zaharah didn't strike Sze-yin as a recluse. Zaharah had a reassuring solidity about her. The children responded to her firm approach. If she said no balls in the house, Kamil took his toy outside, knowing his grandmother would snatch it up on the first bounce, not with anger or recrimination, but with decision. She reminded Sze-yin of her stepmother, an imposing matron who sanctioned no weakness.

Anna was harder to decipher. She could be impassioned, overly emotional at times. Kamil could bring Anna to tears with his tantrums or make her misty-eyed with his charm. But when the situation called for composure, Anna could rival her mother in her strength.

Little Rozi had wandered away from the house one day. Everyone had spread out, looking for her. Somehow Sze-yin had ended up alongside Anna as they headed to the stream. Rozi had been warned many times not to venture near the creek, but she couldn't resist playing with the cats that hung around the water.

Anna had seen her first. She had waded into the water and dragged the limp body out. 'Go get Tong,' she had shouted as she had knelt down and put her mouth to the girl's blue lips. By the time Tong had arrived, Rozi was sitting up, tears streaming down her face.

'What happened?' he had asked.

'I did what you taught us in the first-aid session about the breathing.'

Tong had examined the girl, who by then, was a healthy shade of pink from all the crying.

They had carried her inside and tucked her under the blankets. Zaharah had scolded the child for wandering too far. Mina had sat by the bed all night, hovering over her little girl.

Anna had taken Rozi and Kamil to the stream, the next day, and begun their swimming lessons.

10

Rizal finally found a merchant captain who was willing to put his whole crew at risk for the right price. The captain refused to accept Straits dollars or Japanese notes, but jumped at the offer of Zaharah's diamond brooches—such was the nature of wartime commerce.

The plan seemed simple enough. They would load the car with a raft and pump. Rizal would leave them at the beach with his fishing rod. A Chinese family catching their evening meal on the edge of the sea wouldn't attract any attention. After dark, they would blow up the raft and row to the waiting ship. Then up the ladder, into emptied crates, and off to Sumatra, assuming, of course, that the ship wasn't searched.

Sze-yin spent the last day clinging to her baby. Tong felt more relief than despair. His only purpose in attempting the long-shot escape was to put as much distance between himself and his child as possible.

His son would have a good life here, growing up with the other children among the fruit trees. Anna would cherish this child as her own. Teng Chaun would be safe and loved in this little paradise. And Tong was pleased to be leaving a piece of himself behind with Anna. He hoped she would think of him whenever she embraced the child.

On their last day, his final wish came true. Anna appeared in the doorway of the room behind the garage.

'Could I speak with you for a moment please, Tong?' she said.

Sze-yin was too absorbed in her son to notice the lovers wandering off. Anna took Tong's hand and led him to the little bank beside the stream.

Anna had been walking on eggshells for the last two months, wondering how to conduct herself. She was wracked with guilt every time she saw Tong working in the garden, like a hired hand, perversely attired in that driver's old clothes. Sze-yin had found the musty box in their room and suggested that at least Tong should be able to have a change of clothes, as if Anna had not continually offered her own wardrobe to Sze-yin. Neither Anna nor Rizal could come up with a reason why he shouldn't borrow the clothes. So Tong had spent the last eight weeks living in their servants' quarters, tending their garden, dressed in her husband's lover's rags. The situation was so ridiculous, she would have laughed if she didn't want to cry. And poor Rizal moping around, doing his best to play the dutiful host, as if the doctor and his wife were simply stopping by for an extended social call. Why did she bother about his feelings anyway? What right did he have to sulk?

And then there was the presence of the wife. Sze-yin seemed to be a reasonable woman. She was devoted to her child, Tong's child. Why couldn't he just love his wife? But that romantic notion, a husband in love with his wife, seemed like a silly childhood fantasy now.

She realized now that they would never be together. She had loved him once with all the passionate feelings that a naïve girl could muster. And maybe they would have been happy together. If things had been different. If they had run off to Singapore and married. But they hadn't. He had married Sze-yin and she had married Rizal. Tong was a kind, generous, passionate man. But she didn't love him anymore.

Anna couldn't let Tong leave without trying to set things right. She couldn't stomach the idea of misleading such a kind man. She had promised herself that she would never again deceive. Now was her opportunity to come clean. They walked hand in hand to the garden as Anna prepared her explanation. She would tell him how she felt so they could make a fresh start after the war. Whatever happened between her and Rizal, Tong needed to know the truth.

Before she could speak, Tong took her in his arms and pressed her against his chest.

'I'm so happy to hold you again,' he said. 'I didn't think that I'd get the chance to say goodbye.'

She tried to wiggle free without offending him, just enough to at least look at his face.

'You don't have to say goodbye,' she said. 'We'll see each other again.'

'No, I don't want to pretend.' He shook his head. 'We'll never see each other again. I need to tell you how I feel.' He had prepared his own speech. 'You've been everything to me. I've loved you from the moment I met you. I only wish that I'd had the courage to marry you. I'm so sorry.'

She wanted to discourage him from such futile regrets. 'It would never have worked out,' she said.

'Yes, it would have. We could have had a wonderful life together. I'll never forgive myself for letting you go. I need you to know that I never stopped loving you. I'll think of you till my last breath.'

Anna looked into his earnest eyes. What could she say? Of what use could the truth be to him now? Surely, Allah would forgive one little lie if it could provide comfort to such a good man. These harmless fibs we tell ourselves—'your dress is lovely', 'your brother did not suffer', 'your husband loves you'—these delusional lies can mean the difference between hope and despair. Sometimes, it was better not to know the truth.

'I'll always love you,' she said.

He drew her to him and kissed her as if he wanted to consume her. And though she did not love him, she savoured the overpowering sensation of his desire. Rizal would never kiss her this way. He would never embrace her as if his life depended on it.

In the end, it was Tong who pulled away.

11

Rizal had endured the presence of his wife's lover for eight weeks. Like a painful mosquito bite, the sting subsided if it wasn't scratched. He could endure the theoretical concept of Anna in the arms of another man. He just couldn't stand encountering that man every day, under his roof, dressed in Arun's old clothes. He felt an involuntary shudder every time he saw those familiar shirts hanging on Tong's lanky frame.

He wasn't worried about the trip this time. All he had to do was drop them off near the water and then go about his business. Tong and his wife would probably even get out safely. The ship's captain seemed competent and the Japanese had reduced their patrols of the harbour to the occasional random search. Finally, they would be gone, to whatever fate awaited them. He wished them well. He had risked his life, endured their presence and wanted the sacrifice to be worth it, if only for Anna's sake. He hoped that they would survive the journey and settle down into a comfortable life in Sumatra. So comfortable a life, they would stay away forever.

But if Tong didn't return, Anna might spend the rest of her life pining for him. Or, now that she had fulfilled her duty to her lover, she might take the children and move back to Rumah Merah with her mother and sister-in-law. He had kept silent long enough, fearing her response. But now, he needed to know her intentions.

Rizal dug through the garage. He pulled out the rubber raft and fishing tools and laid them on the grass. Then he set to work, cleaning his rifle. He was sitting on the front steps, wiping the excess lubricant from the barrel with a washcloth, when he heard the warning whistle.

He looked up to see Seiko's car pulling up the drive. Damn. It was too late to hide the gun or cover up the debris on the front lawn.

Seiko walked up the path, ignoring the raft, the fishing implements, and the illegal shotgun.

'Selamat tengah hari. Apa khabar?' Seiko greeted him.

Rizal put the gun aside and walked toward Seiko while attempting to put on a normal face.

'Khabar baik, terima kasih. Have you finished your book already?'

'Yes, sorry to disturb you so soon. But it seems I have run out of pages. May I peruse your bookshelves again?'

'Of course.'

He invited Seiko back into the house. This time, the servants didn't even bother to scamper. Elsie brought them tea. Mina remained frozen on the couch. Seiko chatted, and if Rizal wasn't mistaken, possibly flirted with his sister-in-law for almost twenty minutes before rising to take his leave.

The whole visit resembled a French farce. If only it were. They were beyond saving now. He followed Seiko back out to the car. Someone had cleared the lawn of the suspicious items.

He almost had Seiko back in the car when Tong and Anna came strolling down the path, heading right for them. Hadn't they heard the whistle? As soon as Tong and Anna saw Seiko, they stopped and tried to turn back toward the garden.

'Is that your wife? I'd love to meet her.' Seiko asked.

'Yes, that is my wife Anna with Ling, our gardener.'

Where had he come up with that name?

Seiko bounded toward the startled pair.

'Oh, how delightful.' He bowed. 'I am Seiko. Selamat tengah hari. Apa khabar? I would love a tour of your garden.'

And so the Japanese subjugator, the Chinese fugitive, and the hapless couple went strolling through the garden discussing the care and feeding of the vegetation in broken Malay. Tong was remarkably knowledgeable about the garden. He pointed out the many layers, colors and textures accentuating each corner, though Rizal was sure he was making up most of the names of the plants.

Finally, Seiko seemed satisfied that he had absorbed the whole tour.

'Well, I must be getting back. Thank you so much for showing me around.'

Thanks be to Allah he was leaving. The sun would soon be starting its descent and they needed to get to the beach in time to make their rendezvous with the ship.

Fortunately, Tong and Sze-yin didn't have anything to pack. The wealthy Khoos were leaving with only the clothes on their backs and a few coins. Tong went inside to collect his wife and maid and say a final goodbye to his son. Rizal watched Anna as her eyes followed Tong through the door. He couldn't remain silent anymore. He had to know what she was thinking.

'Will you wait for him?' Rizal asked.

Anna gazed at the door, as if addressing its question. 'He won't be back,' she said.

'You never know. If you want something badly enough, sometimes it can happen.'

'He belongs with his wife,' she said. 'I want them to be happy.'

'But if you love him?'

'I don't love him.' She turned to look at him. 'All my life, I dreamed of marrying for love. I watched my sister and my friends succumb to the pressures of arranged marriages but I was going to be different. I was going to marry a man whom I loved. And I did. I succeeded, except for one fact. My husband never loved me. Do you know how it feels to be so betrayed? Our life together has been a horrible lie. What am I supposed to do? And the worst part is that I still love you. Despite everything, I can't get rid of these feelings. Tong is a good man, but I couldn't love him because of you.'

'I do love you,' he said. How could he explain the many shades of love, duty and affection he was capable of feeling?

'But not the way a husband should love a wife.'

'I think I love you more than most men love their wives.'

'I'm not most wives. You should have married someone like Sofiah or Mina.'

She might be right. With most women, there would be no conflict. They would accept his affairs and he would feel no guilt. But life with such a woman seemed unbearable.

'If I could change for you, I would.'

Her friends accepted all sorts of compromises—mistresses, second wives, dull and unaffectionate husbands. How did they cope? Could she accept this half marriage with compassion and respect, but no passion? Now that she had tasted true passion, could she live without it?

In their household, there were now five children who needed a father. But the children would survive without him. She would survive without him. She just wasn't sure that she wanted to.

They ran out of time for a resolution. Tong, Sze-yin and Elsie came out of the house, ready for their journey. Further discussion would have to wait until their guests had been escorted to their destiny.

Sze-yin walked over to the couple with dry eyes and a sombre face. Her hands remained steady as she cradled her child. Sze-yin had thought she was beyond the reach of sentiment, yet these few months of motherhood had taught her otherwise. She had wanted a son to bring her respect in this life and security in the next, but he had given her so much more. She had never expected to feel such overpowering love for anyone. Life may be short and of no consequence compared to the afterlife, but it was a gift to be cherished, all the same. Her son had taught her that.

Leaving Chaun in the care of this family was the best option for her child and that was all that mattered. She would be reunited with him someday after his death, but in the meantime, she wished him a long and happy life filled with affection. She didn't care if he achieved any accolades or honour in life, as long as he was cherished.

Nobody tried to speak, their emotions were too raw for mere words. Anna's eyes told her that she would love and care for Chaun as if he were her own and that was all Sze-yin could ask for. She handed her baby to Anna and turned to the car, ready to accept her fate. Tong followed, nodding his goodbyes to Anna and his son.

* * *

The four drove in silence through the countryside toward a secluded beach at the outskirts of town. Rizal understood that there would be no confrontation, no resolution, no mutual coming to terms with Tong. Even if the opportunity had presented itself, if the women hadn't been present, he didn't have anything to say. Rizal hated the idea of Tong, but he didn't hate Tong. He understood the impulse that would drive a man to follow his heart, without regard for the people who might get trampled along the way. The socially acceptable response would have been a challenge to a duel or some other manly contest to defend his pride and honour. But the rulebook for civil society seemed naïve and ridiculous under the circumstances. There were no social protocols for two men in their situation.

'I can't thank you enough for all that you've done for us,' Tong finally said.

Rizal searched for an appropriate response but all the options seemed nonsensical. He just nodded his head in recognition of the gesture.

'I'm ready to face whatever happens to us because I know that you and Anna will take good care of Teng Chaun. This thought gives me more peace than you can ever imagine. I can die happy knowing that they will be happy.'

The use of the plural pronoun did not escape Rizal's notice. He was speaking of his son, but also Anna. What a demanding expectation to throw at Rizal's feet. 'I'll do my best,' he said.

They pulled into a spot a few hundred yards from the water. Tong, Elsie and Sze-yin got out of the car and walked toward the water. The sun was already setting in the overcast sky. Rizal watched them until he could no longer make out their silhouettes. He wished them luck. He could do no more.

He got back in the car and waited for the morning. A curfew was in place and automobiles were not allowed on the roads after dark. So he closed his eyes and tried to get some sleep.

In the black of the night, he didn't see Tong inflate the raft and paddle silently to the cargo ship drifting on the darkened sea. He didn't see them climb aboard and hide in the empty crate. He was still asleep when the patrol boat pulled alongside and the soldiers motioned to be let aboard.

12

Heavy boots tromped down the wooden stairs to the hull. Rubber soles flickered in and out of view between the slats of the crate. From the moment Tong had seen the conspicuous crate, large enough to hold the three of them, he knew that it wouldn't escape an inspection. He held his breath and embraced the girls, as if his frail arms could provide any protection. The soldiers pounded on the lids of surrounding crates. Most yielded a solid thud, indicating they were filled with goods. Their crate offered only a hollow reverberation. Two eyes peered through a crack in the slats and a man let out an excited cry at his discovery. The soldiers rushed forward, like wild boar to a kill.

They pried open the lid and pulled Tong and the women out. The sharp point of a gun pressed into Tong's shoulder blade, urging him up the stairs to the open deck. The soldiers had no idea who they had captured; but their commander would be quite pleased when he discovered their identities. It might be better to be killed right away. Tong couldn't go back to his own house to be tortured, not after so many weeks in paradise.

Perhaps Sze-yin had the same thought. She pulled away from the soldier who held her arm. 'Don't touch me,' she shouted in her childhood tongue. When the startled soldier moved to take her arm again, she slapped him in the face. The others snickered at their humiliated colleague. The red-faced soldier lifted the barrel of his gun and pulled the trigger. With the instincts of a doctor, Tong lunged forward to break her fall. He didn't hear the next shot, but felt the piercing stab strike his chest. His legs, suddenly the legs of a rag doll, yielded to the force of gravity. He landed on his back, staring at the sky. Another scream, another shot, a third body crumpled on the deck next to him.

The sun peeked over the horizon, bringing the endless night to a close. A streak of light appeared at the horizon. He felt no pain, only a mild tingling in his limbs. The sky turned a brilliant orange, then purple, and finally black. The shouting voices quieted and the tingling ceased. He felt as light as the ocean breeze.

13

A lone cock sounded the morning alarm, alerting the world to the start of a new day. The call to prayer echoed through the trees, a silvery tune gently reviving the faithful from their night's slumber.

Rizal smoothed his hair and then took a razor from the glove compartment and gave himself a dry shave in the mirror. When he arrived at work, a little early that morning, two of his men were already at their desks filing and stamping papers.

'Morning,' he greeted them, then closed the door to his office and collapsed on his desk, hoping to get a little more sleep before the day began in earnest.

He woke to the sound of his door being kicked open. His eyes, still bleary from their long night, widened at the sight of four soldiers, fully armed, charging toward him. They grabbed him and pulled him out of his chair and paraded him out the door, past his gawking staff, to the police station.

He had been to the station once, years before, to make a report about a warehouse theft. Back then, he had been greeted warmly and told to sit down while a polite lieutenant listened to his complaint and filled out forms. The office no longer had the same smiling clerks and the neat rows of desks. The furniture had been cleared to make room for soldiers, who stood around waiting for orders.

They shoved him through the entrance and down the hall toward the holding cells. A group of ragged men huddled in the corner of one of the cells looked up as he passed by. They watched him wordlessly as he was whisked past them and thrown into what must have been an empty closet. His head hit a hook at the back of the closet and he blacked out.

When he woke up, he had no idea how long he had been out. There were no windows in the tiny room to indicate the time of day. His head throbbed from what he could feel was a laceration near his ear. His shirt clung to his shoulder, where a pool of blood had glued the fabric to his skin. He sat on the floor for what might have been an hour or many more.

The door was opened and a sudden shaft of light flooded the room. Two soldiers pulled him off the floor and escorted him down the hall to an office behind the holding cells, that had been turned into an interrogation room. The soldiers put him in a chair without explanation.

At least this room had a window revealing the afternoon sunlight. A pigeon perched on the sill, taunting him with its freedom. The cane chair he sat in faced a black lacquer desk and two wooden chairs with matching plaid cushions. The soldiers stepped back and stood like bookends on each side of the open door.

Did his family know he was here? His staff had seen him carted out. They would probably have sent a message to his family. Something had gone wrong with Tong's escape. Maybe they had been captured or maybe the captain had turned them all in. Had his family been implicated too? Were they in trouble?

Seiko and the other officer who had taken his inventory walked into the room and sat in the waiting chairs. Without greeting, Seiko pulled a picture from a manila file and placed it on the table.

'This man was found trying to escape today.' It was a picture of Tong in formal attire, maybe his wedding photo. 'Do you know who he is?'

Why was Seiko asking him this? The presence of the photo meant they knew exactly who the man was. He was Khoo Boo Tong, member of the Khoo clan—ardent supporters of the Aid to China campaign. He was also the gentle gardener who had taken Seiko on a delightful tour at Rizal's house yesterday. If it had been any other officer, Rizal might have tried to get away with it. Most of the soldiers probably thought all Chinese looked alike. But Seiko was an intelligent, astute observer; he knew exactly who this particular Chinese man was, and he had probably already pieced together the full story.

And yet, something made Rizal take a chance. If he could pretend they were simply having another friendly chat in his living room, he might be able to keep his voice steady and make it through the interrogation. They'd probably kill him whether he told the truth or not, so why not buy some time and make Seiko tell him what he knew. If nothing else, he might be able to protect his family.

'Yes, I know who he is,' he said to Seiko. 'Everybody knows Khoo Boo Tong, he is a very popular doctor in town.'

'He was captured today with his wife and sister, trying to escape in one of your family's ships,' Seiko informed him. 'They were executed on the spot. So I'm asking you if you know anything about them and how they managed to escape our round-ups.'

Rizal was willing to continue with this charade. Imagining it to be a game gave him the courage to press on. What harm would it do? The truth these days could be whatever you wanted it to be.

'No, I don't know anything about it. I thought that the Khoo family had fled to Singapore. I don't know how they ended up on one of my ships. Did you ask the crew?'

'The crew has been killed. The captain tried to flee before we could question him,' Seiko informed him. 'He was one of your captains.'

'The merchant captains are mercenaries,' he replied. 'They don't work for anyone but themselves. He was probably bribed by the Khoos to let them on board.'

The actor Seiko seemed satisfied with this answer. He and the other officer leaned together and appeared to discuss his response.

'We questioned your staff,' Seiko finally responded. 'They have vouched for your integrity and your unwavering support of the Japanese war effort.'

Well, it was good to know they could lie as well. Seiko again consulted with the other officer. Whatever he said made the other officer nod his head and pick up the photo. The two stood in unison.

'You are free to go,' Seiko announced.

Rizal stared at Seiko's impassive face, trying to read what to do. What was going on? Was he really free to go? Seiko responded with only an absent stare.

'Thank you for your time,' Seiko added with more firmness than civility.

'Thank you.' Rizal infused the words with perhaps too much emotion. He rose without resistance and stepped unaccompanied out of the police headquarters into the blazing sunlight.

Anna was standing outside the police entrance, waiting for him. She threw her arms around his neck. He had never felt more alive than on that sweltering afternoon day, standing outside the police station in Anna's embrace. With each new threat, he had tried to convince himself that he was indifferent to the outcome. But now he realized how desperately he wanted to live.

They hiked together almost a mile in the general direction of home before they were able to hitch a ride on the back of a bullock cart. They watched the city fade to the lumbering rhythm of the animal's stride.

'Promise me one thing,' Anna said.

'Anything.'

'If you ever fall in love with someone else again, I want you to tell me.'

He made her a promise he knew he would never keep. If he did fall in love again—and the possibility seemed as remote as the end of the war—he wouldn't tell her. He would never risk losing her again. And for his part, if she fell in love with someone else, he was sure that he wouldn't want to know.

Epilogue

The burst of an impatient horn startled Rizal from his slumber. He took a moment to reacquaint himself with his bedroom, which was still draped in the shadows of the diffused morning light drifting through the lace curtains. In the fog of his muddled sleep, he heard the distant sounds of voices from the kitchen mingled with the occasional clang of a cast-iron pot striking a metal burner. A hazy impression formed in his mind—she must be up already, preparing breakfast. But as he opened his eyes to the reality of the scene on the other side of the bed, the sheets pristinely constricted, the side table missing a water glass, and the bare post missing its familiar robe, he remembered with the sudden flash of despair that still struck him in the half-conscious moments as he roused, that Anna was not resting beside him in the bed, rustling in the kitchen, or washing in the bathroom; nor would she be present today for her son's bersanding. He laid his head back on the pillow and closed his eyes, reluctant to embrace the waking world.

'Chaun is getting married today,' he reminded her.

She answered with a slight upturn in her eyebrows, as if to say that of course, she had not forgotten.

'Both boys seem to have selected brides with a hint of your temperament, strong-willed but sympathetic, exactly what they need, I think.'

He imagined Anna's nod, conceding the characterization and the comparison.

'You should get downstairs and see what's going on in the kitchen,' she would have chided.

He rose from the bed and made his way to the sink. A splash of cold water on his face removed the last traces of his tranquil repose. He inspected the mirror and frowned at the encroaching groves across his forehead and around his eyes. His reflection was becoming a stranger to him. Others probably thought his countenance perfectly suited to his evolving status as an ageing patriarch, elder statesman, doting grandfather, and serene widower. But he struggled to reconcile the image of himself as a man with gray hair, a slight stoop, or lined eyes. He did not feel old enough to be a grandfather and certainly not a widower. And yet, somehow, fifty-six years had slipped by. He was already beyond the age his father had achieved.

After dressing in his plaid sarong and cotton shirt, Rizal stepped out of his room. He stood at the top of the stairs and surveyed the parlour below, the familiar tableau that had been etched over time with the traces of their busy lives; the wall near the kitchen door marked with the annual progress of each child's height, the teak dining table dented by the pounding of little fists on forks, and the stained glass panel cracked by a toy plane. It was easy to become overly attached to these inanimate objects, imbue them with all kinds of meaning. But he did not need to stare at the photos lining the stairs to remember all the birthdays, weddings and celebrations he and Anna had enjoyed. He did not need to walk through the garden to feel Arun's presence. He did not require the house and the furniture and all its trappings to justify his ample life. Rizal understood that life is not measured in the objects left behind, but in the imprints we make on the people we love.

He followed the aroma of simmering stew emanating from the kitchen. The aunties must have arrived early to start cooking. A caterer would bring the lamb, biryani, sautéed vegetables, and iced desserts. But the rendang, scented rice, achar and sambal would all be made from scratch with loving hands in order to ensure that, despite the uncertainty of world events, the moral depravity foisted upon them by the television, and the low necklines prevalent in the current fashions, Penang had not changed beyond recognition.

Chaun and his bride had wanted a simple wedding. Like all young people, they were eager to leave behind the stifling customs of their parents and recreate the world according to their own imaginations. But just as Rizal and Anna had compromised for their ceremony years ago, the young couple had managed to strike a balance, preserving enough tradition to appease the aunties while adding modest modifications to ensure they felt suitably empowered as they embarked on their modern union.

Rizal opened the kitchen door and was greeted by his daughter, standing in front of the stove with her youngest daughter on her hip.

'Good morning, Bapa,' Nura smiled with her mother's grin. 'The rendang is almost ready.'

'It smells wonderful,' he said as he planted a kiss on his granddaughter's dimpled cheek. 'Why didn't you wake me?'

'You needed some rest,' Nura informed him. 'You haven't had a moment's peace since the wedding festivities began.'

'True, but neither have you.'

'I was up already, so I came over to get started. Selima's just left for the market.' She took a kettle from the stove and poured steaming tea into a porcelain cup resting on the counter.

'Is Chaun awake already?' he asked.

'Don't you mean Shaun? Remember, he thinks he's an American now,' she laughed. 'He left a few minutes ago to meet Sheila for breakfast in town.'

'They aren't supposed to see each other before the ceremony,' he said.

'Try telling them anything,' Nura sighed, handing him the teacup. 'Young people these days have no respect for tradition.'

Now it was Rizal's turn to laugh.

'Why don't you take your tea outside and rest a bit,' Nura suggested. 'The delivery boys won't be here for another hour.'

Rizal put on his slippers and walked across the dewy grass to sit on the bench under the rambutan tree. He sipped his tea and listened to the morning songbirds, who were doing their best to compete with the sound of whizzing cars. Their once-secluded bungalow was now located on a major thoroughfare, the road clogged with commuters rushing to and from the city. The stream where Arun had caught his fish had long since dried up. But the walled compound with its abundant fruit trees, flowering shrubs, mature palms and towering ferns still provided a tranquil setting in which to enjoy a few moments before the day started in earnest. Anna had not lived long enough to see Shaun's bersanding, but Rizal could still feel her presence everywhere this morning.

Her diagnosis had come just before Shaun was due to begin his first year overseas. Rizal had been incredulous. After all they had been through, such a meaningless end seemed unjust. He had been furious. How could Allah have been so thoughtless? And then he had been resigned as he had prayed for an end to her suffering.

Shaun had begged to be allowed to defer his departure for college but Anna would not hear of it.

'He must go to school,' she had insisted as she had attempted to climb out of her sickbed to pack his bags herself. Rizal had urged her to rest.

'He will,' he had said. 'I'll talk to him.' He had tried to get her to lie back down, but she had resisted.

'The children are going to need your help. I don't want to be the reason anyone fails.'

'Please don't worry yourself.'

'And once they're through school, you'll need to guide them as they each select a suitable spouse.'

'I hardly think I'm a qualified authority. Your sister will be here, and Mina. They can help.'

'No, it has to be you. They'll marry whomever they choose, of course, but they'll want your approval.'

'I'll love whomever they love, I'm sure.'

'We were terribly naïve when we decided to get married, like children, really, with no understanding of the consequences. We were lucky that things worked out the way they did. And we've been happy, haven't we?'

The tears had choked his breath. He couldn't muster a response. They had always held to their unspoken agreement. He had never asked her where she went or whom she saw, and she had never mentioned or even alluded to his activities. They had honoured the delicate veil that had held their lives together. And they had been happy, she had said so herself.

When Anna finally succumbed, Rizal had mourned her with a depth he had experienced only once before in his life. As before, it was his responsibilities to his family that had pulled him through.

Sofiah and Mina would be arriving soon with their daughters, surprised to find the rendang already prepared. Sofiah would fret that there might not be enough food, Mina would insist that she was wrong, and Rozi, with her father's aversion to family friction, would suggest they ask the caterer to bring extra portions of biryani, just to be sure. Kamil would drive up in his new Mercedes, frazzled and distracted, but eager to help. His wife would apologize for their late arrival and complain that her husband lacked any sense of time. The men would set up the tables and assemble the dais, the women would dress the young couple in matching rented robes, and the children would soil their clothes with curry sampled from heaping platters cooling on the banquet table.

The house would overflow with the family and friends that Rizal and Anna had collected over the years: the neighbours who lent them a bag of rice or an extra hen during the Occupation; the men who had served with Rizal on the committees and councils that had steered the country through the unsettling postwar years, to independence; the women who had helped Anna nurse her children and celebrate their birthdays, and who sat at her bedside during her final hours. These friends who had stood witness to every milestone in Rizal and Anna's life would raise their glasses in toasts and comment wistfully on the unwavering and unrelenting march of time.

The newlyweds would sit on the dais surrounded by this gathering of loved ones. They would stare wide-eyed into the crowd with excitement and trepidation as they contemplated the life they would have together. Rizal wished that he could allay their fears. He could not tell them that they were making the right decision. Nor could he predict what obstacles they might encounter. Of course, their lives would not unfold in the way they expected. But he wanted to urge them, just as Faisal had tried to tell him, so many years ago, to savour each moment, because regardless of the twists and turns their journey might take, it was certain to be wondrous and all too brief.